THE GREEN BAIZE DOOR

ELEANOR BIRNEY

PARLOR & DOCK PRESS
EST. 2012

THE GREEN BAISE DOOR

Published by Parlor & Dock Press

http://read.eleanorbirney.com

eBook ISBN: 979-8-9934317-3-4

Paperback ISBN: 979-8-9934317-0-3

This novel is a work of fiction inspired by a real life historical events. For the purposes of storytelling, the author has altered timelines, invented characters, changed people and place names, and dramatized incidents.

Cover design: Parlor & Dock Press

ACKNOWLEDGEMENTS

My deepest thanks to Kamil Gagala, Allan Krenitsky, Adriana Dvorska, Heather McLeod, and Michael Sheehan for their generous input, sharp eyes, and extraordinary patience along the way. This book is better for your time and candor.

And to my children—Kazi, Benny, and Eli—thank you for your love, your humor, and the reminder that stories matter.

THE MUSTACHIOED MAN

NOVEMBER 24, 1899. SIX WEEKS BEFORE
THE MURDER

The carriage was a country vehicle in the least flattering sense of the word. Wind and wet sputtered through great gaps between the windows and doors, and the cabin contained several well-used fur blankets that reeked of mildew and wet dog. The exterior had once been painted beetle-black, but rust from the undercarriage was gradually overtaking it, mapping the darkness with winding orange rivers and flaking continents.

James Lett, Jamie to his friends, wiped at the foggy window pane with his handkerchief and peered outside. "At this speed," he said, turning to the carriage's only other occupant, "we may as well have walked from the station. Does the fellow think he's being paid by the hour?"

Manassas Edmunds, Chief Financial Officer of the Keystone Lumber Company, shrugged. "Better to go slow than to get stuck in the mud and have to wait for rescue."

Jamie frowned. The old fellow wasn't wrong; the rain, which was coming down in torrents, had saturated the iron-rich embankment, and with each step, the horses sank to their fetlocks in mud as thick as potter's clay. Jamie sighed and slumped back into his seat. "Remind me, what's our itinerary?"

"We ride to Conifer tomorrow morning," Manassas answered. "You do the inspection tour while I review the ledgers."

"Mph," Jamie grunted. Inspection tours were typically less inspection and more tour, as it took a special kind of idiot to show the owner's son their blunders. It would be awkward, but at least it would end with a feast—they usually did. Famished and half-frozen as Jamie was, the thought of a hot meal could tempt him almost anywhere.

"You'll be fine," Manassas reassured him. "Your father just wants you to show your face. Let the men see the heir apparent."

Jamie turned back toward the window to hide his annoyance. He knew perfectly well what his father wanted, and, if you asked him, the *Captain*, as the men called him, was being damn foolish. Union agitators, and the rash of strikes that followed them, had been splashed across the front pages of the newspapers for months—first with the miners in Idaho and now with the newsboys in the City. It had the old man spooked, but if trouble was brewing, giving the millworkers a glimpse of his face would hardly hold it at bay.

If anyone else had been in the carriage, Jamie would have said as much outright, but Manassas was a company man to the marrow. He had been his father's friend and bookkeeper for as long as Jamie could remember and was incapable of entertaining the notion that the Captain could be wrong.

For the hundredth time that morning, Jamie wondered how he had allowed himself to be talked into this trip. A man whose appetite for nature was sated by a half-hour's walk in Central Park had no business boarding the eight o'clock *Mohawk and Malone* for an expedition into the wilds of Upstate New York. And yet, here he was, inching through a muddy wasteland in a carriage that should have been sold as scrap a generation ago.

Jamie sighed and settled deeper into his seat. There was nothing to be done for it now, and he would have to get through the next few weeks as best he may.

Some twenty minutes after they'd left the station, their carriage pulled up in front of the inn: a modest building located in the center of what passed for Tupper Lake's downtown. Climbing gingerly from the cabin, Jamie was pleased to discover that no lasting damage had been done to his person. Resisting the urge to dash inside to get out of the wet, Jamie watched with begrudging admiration as Manassas stepped down lightly, righted his hat, and started for the door. After two decades of these inspection tours, the old man must have grown accustomed to being tumbled about like an apple in a barrel.

The inn's darkly papered lobby was empty, and the innkeeper, who Jamie suspected was used to receiving guests in the early stages of hypothermia, confirmed their reservations and proffered their room keys in record time. Bone-tired, Jamie was grateful when a uniformed bellhop, a dark-complexioned boy with keen brown eyes, appeared and hoisted his luggage onto a brass trolley with a squeaky wheel.

Jamie turned toward Manassas. "Meet you back down here in an hour for dinner?"

Manassas shivered, his attention fixed somewhere in the distance.

Jamie followed his gaze but saw nothing of interest. "Uncle Manny?"

Manassas jolted. "I'm sorry. Did you say something?"

"Meet here for dinner at six?"

"Of course," Manassas mumbled, then shuffled toward the stairs, his gouty limp more pronounced than usual.

Jamie watched him go with a vague stirring of unease. The ride must have been more fatiguing than the old fellow had let on. Still, it was nothing a change of clothes and a shot of whiskey wouldn't set to rights.

The bellhop deposited Jamie in his room, and after a hot bath and a few minutes in front of a mirror with a comb and razor, he felt almost human again. When six o'clock rolled around, he descended the stairs feeling a good deal sharper than when he'd trudged up them.

The bellhop who'd helped him with his bags spotted him coming through the lobby door and made a beeline for him.

"Sir, there's a message for you."

"For me?" Jamie asked, surprised. It was too soon for a letter from home, and information concerning the mills would be addressed to Manassas.

The bellhop nodded and handed him a small envelope. "Your friend asked me to give it to you when you came down."

Jamie handed the kid a nickel, then opened the envelope.

My dear boy,
There has been a change of plans. I am needed at the Vermont yard immediately. I will explain all when you arrive.
Manassas

This had to be a joke. Jamie glanced around the lobby, half-expecting to see an old school chum crouching behind a potted plant, but, except for him, the place was deserted.

"Has Mr. Edmunds checked out?" He asked, incredulous.

"He did, sir. Shortly after you went upstairs."

"And there are no other messages for me?"

"None."

"Thank you." Jamie wandered distractedly to the Oriental rug in the center of the lobby and studied Manassas's note. It was the old fellow's handwriting, alright. What the devil was he playing at? Why set off in such a hurry? And in this weather? It was damnably odd.

No sooner had these questions flitted through Jamie's mind than the answer came to him. This was his father's doing—an ill-conceived ploy to force Jamie into taking a more active role in the family business.

Well, if that was the case, the Captain was in for a serious disappointment. When he'd asked Jamie to make this trip, he had assured him his role would be strictly ceremonial: a little glad-handing and a few friendly nudges to help increase production. *That* Jamie was equipped to do, but if someone asked a question of substance, he would be hard-pressed to answer it. The old man knew that, or damn well should have.

He lit a cigarette and was puffing angrily at it when the walls of the lobby shifted unaccountably, reminding him that he hadn't yet eaten. That, at least, was a problem he could solve. He located the inn's dining room and ordered a steak dinner with all the trimmings and a bottle of their best whiskey.

The small room smelled not unpleasantly of burnt sugar, onions, and roasted beef. He was the only patron, and it wasn't long before the hostess, a plump, genial-faced woman in her early thirties, reappeared and placed a steaming plate and a jug of George Dickel in front of him. She remained standing by his table until he looked up, then flashed him a toothy smile and flounced back to the kitchen. His eyes followed the sway of her hips until she rounded the corner. No, he thought with a sigh, there wasn't time for any of that.

He was chewing the last bite of sirloin when a man with foreign-looking mustachios appeared at his table.

Jamie assumed the man was a member of the dining room's waitstaff until he cleared his throat and asked, "Do I have the honor of addressing Mr. James Lett?"

The fellow was short and wiry with sharp features unrelieved by a slick of ebony hair. A heavily waxed mustache dominated his face, which, rather than being curled at the ends, was trained into menacing little points. All in all, he put Jamie in mind of a rodent.

Thinking that the man was perhaps someone from the mill, Jamie forced a half-smile and lit another cigarette. "You do."

The fellow slipped into the chair across from him. "I'm an associate of Mr. Edmunds. After he missed our appointment, I made inquiries, and the clerk informed me he'd gone but that his traveling companion—" he nodded at Jamie "—was still a guest of the establishment."

The man's voice held the hint of an accent. South American, if Jamie were to guess.

"You've been informed correctly."

The fellow glanced around the room then leaned across the table, and in a voice so low it was almost a whisper, asked, "Do you have the bonds with you? In your room?"

Jamie could smell the fellow's hair tonic and small clumps of wax speckled his black mustache. Pushing back into his seat, Jamie raised an eyebrow. "Bonds?"

The man nodded. "As I told Mr. Edmunds, it is impossible for me to hold out any longer. These people are not to be trifled with."

Jamie examined the man with more interest than he'd hitherto felt in him. He didn't appear drunk, or mad, but his eyes were luminous with excitement—or was it fear? Jamie stiffened. "I'm afraid I don't have the foggiest idea what you're referring to."

"But Edmunds must have told you." The man's accent was more pronounced now. "Why else would you be here?"

Something in that voice penetrated Jamie's liquor-dulled mind. Whatever trouble this man was in, Jamie wanted no part in it. "I'm afraid you are mistaken." Jamie drained his glass and rose. "Now, if you'll excuse me, it's late, and I have business to see to in the morning."

The stranger leaped to his feet and seized Jamie's elbow. "Stay, sir. I beg you. My very life may depend upon this."

Jamie pulled his arm free. "Get ahold of yourself, man."

"I apologize," the stranger said, straightening. "I'm... I've been under a great deal of strain. I don't wish to be a nuisance, but, as you are Mr. Edmunds's partner, you are the only person who can assist me."

Uncle Manny's partner? A suspicion that this man did not know Manassas at all, but was one of those lunatics the papers were always warning the public against, flickered through Jamie's mind. "Perhaps some other time," he said curtly. "I've been traveling all day and have an early start in the morning. Good night."

The man moved as though to block him, and Jamie found himself drawing reflexively into a boxing stance.

The stranger stepped back, raising his hands, palms outward. "I apologize, sir. It is late and you must be tired from your trip. Please, may I call on you in the morning?"

Jamie's first instinct was to tell the little fellow to go to the devil, but it occurred to him that arranging a future interview might be the easiest way of dispensing with his company. "I will be in the lobby at nine-thirty. If you're there, we can talk then."

"Thank you, sir. Thank you." The mustachioed man bowed low and long.

Jamie shook his head and strode past him. He could feel the man's desperate eyes burning into his back as he walked out of the dining room.

Back in his room, Jamie bolted the door. The fellow made him uneasy. This whole trip made him uneasy. Perhaps he really should forgo the tour and catch the next train home? The idea appealed strongly—at least until he imagined breaking the news to his father. The Captain hadn't been himself lately. He never complained, but he'd seemed tired and listless the past few months. Ill or not, if Jamie left now, his father would be on the next train to Tupper Lake to complete the tour himself.

Jamie sighed. There was no escape.

Making an effort to push the day's strange events from his mind, Jamie scribbled down talking points for the impending tour. When, after forty-five minutes, he'd come up with nothing more than a few pleasantries about a successful nation's dependence on finished lumber, he gave up and went to sleep.

When he awoke the following morning, the immediate effects of last night's irritation and alcohol had subsided. He even began to wonder about the odd little fellow and what, exactly, his connection to Manassas could be.

Dressing with less fastidiousness than usual, Jamie went downstairs, but the mustachioed man was nowhere to be seen. The town had awakened after the rain and was busier and noisier than he'd expected. He had his shoes shined by the bootblack and flirted with the little blonde selling tobacco in the lobby. When the clock read a quarter to ten, Jamie could wait no longer. Feeling foolish, and not a little annoyed, he signaled that he was ready for his carriage and stepped outside.

A noisy crowd was gathering down the street. Something about their placement and the pitch of their voices communicated tragedy. A coldness spread through Jamie's chest as he strode toward the group. When he drew near, a large fellow with the look of a blacksmith shook his head and backed away, leaving a gap through which Jamie saw the body.

Even before Jamie drew close enough to see the unfortunate fellow's face, he knew it was the mustachioed man. He lay on his back, his head turned too far to the right, as though trying to stare into the earth; one tip of his waxed mustache projected obscenely into space. Jamie's stomach lurched, and he forced his eyes away.

"What happened?" he asked a portly man in a leather apron.

"Poor devil was struck down while crossing the street."

"Was his own fault," volunteered a newsboy. "He dashed right out—ran straight under the horses' hooves."

Swallowing back the bile in his throat, Jamie retreated to the waiting cab.

"To the mill," he croaked at the driver.

Jamie turned his head resolutely away as the carriage rolled slowly past the body in the street. It was an accident. A tragic accident. What else could it be?

He shivered as he recounted the stranger's desperate plea, *my very life may depend upon this.* Depend upon *what?* If only he had been a little less tired last night, or just more courteous. This pang of conscience was immediately extinguished by a fresh wave of irritation with Manassas. If the old fellow hadn't run off as he had, none of this would have happened.

This thought unsettled him even more than the others. What had Manassas to do with that strange, tragic little man? The mill was at least forty minutes from town, and, try as he might to focus his mind elsewhere, it was this thought that most occupied him as the miles rolled by.

When the hack at last rolled through Conifer Lumber Mill's arched gateway, Jamie's nerves were still prickly and bilious, though he had regained a semblance of composure. The manager, foreman, and several assistants met his carriage in the yard. They puffed out their chests and spoke in loud voices while Jamie feigned interest.

After an hour or so, he was shut into a little room with Mr. Collins, the bookkeeper, to sign off on the accounts. This was typically Manassas's job, and it was all Jamie could do to pay attention as Collins talked in a steady drone and leafed through books filled with interminable rows of numbers.

Jamie was idly skimming the columns in one of the books Collins had set before him, trying to look like he knew what he was about, when one of the entries caught his eye. It was a large deposit made under a name he didn't recognize. He flipped through several pages and found another. The entries were both sizable and marked as payments from one Rodrigo Vincente Alvarez. While ignorant of the minutia of his family's business, Jamie had been dragged to so many board meetings, conventions, and business dinners that the names of the large accounts were at least familiar to him. This one, however, he had never heard before. It was probably a coincidence. And yet, it made Jamie think of the dead South American whose name he hadn't bothered to ask. Jamie gestured to Collins, who was standing alongside him, bemoaning the deleterious effects of the Sherman Act, and pointed at the entry. "What's this?"

The bookkeeper straightened his wire spectacles and stepped in closer. "Let me see, entry three-hundred-and-seventy-two. That's the Alvarez Account."

"What is the Alvarez account?"

Collins blinked and his jaw slackened. "I couldn't rightly say, sir. It's not one of my accounts. You'd have to ask Mr. Edmunds, he's the one who handles those payments."

"Personally?"

"Yes, sir."

Jamie picked up a small, spiral bound notepad and copied the transfer into it, then he tore the sheet out, folded it carefully, and placed it in his shirt pocket. He didn't know what he would do with this information—probably nothing—but some quirk in his nature insisted that the least he could do for the poor, dead gentleman was write it down.

VISITING MÉMÉ

DECEMBER 24, 1899. SEVEN DAYS BEFORE THE MURDER

"Do hurry, Eliza. We're going to be late." Marie Chevalier stood poised to exit the apartment, her hand firmly gripping the handle of the front door. Her attention, however, was directed toward the bedroom behind her. After waiting impatiently for what seemed an eternity, Marie had been seized with the notion that the act of turning the knob would, through a supernatural process obscure to mortal minds, impress the need for haste upon her sister. It hadn't worked, but having started down this path, she was reluctant to give ground.

When no promising sounds of movement reached her, Marie forced herself to let go of the handle, marched to the bedroom she shared with her sister, and pushed inside. "You do realize Mémé expects us at one."

Eliza, clad in the one serviceable frock she owned, was on her knees rummaging through the clutter under her bed. She glanced up and a lock of wispy dark brown hair fell across her lightly freckled face. "You go on ahead and get our coats. I'll be along in a moment."

Marie narrowed her eyes skeptically.

"I promise. I'll be right down," Eliza mumbled, already half under the bed again.

Leaving the bedroom door open, Marie paused in front of the mirror to adjust her bonnet before heading downstairs to the apartment house's small foyer. She pulled their winter coats from the closet and gave each a thorough brushing before slipping hers on and buttoning it to the chin. Folding Eliza's over her arm, she drifted to the front window to peer as far as she could down the street.

Mr. Griggs, their landlord, was probably stumbling home this very moment. Night watchman for a privately owned stable, it was his habit to stop by a local saloon after finishing his shift to enjoy a little "jollification". Far from a pleasing man at the best of times, drunk, he was unendurable.

Thinking of Griggs increased Marie's impatience. She strode to the stairs, prepared to retrieve her sister bodily if she had to, when a door banged shut overhead and Eliza's distinctive foot-steps sounded in the hall.

"Sorry," Eliza muttered, finally emerging. The holly-green ribbons of her untied bonnet danced around her rosy face as she tromped down the stairs as fast as her leg brace would allow. She took the coat Marie held out to her. "I couldn't find my copy of *Cyrano* anywhere, so I decided to take *Martin Chuzzlewit* instead, but then I couldn't find that either. I was searching for my copy of *Futility* when I spotted *Cyrano* in the sewing basket. So, you see, it all worked out."

Marie shook her head despairingly. "You'll ruin your eyes with all this reading, and then where will you be? Men do not want bookish, bespectacled wives."

Eliza cast her a wry look before thrusting her arm into the coat and swinging the front door open. "If all men are truly such shallow, spiritless creatures, I can't think why any woman would want to marry one. I know I wouldn't."

Marie suppressed a smile. "It's fine and well for you to talk that way now, but give it another five years and you'll—Oh! Confound it!"

The moment they stepped onto the porch, Mr. Griggs's swaggering bulk came into view. Marie seized Eliza's wrist and pulled her in the opposite direction. With any luck, the old reprobate would be so drunk he wouldn't notice.

They made it to the walkway before Griggs called out, "Not so fast, the pair of ya! I'm wantin' a word!"

Marie's stomach lurched, but she pasted a smile on her face and turned to wait. She avoided Griggs whenever possible, but given the rarity of decent rooms at a price her family could pay, incivility was not a luxury she could afford.

Blunt-featured and red-faced, Mr. Griggs's bulbous nose and bloodshot eyes announced him as a man who liked his drink even before he drew close enough to catch the scent of horse manure and ale peculiar to him.

"Mr. Griggs, how pleasant to meet you like this, but I'm afraid we cannot stop. Eliza and I are on our way to dine with Grandmother on *Chestnut Hill*." Marie emphasized the last two words, hoping the reference to their affluent connections would encourage him to exercise a little forbearance.

"I don't care if yous were on yer way to Hades to sup with the devil himself, I'm wantin' a word!' Griggs wagged a filthy finger in her face. His nail was a dark line, as though it had been drawn on in India ink. "Where's that good-fer-nothin' father of yours gotten himself off to, huh?"

"Father?" Marie echoed, her throat tight. "I believe he's out looking for work."

"Work?" Griggs spat. "That no account's never done a day's work in his life. And now he's a week behind in the rent."

Marie managed a stiff smile, but the insult stung—all the more because it was true. "He settled our account with your good wife earlier today."

Settled their account, indeed. She and Eliza had spent the whole of the morning on their hands and knees scrubbing the old woman's kitchen from top to bottom with a detergent so caustic Marie's fingers had blisters. And while they had been toiling over the landlord's old wood-fired stove, Mrs. Griggs had been in the back room with Father, hooting and laughing obscenely.

Griggs waved her words away as he might shoo a horsefly. "It best be like ya say, 'cause I ain't gonna stand fer no more of yer father's empty promises. So, he's gonna get rich investing in that South America prospect, is he? Fie! Tell him to save his fairy stories for them that's daft enough to believe 'em."

Marie examined the seam of her glove while he spoke. The wool had begun to pull apart near her thumb—close to where she had mended it last time. His words could only hurt her if she let them, and she was determined not to give him that sort of power.

"Putting on fancy airs, struttin' about like a peacock. Hell," Griggs continued. "It's plain to anyone with eyes that muck-snipe's got all the breedin' of an alley cat—and half the scruples. Mark my words, Missy, if that puffed up do-nothin' falls behind just once more, it'll be the boot fer the lot of ya."

Marie looked up, and in as calm a voice as she could manage, said, "I'm sure it won't come to that. Now, if there's nothing more we can do for you, we really must be off. Good afternoon, Mr. Griggs, and Merry Christmas."

Without waiting for a response, Marie rejoined her sister, who'd wandered a little way down the lane.

"Rent?" Eliza asked, her expression knowing.

Marie gave a quick nod.

"You can always tell when Papa has been going to the fights. He has the worst luck." Eliza sighed, then added, "We'll have to hurry if we don't want to be late."

Marie gave another nod, too angry to speak. How she hated

drunkards! Times like this, she was in perfect sympathy with those imperious temperance folk who stood on street corners handing out broadsheets and singing old-fashioned hymns. It would serve Papa right if she joined the local league and plastered the house from floor to ceiling with leaflets and hand-scrawled psalms. She'd do it too, if she thought it would do him one ounce of good.

Eliza opened her book the moment they found seats on the trolley, leaving Marie with her thoughts. The muddy roads, crowded with last-minute shoppers and merrymakers, gave way to long tree-lined avenues and parks. Cheerful scarlet and emerald ribbons appeared on gaslight posts and the voices of carolers lilted on the winter air. Never having possessed the ability to maintain her anger, be it ever so just, Marie's mood improved with her surroundings. By the time they neared Chestnut Hill, she felt sufficiently recovered to smile at passers-by and hum a few bars of "It Came Upon the Midnight Clear".

The streets on Chestnut Hill were lined with ancient trees. Their outstretched branches, now clad in freshly fallen snow, created a delicate crystalline canopy over the lane. Marie pulled the cord for their stop, and they walked the remaining distance to the house. Before making their way up the cobbled path, Marie stopped Eliza and inspected her. At fourteen, her sister was seven years her junior. A childhood bout of polio had left her right leg weak and underdeveloped. The metal braces the doctor fitted her with were burdensome, and the leather straps rubbed her skin raw, but Eliza never complained and had learned to get around as well as anyone. Since their mother's death, eight years ago, Marie had done her best to care for her.

Marie fixed the collar of her sister's coat, flashed her a reassuring smile, and led the way to the servants' entrance. The Lett mansion was magnificent, easily the finest in the neighborhood, at least in Marie's estimation. Through gaps in the heavy blue velvet curtains, she caught glimpses of modish furniture and elegant gilt-framed paintings. A familiar pang of longing tugged at her heart, and she consoled herself by vowing that one day she too would be surrounded by beautiful things.

At the rear door, Marie knocked twice and waited. When no one answered, she opened the door and ushered her sister inside. "Mémé must be downstairs."

The Letts spent most of the year in New York City. While the family was away, the house was staffed only by a butler and their grandmother, the housekeeper—both of whom were hard of hearing.

Marie and Eliza removed their coats and tramped through a small storage room that skirted the kitchen, then down a long corridor that, when followed to its termination, led to the dining hall, but they weren't going that far. Marie paused briefly before passing through a narrow door covered in emerald green baize. She had never seen another like it, but Mémé assured her that all the best homes had one: a clear separation between the *upstairs* and the *downstairs*, the borderline between the masters' world and the servants'.

Mémé sat before the fire in the servants' hall: a large, open room with whitewashed walls and a cedar floor. The air was thick with the pleasing aroma of sweet spices and roast turkey.

Marie smiled and called out, "Merry Christmas, Mémé."

Their grandmother looked up from her knitting. "*Vous êtes en retard.* You're late."

Eliza stepped forward. "Terribly sorry, Mémé! Papa fell behind on the rent again, and that awful Mr. Griggs stopped us as we were leaving. The man's a dreadful swine and an awful bore." Eliza paused, her heart-shaped face breaking into a broad grin. "I'm not sure which is worse."

Grand-mère Alozia stood. She was a short woman whose regal carriage made her seem several inches taller than she was. People said Marie took after her, which was a rare compliment indeed. In her prime, Mémé had been one of the great beauties of New Orleans: a copper-complexioned Creole woman with sea-green eyes and wild, curling raven hair.

Mémé's father had been a prosperous merchant, and, according to John, Marie's father, Mémé had once had her choice of husbands. John also never failed to add that their family's current, deteriorated situation was due to Mémé Alozia's failure to choose wisely.

John meant this as a cautionary tale, no doubt, but it had invested her grandmother, who was in all other respects the most punctilious woman Marie knew, with a hint of the dangerous, of the romantic.

After exchanging more pleasantries, Mémé ushered the girls to the already set table. "It's just us this year, I'm afraid. Mr. Candler's sister married last May, and she invited him to her house for the holidays."

"Oh? Good for her," Marie said, genuinely surprised. Even allowing for an age gap of ten years or more between the siblings, the bride must have been ancient.

"Has my son found employment yet?" Mémé asked once everyone's plate was full.

"No, but he says —," Marie began.

"He says!" Mémé cut her off. "*Sa bouche n'a pas de dimanche.* The man's mouth never takes a day of rest. What does he *do*?"

"Nothing," Eliza answered quickly. "Unless you count going to saloons with Charlie and William."

Mémé looked up sharply. "Not William Jones?"

"The same," Eliza confirmed.

Mémé's lips thinned and two spots of color appeared on her cheeks. "When I think of all the trouble Mr. Lett went to, getting our Charlie hired on at the attorney Duncombe's, and what that dreadful friend of his did. Ah! The shame of it." She shook her head, as though physically clearing the thought from her mind. "Never mind. *Ce qui est bien fait, n'est jamais mal fait.* What's done with good intentions can never be wrong. We must remember that—even if the boy is an ingrate."

Marie murmured what she hoped would pass for disinterested agreement. She didn't like to hear people speak ill of William, however he might deserve it.

"What your brother, Charlie, needs is a man about, someone he can look up to, but all he has is your father." Grand-mère shook her head in disgust. "How a son of your grandpapa's could turn out like him, I'll never know. Born tired, he was—just plain lazy. Your Grand-père Jean, on the other hand, was selling artificial feathers out of a suitcase when he was just ten years old, and by the time the good Lord took him, he owned an entire factory down by the river."

"It's too bad Grandpapa didn't live longer," Eliza contributed. "Perhaps Papa would have turned out better."

Mémé stiffened, and Marie broke in, "Isn't this stuffing delicious, Lizzy? What's in it?"

There were many details Marie didn't know, but she'd overheard enough arguments between Mémé and Papa to understand that Eliza's words had struck a nerve. Grand-père had died when her father was still an infant. Mr. Tompkins, Mémé's second husband, had never taken to his stepson. Worse still, he had indulged his taste for gambling and squandered the bulk of the generous inheritance left by his predecessor. Mémé's family, embarrassed by the connection, had severed communication and left Mémé to her own devices.

Papa received a fair education and a small annuity, as that had been set aside for him when he was still in the cradle, but that was all. He grew into a wild youth, becoming, in many respects, evermore like the stepfather he loathed. Tompkins died when Papa was sixteen, but the damage had been done.

With the family's small fortune all but spent, Mémé had been grateful to find a respectable post as a housekeeper, a position she'd held all the years Marie had been alive. Papa, however, had never adjusted to his family's change in station. He spoke—and spent—as though their poverty was a temporary inconvenience.

Mémé Alozia explained the intricacies of stuffing made in the Creole style, after which the conversation stayed more-or-less on track. After dessert, they sat around the fire and chatted until the clock on the mantel chimed four. When the girls rose to take their leave, Mémé Alozia followed them into the hall and withdrew two neatly wrapped packages from the cupboard, pressing one into each of the girl's hands.

"Best open these here," she said.

Eliza's package held a leather-bound book of verse, Marie's a lovely tortoise comb.

"It's beautiful," Marie gasped, throwing her arms around her grandmother's neck. "Thank you, Mémé."

"Don't let your father know about these," Mémé said as Eliza hugged her too. "He'll pawn them, sure as you're born."

Both girls promised, more Merry-Christmases were exchanged, and they started for home. The day had been warm, and the half-melted snow shone brilliantly, reflecting the last rosy-gold rays of sunlight. Marie always liked this time of day. The fading light obscured much of what was unattractive in the world, reducing it to interestingly shaped shadows on a painted sky. A breath of fog appeared in the street. It suspended in the air just above the ground, fingering the bottoms of the shop windows and blushing pink in the gloaming. It reminded Marie of fairy stories she had heard as a girl, of magical kingdoms, ogres, and princesses.

By the time they reached the front door of the Griggs's house, the fairytale had evaporated. Even in winter, the smell of urine and old garbage hung in the air. In the foyer, they shrugged out of their coats and were halfway up the stairs when a hoot of coarse laughter reverberated through the corridor. It came from the Griggs's. When she strained her ears, Marie could just distinguish the rumble of her father's voice.

Eliza nudged her. "It sounds like Papa made peace with Mr. Griggs."

"That's a blessing, at any rate."

The windows had been closed all day, and the acrid smell of stale tobacco mingled unpleasantly with the sharp scent of detergent. Marie fumbled on the table for the matches and lit a small lamp. Eliza lit a candle from it, gave Marie a quick hug, then retreated to bed to read.

Listless, Marie put on the kettle and looked around the dreary room. She had hung some old stockings over the fire, and tonight she would slip a few small gifts into each one: a new thimble and two yards of yellow ribbon for Eliza, some tobacco for Charlie, and a new clay pipe for Papa. It wasn't much, but it was the best she could do. The cheerless sight of the cramped room and the bedraggled stockings in front of the hearth filled her with despair. It was a far cry from the tasteful simplicity of even the servants' hall in the house on Chestnut Hill.

Marie took her mother's old wedding ring quilt from her bed and wrapped it around her shoulders before settling into the window-seat. Her lamp threw a golden reflection on the windowpane, obscuring her view, so she blew it out. The sun had almost set, and the world outside was turning an inky blue.

She pressed her forehead against the cold glass, allowing her mind to wander. The walls were thin, and muffled barks of laughter reached her from the Griggs's rooms below. They must be quite drunk by now. She wondered if Charlie was down there. She listened but couldn't detect his voice. Maybe he was out—with William. She stared into the night, trying to imagine them in it.

The fog was thick in the street now, but she could still make out figures huddled around a gas street lamp. Its flame cast an unnaturally bright glow on their faces. Even at a distance, she recognized them as painted ladies, who, in defiance of the fog and cold, were plying their trade. As she watched, one of them glanced up at the window. For an instant, their gazes met, and, through the distance and the fog, Marie thought she saw the woman's carmined lips twist into a mocking smile.

Marie turned away. Her hands balled into fists, and her fingernails dug into the flesh of her palms. She had to get out of here. She had to.

CAST OUT

DECEMBER 24, 1899. SEVEN DAYS BEFORE THE MURDER

illiam Jones sat across from his friend, Charles Chevalier, at their usual table at Morris's Saloon. The holiday and the early hour kept most of the regulars away, and the always dark room was unusually quiet. The silence made William fidgety, not because he preferred a rowdy atmosphere, but because the emptiness was a constant reminder that other men had somewhere better to be.

He swallowed the rest of the gin in his glass and winced. Some said the liquor here was cut with sulphuric acid, turpentine, and lime oil. It certainly tasted vile. The contents of his cup scorched a path from his lips clear down to his intestines, but it was damn effective. A sign above the bar read "Drunk for a penny, Dead drunk for two".

Tonight, William thought reaching for the bottle, was a two-penny night.

"Wish I could help you, Liam, I really do, but frankly, I could stand that sort of help myself just now." Charlie spoke in that good-humored way peculiar to men who have never been troubled by any problems but their own. "How far behind are you?"

"Five weeks."

Charlie let out his breath in a low whistle.

William shrugged, past embarrassment. His eyes followed a shaft of light that streamed through the saloon's smoky interior. Its source was a small window the shape of a porthole.

"Surely she wouldn't put you out on Christmas Eve," Charlie contributed, the liquor making him speak in exaggerated tones.

William smirked. "I wouldn't bet on that."

Charlie slammed his palm against the table. "Well, that's a fine example of Christian charity for you!"

The noise resounded through the empty room and Otto, the red-bearded barkeep, stopped wiping glasses to shoot them a look of warning.

"What about your little friend?" Charlie screwed up his face in thought. "Cathy or Caroline, whatever her name is, can't she help?"

"Charlotte," William corrected. "She's been out on the Tenderloin every night, but with the weather being what it is, there's no business to be had."

"It's a damn shame." Charlie shook his head. "If only we had a hundred dollars—no, fifty—we could solve all our problems. That South America speculation is a sure thing. John and I are going 'round to see Mémé tomorrow. The old girl is loaded, but wonderful tight-fisted."

William sighed. John was Charlie's father, and Charlie had been going on about his rich grandmother since they were boys. William had even met the old woman once or twice; she was a proud, sanctimonious sort, very much of his own father's ilk.

William picked up his glass but paused before drinking when the burning in his stomach intensified. When was the last time he'd eaten? He couldn't remember. He drained the glass anyway, then rose, somewhat unsteadily. "I'd better be off. Charlotte will be wondering what became of me."

Charlie rose too, pushing heavily off of the table. "I need to be moving along myself. Marie asked me to be home early tonight."

William winced.

Charlie looked at him puzzled, then, realizing his mistake, mumbled a quick, "Sorry."

In the year since Marie had broken off with him, this was the first time Charlie had mentioned his sister's name.

William shrugged.

"See you tomorrow?" Charlie asked as he secured his muffler. The question wasn't really a question, and Charlie lumbered off without waiting for a reply.

William used the facilities, wished Otto a merry Christmas, and stepped outside. The icy brightness of the world temporarily blinded him. His coat, which had once been tailored to his form, hung loose on his lean body, allowing the cold to snake around his ribs and squeeze him like a vise.

Hugging himself to keep out the wind, William fixed his gaze a foot or two ahead and plodded home. By the time he reached his building on East Indiana Avenue, his feet were numb and his eyelashes froze together with every blink. He turned the handle slowly and eased the door open.

"Might as well come in. I know it's you, *Mr. Diaz.*" Mrs. Murch's voice had an accusatory ring to it.

A dull pain radiated through William's chest as he opened the door the rest of the way. His landlady, a middle-aged widow, sat perched on a stool in front of the stairs.

"It wasn't enough for you to cheat me, to play on my feelings, you had to humiliate me as well?" Mrs. Murch rose to her feet, her watery blue eyes searching his. "I went all the way to the bank with that note you gave me, and the cashier near laughed in my face."

"The check didn't clear?" William tried to sound surprised, but a profound apathy had settled over him, draining the emotion from his words.

She shook her head aggrievedly.

Her pale, blunt-featured face wore an expression that spoke more of hurt than anger, and a pinpoint of hope flickered in William's chest. "My dear Mrs. Murch—Moira, I was just coming to talk to you." William's throat was raw from the gin and the cold, and he coughed to clear it. "This business with the check, it's a terrible misunderstanding. Has to be. You can't believe I'd try to cheat you?"

"Stop." She held up a plump, white hand. "I haven't called the law—not yet. I would rather spare myself *that* humiliation. But if you and your wife haven't cleared out by tomorrow morning, I will. I swear it."

Her eyes met his, and he was reminded of the looks his mother had given him when he'd lied as a child. Not angry. Not even surprised. Just … disappointed.

"Moira," he tried again, reaching for her, but she turned and walked away.

"Wait, please." William stumbled after her. "Hear me out."

Mrs. Murch walked briskly into her apartment and closed the door.

For a long moment, William stood staring at the chipped paint around the frame and hinges, his mind empty. When at last he mounted the stairs, he felt like a man twice his age. His lungs burned from the cold, and there was a dull ache in the pit of his stomach.

The door to his and Charlotte's room was unlatched, and he shoved it open. The fading rays of the winter sun filtered through the small window and cast the room in shadowy relief. Charlotte stood by the bed, stuffing clothes into a flour sack. She was twenty-one, but so slight she could have passed for a girl of fifteen. Her hair was a nondescript brown that, when loose, hung in lank waves. She was fair but freckled, and her brows were so fine, they appeared to have been penciled on.

Only her eyes were remarkable; they were unexpectedly large and dark, a rich, emotive shade of brown.

"You've seen her?" Charlotte's voice was soft and slightly husky from crying.

William nodded and hung his coat over the back of one of the room's two rickety chairs. He moved the other chair nearer the fire and sat. The small pile of coals burning on the black iron grate caught his gaze and held it. "You'll have to pawn my coat. Get us a room anywhere you can."

Charlotte, who had moved to put the kettle on the fire, stopped to look at him, her expression uncertain. "Without your coat, you won't be able to go out."

"You think I don't realize that?" A spark of anger ignited inside of him and, just as quickly, fizzled out. "There's nothing else left. Hurry, it's getting late."

He rotated his hands in front of the warm grate, disinterestedly observing the blue veins that traversed their sinewy length. He glanced over at Charlotte, who continued to stare at him, the tea kettle frozen in her hand. She presented such a complete portrait of anxious indecision that, some other day, he might have pitied her. As it was, he turned his eyes back to the fire and said coldly, "Don't just stand there. Pawn the damn thing, and let's be done with it."

❧

*L*ong after Charlotte left with the coat, William remained staring into the orange coals, marshaling his thoughts from one source of grief to the next without analyzing any of them too closely. He was hungry and could not afford food, tired but could not sleep, and the last of the coal flickered and waned in the grate. The various wants and lacks within him grasped impotently into a nothingness so vast that even the enormity of his misery seemed insignificant within it.

He rubbed his jaw and tried to focus his thoughts. Now that he was housebound, he'd have to write to Charlie, let him know his new address just as soon as he had one. It was, after all, possible Charlie's grandmother would relent.

He considered dropping the letter by Charlie's place personally and cringed. He'd sooner starve in the gutter than let Marie see him like this.

Marie. For months after things ended between them, he had lived amidst the corpses of his dreams, tainting every memory he had of her with bitterness and regret. A thousand times, he had struck her from his mind, and a thousand times she had returned. He loathed his weakness even while he relished the completeness of the emotion she stirred: to be hurt, to be angry, to be anything other than hopeless and numb. And so, he allowed his mind to wander, and with ghostlike ease she passed through all the barriers he had constructed against her, and he felt himself gradually transported from his small, darkening room to a summer morning some three years ago when he first discovered what it was to love.

He'd always known Charlie, and, knowing Charlie, had known his sisters. He could not say what had been different about that day. He'd gone to get Charlie and found him sitting down for breakfast. Not being in a particular hurry, William joined him. While handing him a cup of tea, Marie smiled shyly down at him, and her eyes, which were a piercing green, had reached into him with such penetration it made his breath catch. Nothing more passed between them that day, but something new and powerful had ignited inside of him.

For years, Marie had existed in the periphery—a person whose entry into the room at the wrong moment spoiled a good joke, and who fussed and frowned when he had mud on his boots. But from that day forward, he would make any excuse to go by Charlie's just to catch a glimpse of her. All day, his thoughts drifted to her, until even his friends complained that he'd become dull and forgetful. And at night, he'd lay awake, his chest aching as he remembered the way she had smiled when she opened the door, the sun on her face through the parlor window, and her laugh—her glorious laugh—full-throated and unrestrained.

Late that summer, when the world was all sunlight and flowers, he offered to help tidy up after dinner. Charlie, who had an antipathy for housework, made himself scarce. Marie washed and he dried the dishes, while Eliza put them away. The day was hot and the kitchen stifling. When they finished, Eliza sat down to read. Marie smiled shyly at him and said, "I think I'll go outside for some air."

It might have been his imagination, but he thought, or rather hoped, there was a pointed intensity in the glance she cast his way. He followed her outside.

The full moon threw a softening light into the alley. Heat radiated from the bricks, but a breeze blew between the buildings, fluttering the curtains in the open windows and cooling their overheated skin. They stood without speaking, listening to the clattering of the horse's hooves in the street, neighborhood children playing on the front stairs, and the cries of the newspaper boys and hawkers making their evening rounds.

Marie leaned against the whitewashed brick, her head tilted skyward. Strands of her dark hair caught in the breeze and danced across her face, which shone like marble in the moonlight.

"Isn't it beautiful?" Marie said, staring at the little patch of stars above them.

He kept his eyes locked on her. "Very."

Marie's gaze dipped to meet his, and she smiled self-consciously. This smile galvanized him, and only half-aware of what he was doing, he closed the distance between them and kissed her. All these years later, he still wondered where he'd found the courage.

As they kissed, the world narrowed until it consisted only of that alley, the softness of her mouth, and the warmth of her body.

"I love you," he'd murmured, his mouth now pressed to her cheek. The words surprised him, all the more so because they were true.

She'd smiled then, and whispered, "And I love you."

Thus began his life's great romance. It was never an easy pairing. One moment, Marie was all soft supplication, the next she could be as haughty as a debutante or as shrewish as a fishwife. It drove him mad, but it was a delightful kind of madness.

He had maintained his habit of visiting the girls on Eleventh Street but grew increasingly disenchanted with their charms. He wanted Marie more than he'd ever wanted anyone, but she made it clear that nothing short of marriage could win her.

For months, he'd debated the subject with himself. The match, if not unequal, was certainly not advantageous. He was fond enough of Charlie, but Marie's father, John Chevalier, would be an anchor around any man's throat. Too proud to work for a living, and too fond of drink and gambling to subsist on the income he had.

In the end, William came out as he always knew he must. He loved the girl—senselessly, entirely—and there was no reasoning his way out of that.

Looking back, he had to admit that the moment he chose for his proposal was not the most romantic. Months earlier, their grandmother had gotten Charlie a job clerking at Duncombe's law firm, and Charlie had arranged to have William hired on as well. Things had gone swimmingly, until the business with the forgeries.

William's supervisor, a senior clerk, noticed a client statement containing a list of high-value transactions that had never occurred and letters of reference that had not been ordered or approved by the companies in whose name they were issued.

There was an effort made to trace these documents, but it led nowhere. It was, however, noted that they had all crossed either William's or Charlie's desk. William was fired at once, and Charlie was let go a week later.

Finding another job had proven to be more of a nuisance than William had anticipated, but it wasn't until he heard the police were looking for him that he became truly afraid. Assuming his mother's maiden name, Diaz, he'd decided the only sensible course of action was to keep his head down and wait the trouble out.

One night during this period, he and Charlie stayed out until morning letting off steam. Marie was still scowling her disapproval at him the following afternoon when, all at once, he made up his mind to propose. For months afterward, he asked himself why he'd chosen that moment, and there was no satisfactory answer. He remembered having some idea that it would stop her being angry. He thought too that the Duncombe affair had them living under a cloud, and it would be pleasant to have something to look forward to.

Whatever his reasoning, once the idea took hold, he was determined to have the thing done. He took her limp hand into his, and said with real tenderness, "You think me in need of reform, and you're right. I suppose we will have to marry, so you can make an honest man of me."

Marie's eyes widened, then narrowed as the color rose in her cheeks. "Not if you were the last man alive."

Her response was too strange to credit. He studied her face and decided she must think he was teasing. Smiling, he stepped closer to her. "You think me beyond redemption then? In all seriousness though, I love you, and I want to marry you."

She turned to face him fully, her eyes flashing fire. "I wonder how you dare!"

He stepped away, too surprised to be angry. "Have you run mad?"

"I must be mad to love you," she said. Her voice was low, but her eyes were half-wild. "After what you did at Duncombe's, and how you've behaved since."

For a breath, he went numb and could hardly move. He waited for her to laugh, cry, do something, anything, that would let him know it was all a joke or a horrible misunderstanding. When she continued to glare at him, rage and shame flared inside of him. "Be sure you mean what you say, woman. You'll not get another chance."

She had locked eyes with him then and intoned distinctly, "Never have I been more certain of anything."

His stomach had lurched, and he'd wanted to shake her, to break the horrible spell she was under, but he didn't dare. If he'd set hands on her at that moment, he could have killed her. So, instead, he turned and fled.

The next few weeks passed in a haze of half-conscious expectation as he waited in his increasingly claustrophobic room for word. When the initial sting of her rejection dulled, he began to miss her. He sent her a carefully worded letter expressing his willingness to overlook their quarrel and move forward.

There was no response.

Her silence was crueler than any hate-filled words she could have penned. He sent another letter, less carefully worded, that expressed his love and need for her. What followed was a void, a black emptiness more terrible than anything he'd known.

Swallowing what little remained of his pride, he turned up at her door, prepared to throw himself at her feet if necessary. Her sister answered and told him that Marie did not wish to see him again. *Ever.* Before he could get his mind around what was being said, much less form a response, the girl slammed the door and bolted it. The click of the bolt exploded through William like a shot. It carried with it a grave insult, a wordless accusation, as though he were a mad dog or other loathsome beast.

Being treated like an animal, he began to feel like one. He pounded the door, rattling it on its hinges. Vacillating between fury and desperation, he called out Marie's name again and again. A curtain in the upstairs window jerked closed, and he knew instinctively that the hand moving it was hers. Never in his life, not even after his father's most vehement sermons, had he felt so small. He pulled himself together as best he could and slunk home.

Weeks and then months passed in a haze. Sometimes he missed her so much he felt he would die of it, but then he remembered the tug at the curtain and the coldness of the heart that had moved it. When he conjured up the image of Marie's face, he began to detect an arrogance, a cruelty in it, he had never noticed before.

That well-known apparition appeared to him again now, her sharp green eyes glaring hatred at him. The image was so vivid that he felt a momentary unsteadiness, a recoiling inside of himself. This pang was consumed by a wave of anger so intense it made his head pound and left his limbs weak and weightless.

He grabbed the poker and prodded the dying coals. His careless ministrations sent sprays of bright orange sparks into the now dark room where they glowed on the wooden floor before fading to ash. He no longer cared if Charlie knew he was moving. As far as he was concerned, the entire Chevalier family could go to the devil.

He might be down now, but it would not always be so. He didn't care how long it took, or what he had to do to achieve it, one day, Marie would regret what she had done to him.

GADSBUDLIKINS

CHRISTMAS DAY. SIX DAYS BEFORE THE MURDER.

"*S*tingy old bag!"

Charles Chevalier winced as his father, John Chevalier, shouted the insult at the freshly bolted door of number eleven Chestnut Hill. Charlie withdrew further into his hiding place behind the oak tree in front of the house as John rounded, hurling a bouquet of hothouse flowers into a nearby snowbank and strode down the cobbled path toward the road.

When Charlie was sure no one inside the house was watching, he jogged after his father.

"Gadsbudlikins!" John shouted, barely sparing Charlie a glance. "Who does that stuffed-up prig think he is? A butler—what sort of job is that for a grown man?"

Charlie dropped a half pace back, long experience having taught him it was best not to be too handy when John's blood was up.

"And my mother! That woman wouldn't part with a fiver if it was all that stood between me and the hereafter. But on Christmas—Christmas!—you'd think she'd at least come to the door."

"Watch where you're going!" John yelled at a short, spectacled man ahead of them on the walk. The little fellow scrambled over a snowbank and into the street to avoid being knocked over. The stranger opened his mouth to protest, but, getting a better look at John, changed his mind.

Charlie smiled. His father might dress like a dandy, but he had the bulk and strength of a dockhand.

"Oh, I knew I'd have to sit through her glowering at me while I suffered through her self-righteous preaching." John continued. "But, no, she couldn't even manage that. I show up, hat in hand, ready to pay my respects to my mother on this most Christian of holidays, and what happens? That mutton-monger of a butler tells me that, in light of my *disgraceful conduct,* she's not at home to me. Not at home to me! On Christmas! And then—" John pounded his fist into his palm for emphasis. "He slams the door in my face. What I'd give for just five minutes alone with that meater! He'd rue the day he ever set eyes on old John Chevalier."

Charlie said nothing, as no response was expected, but mentally he congratulated himself on convincing John to go it alone. They'd planned to arrive together, but, on the walk here, it had occurred to Charlie that if Mémé had her nose out of joint with his father, as she often did, it would ruin both their chances. Divided, they would get two bites at the apple instead of one.

A stiff wind blew between the brownstones on German-town, hurling little flecks of ice and snow into Charlie's eyes. He pulled his coat tight and sunk his chin into his navy muffler. When he spoke, his words were half lost in the wool and the wind. "I told Liam we were trying for the money today. We should let him know how we came out."

"What's that?" John asked, his face red with anger.

"We should let Liam know how we came out."

John grunted.

Charlie tried again. "He's moved to new rooms. He sent over the address last night."

"Do what you must," John grumbled. "I'm off to Morris's. I want to see if there's any news on the war in Colombia. General Herrera's on the move."

They parted company a few blocks later. Once alone, Charlie noticed how empty the streets were. It made him uneasy until he remembered it was Christmas, then it made him angry.

Everyone knew Mémé had held on to a sizable portion of her first husband's estate. She had also been living rent-free, saving up her pay, for the better part of two decades. Meanwhile, her only son and grandchildren were forced to live on the brink of poverty. John was right, she was a stingy old bag.

Mitre was the filthiest street in a lousy neighborhood. Muck and garbage lay strewn across the yards, half-frozen. The whole block gave off an odor: a combination of coal smoke, sauerkraut, and an overused outhouse. It was faint now, but come summer, the place would stink to high heaven. Charlie wrinkled his nose. He'd lived on the ragged edge of poverty his entire life, but nothing like this. Things must be bad if William was forced to put up here.

Charlie located number thirty-five and knocked firmly. The door, which was covered in peeling black paint, was opened by a woman with wispy blonde hair wearing a stained blue house robe. In her right arm, she clutched a wailing infant.

"Hello, Mrs...." Charlie paused, waiting for the woman to introduce herself.

"The name's Stapleton. Who're you here for?" She shifted her whelp onto the other shoulder.

"Mrs. Stapleton," Charlie continued. "I'm looking for my friend." He hesitated a fraction of a second, remembering the name William was going by. "Mr. William Diaz. Is he lodging with you?"

She turned and hollered, "Diaz! Visitor!"

Mrs. Stapleton returned the baby, who was crying louder now, to the shoulder it had started off on and swung the door wide.

Charlie stepped past her and blinked. The room was dark. He could just make out wood floors, gray and mottled with dirt. Ahead to the right was an ancient stairway. The banister had broken clean away toward the bottom, so that it terminated in a sinister cluster of feathery spikes.

A shadow moved at the top of the stairs. At first, Charlie thought it must be one of Mrs. Stapleton's brats—judging from the ruckus coming from the open door to his left, she must have quite a brood—but when the figure raised its hand in a gesture of familiar greeting, he guessed it was Charlotte.

Charlie climbed to the second landing. He smiled down at the waifish figure and said, "Merry Christmas."

The girl mumbled something incoherent, and scurried down the hall. Frowning, he followed her into a musty room. The only light came from two meager lamps. On the far wall, a glassless window had been boarded up to keep the weather out.

"Merry Christmas!" Charlie tried again.

"Charlie. Have a seat." William, who was reclining on a straw mattress, kicked at a nearby stool. "You'll have to forgive this rat hole. It was the best Charlotte could find on Christmas Eve."

Charlie perched on the edge of the stool. "I've been in worse."

William gave a small laugh.

"Tea?" Charlotte asked.

"If it isn't a bother," Charlie answered.

Charlotte retreated to a small table in the corner.

Nothing had ever been said, but Charlie knew Charlotte didn't like him. The sentiment was more than mutual. On the surface, the girl was as timid as a mouse, with a blushing disposition better suited to a novitiate at a nunnery than a prostitute.

But there was something about that contradiction, and the girl's absurd fragility, that felt wrong to Charlie—performative. Like the stage girls who play the innocent-maiden at the two o'clock then run riot at sundown. Still, she wasn't *his* girl, and William had so many, it didn't much matter.

Charlotte put the kettle over the fire. While they were waiting for it to boil, Charlie tried to dispel the tension by making a few casual remarks on the beastliness of the weather and the even fouler temperament of landlords. The room was dim, in spite of the lamps, and the stink of cheap kerosene was already giving him a headache. He would stay fifteen minutes, just to be polite, then deliver his news and leave.

The unreliable light deepened the shadows under William's eyes and mouth. He hadn't been this sickly yesterday, had he? Laying on the bed, with his lips pale and parched, and his undershirt hanging off of him in limp folds, he looked like a lunger.

Charlotte handed William a mug, then gave one to Charlie. When the tea touched Charlie's tongue, his throat seized. The leaves must have been used a dozen times, and the brew tasted like warm mildew. He forced himself to swallow and concentrated on the warmth of the mug in his hands.

William sipped his without even seeming to notice. A pity so profound it was almost disgust gripped Charlie. "Dammit," he said. He'd spilled some of the tea on his best pair of trousers. When he fished his handkerchief from his pocket, he felt the two silver dollars Marie had given him earlier in the evening. She'd made him promise to pay the grocer, but he had a better use for the money now. "How about we all head over to Morris's, my treat? John's there already, and we can make an evening of it."

"That's good of you, Charlie, but you see how it is with me." William gestured to the room. "I pawned my only coat to get the money for this place."

Charlie's spirits, which had risen at the thought of escape, crashed back down. "Have you tried writing to your father?"

William's expression hardened.

"I only suggest it 'cause I saw his book of sermons in the window of that bookshop on Mulberry. Looked like they were selling."

"They always sell. You'd be surprised how much people will pay to read about how their employer, their neighbor, their friend will suffer in the hereafter. And no one is better at conjuring hellfire than dear old Dad." William stared at a spot on the far wall, a wry smile twisting his face. "By now, the old bastard must be richer than Croesus, for all the good it does me."

Charlie nodded because it was the polite thing to do, but on this point, at least, he and William would never agree. He had never understood his friend's tendency to wallow in life's disappointments. What was the use of having rich relations if you didn't ask them for money? Sure, they might say "no" four, five, even a dozen times, but if you kept at it, sooner or later, they'd give you something—if only to get rid of you.

"Remember at school," William went on, his gaze still fixed in the distance. "I was the only boy who started every year with holes in his shoes. In the winter, my feet froze, and by the time summer rolled around, my toes were so pinched I could hardly walk."

"Maybe you can try your mother, or your sister?" Charlie said hopefully.

"I must have written them a dozen letters last year, told them I was nigh on dying...nothing." William shrugged. "Like as not, the good reverend is monitoring the post box."

Charlie bit back his disappointment. He couldn't leave now, not after he'd as good as told them that he had both time and money. This is what he got for trying to help. He stretched his legs, which had started to cramp in the cold. The stool underneath him wobbled and he leaped to his feet. Standing now at the foot of the bed, he was going to say something smart to cover his embarrassment, when he realized they hadn't even noticed. William lay on the bed, lost in thought. Charlotte sat on a small chair next to him, her worried eyes glued to his face.

They couldn't sit like this all night. He'd go off his head. "How about," Charlie said, saying the words as they unfolded in his mind, "we send your proprietress, or one of her brats, for some cold cuts and gin? We can celebrate here. Look, I'm rich."

He deposited the two silver dollars on the bed. The metal gleamed brilliant and clean against the stained bedsheet.

"Well, I'll be damned." William managed a smile.

"I'll go make the arrangements," Charlotte said, hopping to her feet. She scooped up the money and made a beeline for the door.

"You're welcome." Charlie flung the words at her back.

"Charlotte," William said, and his voice held a hint of reprimand.

Charlotte stopped immediately and turned to face them. "I'm sorry, I'm just so happy, and so relieved, So, very, very relieved...." Her voice, always soft and tremulous, died off completely. She looked to be on the verge of tears, but Charlie noticed she kept the money tightly gripped in her fist.

"Never mind," William said consolingly. "Go on."

When she returned a couple of minutes later, she had enough decency to flash a smile at Charlie before resuming her perch at William's side. "We're in luck," she said. "Mrs. Stapleton says there's a place open on Callowhill."

The prospect of food and gin lightened everyone's mood, and conversation came easier.

When the liquor arrived, and they had all enjoyed several mugs of it, Charlie decided the time was ripe to relate this morning's episode. To his surprise, when he came to the part of his story where the door was slammed in his father's face, he was choking with laughter.

The little company, enlivened by the gin, allowed themselves to be entertained. Charlie even did an impression of John, mimicking his great ape frame and flaring his nostrils in simulated rage. When he finished, he collapsed onto the foot of the mattress and laughed until tears streamed down his cheeks.

William spoke then, his voice wistful. "It's a shame she won't lend the money. It would be an end to all our troubles."

"Oh, we'll get it alright." Charlie took another swig of gin before standing, a little unsteadily, to refill his glass. "I'll have a go at her next week, and who knows? I might get it then." He poured carefully; the bottle was getting low. "If not, you can be sure I'll get it soon." He reseated himself and leveled a crooked grin at William. "After all, the old bitch can't live forever."

BREAKING IN

CHRISTMAS DAY. SIX DAYS BEFORE THE MURDER.

amie stretched down the length of the velvet divan and yawned. Sitting in chairs on either side of him, his mother and sister were debating the virtues of goose stuffed with apples and caraway as opposed to goose stuffed with rosemary and mushroom. The savory smell of roasted meat wafted through the house, and Jamie felt certain his appetite would do justice to any bird they set before him.

The newspaper he'd been reading slipped off its perch on his chest and slid to the floor. With a sigh, he sat up and retrieved it.

"Enjoy your nap?" There was a playful note of reprimand in Melly's voice.

"Very much," he answered his sister, looking around the room. "Where's Father?"

His mother frowned. "In the library. I do wish you'd persuade him not to overwork himself. He's still recovering."

Jamie stood, then stooped to give her hand a reassuring pat. "Leave him to me."

The Captain sat in the library, hunched over his mahogany writing desk. Jamie rapped briefly on the doorjamb, and his father glanced up and waved him in.

"So, this is where you've hidden yourself," Jamie said, taking a seat in one of the winged-back leather armchairs.

"Hm? Oh yes, just a moment. I've almost finished."

Jamie let his gaze travel around the familiar room. With its smell of leather, cigar smoke, and wood polish, this little library was the backdrop of many a happy boyhood memory. How many times had he sat here, at his father's desk, leafing through a gilt-edged book filled with fantastic etchings of strange peoples in distant lands? Back then, all the knowledge in the world seemed to be housed within this room's emerald walls.

His father coughed, a dry, wheezing sound, and Jamie watched him anxiously until the spasm passed. Jamie had been in Vermont only a day when the telegram informing him of his father's illness had reached him. He'd rushed home to find his father in a state very near death. For the better part of a week, the Captain lingered there.

When he finally began gaining ground, Jamie had been giddy with relief, but two weeks had passed, and his father's return to health remained unnervingly slow. He seemed unable to regain the weight he'd lost, and walking from one room to the next tired him. The Captain, always a stout, vigorous man, looked so different now, so *old*, it made something deep inside of Jamie ache.

"There." His father blotted the paper and looked up. "What is it that you wanted?"

Jamie masked his gloomy thoughts with a quick smile. "Mother's afraid you're overworking yourself."

"Tut, tut! Your mother worries too much. I was writing to the upholsterer about the house on Chestnut Hill. Since you've agreed to spend some time at our head office, they'll need to rush their work."

"You needn't on my account. I don't expect to be in Philadelphia until well after the start of the new year. You haven't told anyone of my plans, have you?" Jamie studied his father with an interest at odds with his casual tone.

His father, who knew nothing of the events in Tupper Lake or of Jamie's half-formed investigative designs, arched a brow at him. "I wasn't aware they were a secret."

"It isn't a secret, exactly. Only, I would rather it didn't get around that I was going to be in Philadelphia just yet." Jamie assumed a cavalier tone. "You know what a nuisance all those supper parties can be. Every woman with an unmarried daughter between the ages of sixteen and thirty won't be able to pour a cup of tea without first issuing me an invitation."

His father leaned back in his chair and folded his hands on his desk. "What a terrible burden that must be for you."

Jamie laughed self-consciously, wishing he'd thought of a less ridiculous excuse. "I know it sounds foolish, but it does rather get to be a nuisance."

His father stood, walked over to him and patted his arm. "You may keep yourself a secret if you wish, but mind you don't overplay your hand. Avoid society too long and you may end with society avoiding you. Nuisance or no, I shouldn't think you'd care to see some other lad usurp you as darling of the drawing room."

Jamie grinned and rose to his feet. "Perish the thought."

~

*B*ack in his bedroom, Jamie leaned back in a chair he'd placed before the fire and closed his eyes. He'd meant to give more thought to his nascent investigative plans, but he'd eaten so much at dinner that both his mind and body felt leaden and dull. He must have started to doze, because a light knock at the door caused him to jump. Not waiting for a response, Melly cracked the door and stuck her head in. "Good! You're still awake."

Before he could inform her that he didn't plan to be for long, she disappeared. A moment later, the door pushed open and she glided in, carrying a crystal brandy decanter in one hand and a pair of snifters in the other.

"I thought you could do with a nightcap," she said, gently pushing the door closed with her bare foot.

He could, at that. He rose to help pour.

Cupping her snifter in both hands, Melly curled into the thickly cushioned armchair Jamie had just vacated. He shot her a mildly reproving look before drawing up its mate across from her.

Melly waited for him to get settled then said, "Well? Are you going to tell me, or are you going to make me guess?"

"Tell you what?"

"What has been on your mind. Ever since you returned from your adventure in the wilds, you've been skulking about like Hamlet's ghost."

Jamie grimaced.

"Alright, that was a bad comparison," Melly said quickly, wrinkling her nose. "But you know what I mean."

"No, I'm afraid I don't."

She kept her gaze firmly leveled on him until he looked away.

"Dad is on the mend now, isn't he? You and the doctor aren't keeping some dreadful secret from Mom and I?"

"Good Lord, Melly, it's nothing like that."

"Well, I'm glad to hear that at least. What is it then?" She tilted her head to the side, her dark blue eyes twinkling. "Some little lady done you wrong?"

Jamie half-smiled, relaxing back into his chair. "Nothing like that, either, I'm afraid. Really, I don't know what it is—in fact, it's probably nothing."

"Go on, unburden yourself." Melly, sensing that victory was at hand, took a sip of brandy and waited. She was the elder by sixteen months, and, as children, they had whiled away whole summer days catching grasshoppers and emptying the lake of fish. Of necessity, things had changed as they grew. Mother insisted Melly try and act like a lady, a campaign rife with conflict and hard fought on both sides. With her blunt features, fair, freckled skin, and hair the color of damp straw, her very biology seemed at odds with feminine frippery.

Still, Mother had persevered, and the demure appearance of the young lady before him, with her braided coif and elegant blue oriental silk robe, was proof of her gains. But, in spite of these superficial changes, something of the independent tomboy remained—a certain frankness of expression and unembarrassed sharpness of mind. He had heard it said that, even more than her lack of beauty, it was these *masculine* traits that were responsible for her having achieved the advanced age of twenty-eight without finding a husband. Whatever opinions other men might hold, Jamie had always found his sister to be both a worthy confidante and a staunch ally.

As succinctly as possible, Jamie described his meeting with the mustachioed man in New York, the man's tragic accident the following day, and the entries he'd noticed in the account books.

Melly listened intently.

When he finished, he half-expected her to laugh or tease him for worrying over nothing. To his relief, and, paradoxically, his disappointment, she did neither.

"What did Manassas say when you caught up with him?" she asked, her voice as serious as he had ever heard it.

"Not much. Apparently, a union man was stirring up trouble on the yard in Vermont. Uncle Manny claimed to have no idea who the man with the mustache was. When I pressed him, he suggested he was another agitator."

"That sounds ... *odd*, but not impossible," Melly said thoughtfully.

45

Jamie nodded slowly.

"But you didn't believe him?"

Jamie shook his head. "If Uncle Manny was worried about the men striking, why not just come to my room and tell me? Or say so in the letter he left? And the man with the mustache talked like he knew Uncle Manny, like he'd spoken to him."

"Did you say any of that to Uncle Manny?"

"No," Jamie admitted. "Mother's telegram about Father reached me the next day, and I caught the first train home. But I can't shake the feeling that something is off."

"Do you think Uncle Manny is being blackmailed?" she asked.

"Blackmailed?" Jamie almost laughed. "He's the most conservative man I know. What do you imagine he did?"

"How should I know? I'm not the one who spoke with that foreign gentleman in New York," Melly said matter-of-factly. "And what have you discovered since your return?"

Jamie winced, and picked up his snifter. "Nothing."

Melly cocked her head to the side and raised her eyebrows.

"When have I had the time?" he protested. "What, with Father being ill, and you and Mother in a flutter over Christmas—"

"The most logical thing," Melly said, interrupting his defense, "would be to have a look at Uncle Manny's personal files. As I understand it, he's finishing the mill tour without you, and shouldn't be back in Philadelphia until mid-January."

"And how do you propose we do that? Loeffler, his secretary, would be on the telephone to him, and everyone else he thought might be interested, before I'd advanced two steps beyond the threshold."

"*We* will just have to go when Mr. Loeffler isn't guarding the gates."

"And how are we to do that? Don't tell me you've developed the gift of clairvoyance?"

"No, stupid, by going in the middle of the night."

"The middle of the night?" Jamie parroted. "Are you off your head? That will never work."

"Of course it will," she said calmly. "I know Mr. Loeffler is dedicated, but even he has to sleep."

In spite of himself, Jamie smiled. "Let me make sure I'm understanding you. You're suggesting I travel to Philadelphia, break into our building in the middle of the night, and rifle through Uncle Manny's files?"

"No, I'm suggesting that *we* do it."

"Out of the question."

"Why?"

"Why?" Jamie repeated, the blood rushing to his face. One of the things that irritated him most about Melly was the way she asked questions every reasonable human being already knew the answer to, even if they couldn't articulate it. "Because it's a damn fool idea, that's why. The night watchman will probably see us—see *me*—creeping about and shoot me dead, and, if he doesn't, I'll doubtless wish he had once news of our little escapade gets around."

"Do you have a better plan?"

Jamie frowned and took a large swallow of brandy.

He didn't.

∼

"*H*urry! Someone's coming!" Melly's urgent whisper came from close behind Jamie's left shoulder.

"I *am* hurrying," he hissed, jamming another key into the lock and trying vainly to turn it. Cursing under his breath, he selected another from the heavy ring. After two days of watching and waiting, Toby, the boy he'd hired, managed to lift Old Edd's master keyring. It held a key for every door in the building, at least fifty by Jamie's estimate. So far tonight, he'd worked his way through at least twenty.

Melly jabbed him in the back. "Don't you hear that? Oh, do hurry, Jamie!"

He gritted his teeth and wondered for the umpteenth time how he'd allowed Melly to talk him into this. She'd sworn it wasn't a crime—not really. After all, their family owned the business, and Jamie himself had an office in the building, making their late night adventure unusual, perhaps, but not illegal.

This argument had been persuasive when they were snug at home, but he could think of no better way to end up in a padded cell than by trying to fob it off on the policeman who was bound to come around that corner any moment now.

"Damnation," Jamie grumbled, fumbling for another key.

Melly grabbed his elbow and squeezed. She didn't say anything, nor did she have to. The footsteps were growing louder. Offering up a silent prayer, Jamie fit another key into the lock. To his unutterable relief, it turned.

The moment he opened the door, Melly pushed him inside and shut it behind them. They had come through the service entrance, which opened into a small storeroom. It was pitch black. Jamie listened to the footsteps outside, when they faded, he lit a match.

"Here, I brought candles." Melly searched the knapsack she'd insisted on bringing and pulled out two tapers that looked suspiciously like the ones in Mother's favorite candelabra. The knapsack was a grammar school relic, part of the ridiculous costume Melly had assumed for tonight's outing. Aside from the bag, her adventure-attire consisted of an old pair of navy blue trousers and a dark gray coat that was at least five sizes too large for her.

She looked absurd, a cross between a clown and a hobo, and Jamie had taken great delight in telling her as much. She had responded by declaring that either a clown or a hobo would draw less attention on the street at two in the morning than a respectable young lady. Silly as she looked, she had a point.

Melly touched a taper to the flame and passed it to him, then lit her own.

"We may as well get on with it," he said, then began walking toward Manassas's office.

Candlelight flickered along the cold marble walls, and their footsteps echoed down the empty corridors. Jamie shivered, not entirely from the cold. When they reached the office, the door was locked. Sighing, Jamie pulled out Old Edd's ring. The sixth key took. He looked at Melly, and she grinned. They were in.

Filing cabinets lined the walls on either side of Manassas's desk, which was itself stacked high with ledgers. Melly pointed him toward the desk and moved to one of the far filing cabinets. She pulled open the top drawer and started sifting through its contents.

After flipping uselessly through a book the size of an encyclopedia, Jamie turned to his sister. "Have you found anything?"

She looked at him hopefully. "No, you?"

He shook his head and checked his watch, it was almost three. Toby told him that the charwoman arrived around five. Jamie planned to be safely at home in Chestnut Hill at least an hour before that.

Melly must have been thinking the same thing, because she said, "We'll have to look at as much as we can tonight and come back tomorrow."

"Oh no," he said, his voice firm. "My plans for New Year's Eve do not include being arrested for burglary. Besides, Uncle Manny isn't expected back at the office until Monday, the fifth. Rather than risk our necks to read in the dark, I say we take as many files as we can now, look them over, then return them before anyone notices."

Melly looked thoughtful, then smiled. "That's not a bad idea."

"You needn't sound so surprised."

She wrinkled her nose. "I must say, it certainly is a good thing I brought this knapsack. I don't know what I'd do without it." She looked at him meaningfully before shoving a stack of folders into her bag.

Jamie looked at the ledgers and frowned. He wouldn't be able to carry very many, and he'd look a damned fool with them tucked into his waistcoat. He scanned the office for a handy sack or box and spied Manassas's golf bag in the corner. Inspired, he grabbed his candle and dashed down the hall to his own office. There, he dug around until he found the leather satchel with his tennis gear in it. After dumping balls, rackets, and clothing into a desk drawer, Jamie returned feeling vindicated.

In less than fifteen minutes, their bags were full. They slipped out, careful to lock the door behind them. Traffic was thin, but Jamie managed to wave down a cab. As he followed Melly into the compartment, a flood of relief washed over him leaving him almost euphoric.

He glanced at his sister; she was grinning. For no reason he could name, he began to laugh. Melly joined in. Once started, they couldn't stop, and the two of them rocked with senseless laughter all the way back to the house on Chestnut Hill.

OFFICIAL BUSINESS

JANUARY 2, 1900

*M*arie shifted the heavy basket of mending onto her other hip and waited for two muscular bays pulling a Watkin's Dairy Wagon to pass. The winter sun, not yet fully risen, cast an amber hue over the snowbanks and icy window panes. Despite the early hour, the city was already bustling. Tradesmen and factory workers jostled each other on the broad sidewalks, hurrying to work, while vendors selling fresh baked buns, and newspaper boys, their sacks bulging with this morning's edition, sang out their wares. This long-voweled choir of commerce was punctuated by the rhythmic clopping of hooves on cobbled streets and the bell-like jingling of horses in harness. Marie, who stood near the corner of North 8th and Race Streets, could see the alley leading to the rear entrance of the Bijou Theatre. Her arms gave a dull pang, eager to be free of their burden now that the end of her journey was in sight.

Once the wagon had rattled past, Marie hurried across the street and onto the narrow, bricked path that led to the theater's back door. It had taken her half the night to finish all of her orders. Her fingers ached from darning stockings and raising and lowering hems, but when she thought of the seventy cents her work would earn her, her heart swelled and the pain disappeared.

When Mrs. Griggs had asked Marie if she wanted to earn a little money doing mending, Marie had leapt at the opportunity. Her mother had taught her needlework when she was still a small girl, and, in the succeeding years, necessity had honed her skill. She had learned to be precise, to avoid waste, and creative, as she rarely had sufficient materials to sew to pattern.

The mending Mrs. Griggs brought her from other apartment buildings along their street was routine, mostly patching blown-out elbows and knees in oft-mended work clothes. But the deliveries from the Bijou were something different entirely. Gowns, robes, tights, and tutus arrived in a riotous array of colors and materials, each with a short note pinned to them describing what was to be done.

This was the work she delighted in. It was not precision work, as the clothing was often cut down the back and fixed with stays for hasty costume changes, but each and every stitch was an adventure, something wholly removed from the drudgery of her everyday life. Sometimes, when she was alone, she would slip on a gown and swirl across the living room singing a Paul Dresser tune.

Shifting the basket once more, Marie mounted the icy steps to the service entrance and knocked hard at the door. A few seconds passed, then Sam, a gray-whiskered man with lively brown eyes who managed the costume department, opened the door.

"Good morning," Marie said.

Sam gave a brief nod that communicated both a greeting and an invitation to come inside.

Marie followed him through a maze of crates and equipment until they came to a large storeroom with racks of clothing. It smelled of cedar, mothballs, and mildew.

"Put the finished costumes over there." Sam pointed to a

table against the far wall. "There's a fresh order by the door. We'll need these done by Wednesday."

"*This* Wednesday?" Marie asked, her heart sinking. That was two days sooner than normal.

"If you can't do it, tell me now, so I can find someone else."

"I can do it," Marie said hastily.

"Good," he said. Then, after a brief pause, "Do you do all of the sewing yourself?"

"Yes."

"How much does that Griggs woman pay you for it?"

"A dime a garment."

"She charges us a quarter, ya know."

Marie hadn't known this, but she wasn't surprised. Mrs. Griggs was not the sort to do anything that wasn't in her own interest. The money Mrs. Griggs paid her might seem paltry to Sam, and perhaps to most people, but to Marie it was transformative. The ability to go to a matinee, or buy a yard of ribbon for Eliza's new bonnet, without having to beg, scold, or bargain, gave Marie a sense of freedom she had never before known.

Sam was still looking at her, probably expecting a show of surprise and complaint, and Marie began to feel self-conscious that she had none to make.

"Do you ever catch any of our acts?" he asked, abruptly.

Relieved, Marie nodded enthusiastically. "I come as often as I can."

"Which isn't very often," he said knowingly.

"Not as much as I'd like," Marie admitted.

"Shame that you let your free seat go to waste like that."

"Free seat?"

"Everyone who works for the theater can sit in the penny gallery for free. I'm talking about weekday matinees, of course. Don't tell me you didn't know that?"

Marie shook her head.

"Give the girl at the ticket booth your name, and she'll let you right in."

"I'll do that," Marie said gratefully.

"What *is* your name?" Sam asked.

"Marie."

"Marie what?"

"Chevalier."

Sam nodded and hefted the basket with the finished work onto his shoulder. "You see that you get that mending back to me by Wednesday, Marie Chevalier."

"Yes, sir." Marie picked up the new basket, barely noticing its weight, and started for home. A free seat to any matinee? It was too good to be believed. She couldn't come every day, of course, there was too much work to be done. But if she could get a little help with the shopping, and if she slept a little less, she might be able to make it once, maybe twice a week.

Full of such thoughts, the trip home passed quickly. Back in their rooms, she found Eliza at the table finishing a bowl of oatmeal.

"You look cheerful," Eliza said, her eyes brightening in expectation of good news. "Has something happened?"

"No, not exactly." Marie set the basket down in the corner and took her time spreading the gray wool shawl over it. How could she share her good fortune without seeming to rub her sister's face in it? Maybe they could share the free pass between them? On days when Eliza was home from school, she might use Marie's name to get in. Of course, if they were caught, Marie might lose not only the seat, but the work too. She was still considering how to handle such a sticky situation when three loud raps sounded on the front door.

Marie cast Eliza a questioning glance and found her own surprise mirrored back at her. Between the family moving so often, and Papa's habit of pressing everyone they met for a loan, the Chevalier family possessed few friends, and none who were likely to call at this early hour.

It must be a dunner, she thought. But for which bill? The grocer had given them another week to pay, and she'd settled with the milkman last Tuesday.

Marie tugged at her dress to straighten it, then walked to the door, smoothing flyaway hairs with the flats of her hands before opening it.

"Oh," Marie mumbled, taking a reflexive step backward. "Good morning."

The man in the hall did not resemble any dunner Marie had ever seen. He was tall and pale with dark brown hair and narrow eyes. He wore a black serge suit and carried a felt derby with a small gray feather tucked into the band.

"Good morning," he said, his gaze steady. "May I speak to Mr. John Chevalier?"

"I'm afraid he's not at home."

"When do you expect him?"

"Any time now," Marie replied, her curiosity piqued. "If you like, I can take a message?"

"I'd sooner wait for him, if you don't mind."

His tone made what should have been a question sound like a demand. Marie frowned. She was not in the habit of inviting strangers into their home, and being an acquaintance of their father's was hardly a good character reference.

As though reading her thoughts, the stranger pulled a black leather bifold from his pocket and flipped it open. "My name is Detective Gardiner. I'm here on official business. I assure you, you're quite safe."

Marie's heart took off at a gallop. Papa could be rash, and his temperament volatile, but this was the first time the law had ever come knocking.

"What do you want with Papa?" she asked.

"I'd rather discuss that with him."

"I've already told you, he's not at home. Perhaps," she added, in the most unconcerned voice she could muster, "it would be better if you came back later."

"You said you expected him any moment."

Marie shrugged, wishing she'd been more circumspect. "And I hope that's the case, but, with him, there's never any saying."

A door behind her banged closed, and Charlie's groggy voice called out, "What was that pounding?"

Eliza must have told him, because a moment later her brother, still clad in pajamas, pushed in beside her at the door. "What's this about?"

Gardiner inspected Charlie before turning back to her, and there was something discerning about his gaze that Marie shrank from.

"I think," Gardiner said, "that we should wait for your father to return before discussing that."

"He's at Queenie's," Charlie said matter-of-factly. "I'll go fetch him. Won't take a minute."

Marie frowned at Charlie's retreating form.

"May I?" Detective Gardiner gestured at the door she still held.

Reluctantly, she stepped aside, and he entered. As he did, a keen sense of the apartment's shabbiness pressed in on her. She gestured to the carved oak armchair reserved for company.

"Would you like some coffee?" she asked, uncertain how far the normal courtesies extended to policemen.

"Please." Detective Gardiner sat in the seat she'd indicated and took in everything around him with undisguised interest.

The winter sunlight streaming through the stained linen curtains emphasized the room's defects, draining what little warmth and color it possessed. Even the fat pink peonies printed on the shabby green and gold striped wallpaper faded under its glare.

Marie's face burned, and she knew she must be flushing

bright red, but she couldn't help it. She hated this apartment and everything it told this stranger about her and her family.

"Lizzy," Marie said gently, spotting her sister watching from a post near the wash basin. "Why don't you fetch the china."

Eliza shot her a questioning look. Marie arched her brows meaningfully. Her sister shrugged and disappeared into their room just as Charlie strode out of his, one arm already in his coat.

"Back in a flash," he said, and banged out the door.

Marie shook her head. Of all the days for Charlie to be helpful.

She placed the old iron kettle on the fire, then seated herself in the tattered gold armchair while it heated. She licked her lips, which had gone dry, and asked, "Could you give me some hint as to what this is about?"

His hazel eyes flicked to hers. He seemed to be considering something, but said only, "As I said at the door, I think it best we wait for your father."

"But everything is alright, isn't it?" She needed only a little reassurance, why not give it to her?

There was a pause, then Detective Gardiner said, "I believe your sister has returned with the cups."

Marie rose mechanically and helped Eliza serve the coffee. No one spoke, and by the time they were all settled in their chairs again, the silence had stretched on so long, it felt inescapable.

Marie stared down at her coffee and racked her mind for something to say. She doubted very much the detective would be interested in the new chintz at Price's, or in the sleeve pattern in the October edition of Godey's, and it disquieted her to discover how much omitting these topics limited her discourse. She could, she supposed, talk of crime. Old Mr. Jenkins' cart had been stolen twice in the past month, and Mrs. Talcomb was always complaining about the drunkards relieving themselves in the alleyway. These topics, however, didn't seem quite polite.

"It's very cold, isn't it?" Eliza's voice was quiet but strong, and Marie shot her a look of intense gratitude.

"Yes. It is," Detective Gardiner responded flatly.

"Even for the season," Marie jumped in. "I had to heat the water three times yesterday before I could wash the linen clean."

"Indeed." Detective Gardiner spoke with the sort of exaggerated politeness people use when speaking to children or idiots.

Silence settled around them again. Marie was relieved by the slam of the front door and the thud of heavy steps on the stairs. Detective Gardiner stood, and not knowing what else to do, Marie rose also.

Their door opened and Papa entered. He must have still been sleeping when Charlie found him; whiskers shadowed his jaw and creases lined his blue tweed suit.

Charlie slipped in behind him and closed the door.

"Good morning," Papa said a little too loudly, his eyes lighting on the detective. He shrugged out of his greatcoat, and the scent of stale tobacco, whiskey, and cold morning air entered the room.

"Good morning, Mr. Chevalier. I'm Detective Gardiner—"

"So my boy told me," Papa broke in. "What's your business here?"

The lines of the detective's face tightened. He glanced at Marie, then back at her father. "I regret to inform you that yesterday afternoon your mother was found dead at her place of employment."

His words sucked the air from the room. Marie gripped the arms of her chair and looked to her father. Her ears rang as though a bomb had gone off, and a sinkhole was opening inside of her. She willed Papa to tell this man that there had been a mistake, that Mémé couldn't be dead.

Papa's ruddy complexion paled, and his eyes, at first so defiant, grew glassy and unfocused. He stumbled a few paces, then bent down and felt for the settle before lowering himself onto it.

"I'm afraid her death occurred under suspicious circumstances," the detective continued. "There will have to be an inquiry."

"No," Marie whispered reflexively. She turned back to Detective Gardiner and saw him, *really saw him*, for the first time: this tall, pasty man in his neat black suit and his feathered hat. He was a grotesquerie, a figure that inhabited nightmares. "No," she said again, shaking her head. "That can't be true."

"I'm afraid it is." He spoke matter-of-factly, with less feeling than one might discuss the corn crop in Iowa or the rising price of flour.

Marie sank back onto her seat, her head and stomach churning. Charlie, whose presence she had all but forgotten, whispered, "Well, I'll be damned," then turned and strode to the window. All at once, she remembered Eliza and scanned the room for her. She spotted her sister seated at the kitchen table, tears streaming down her cheeks.

"The inquest will be next week," Gardiner said. "We'll provide you with more details as they become available. And, Mr. Chevalier, we will need you to come down to the station and answer a few questions. It's standard in cases like this."

Papa's head jerked up, and an emotion that looked like fear flashed over his face. "Yes, of course. I'll be down this afternoon."

Gardiner nodded then set his still full cup on the rickety side table. "I'll see myself out."

He threaded the short distance to the door and was gone, but the stifling atmosphere remained.

Eliza sniffled, and Marie, feeling as though she were in a dream, stood and went to her, hugging her close.

The room was still quiet when Charlie turned from the

window. "Do you realize what this means? We have the capital to invest in the South America speculation now."

Papa turned his head to look at him, his expression uncharacteristically flat.

"Don't you see?" Charlie continued. "It's the end of all our troubles!"

Before Marie knew what was happening, Papa had charged from his seat and struck his son, open handed, across the face. The slap rang out in the little room, and Charlie stumbled backward and fell.

Marie and Eliza exchanged horrified glances. Not since they were children had their father hit them.

Charlie remained where he landed, his eyes round and his lips parted. Then he blinked several times and scrambled to his feet, his face fuchsia. He snatched his coat and hat from the chair, and Marie expected him to rush out without a word, but he paused on the threshold to face them.

"There isn't one of us who hasn't thought about how much better off we'd be once the old girl kicked off." He tried to sound cheerful, but tears choked his voice. "Well, she finally has, and I'm sorry if I'm not the hypocrite you all are. Go ahead and playact for one another if you must, I have better things to do."

With that, he slammed the door and was gone.

ON THE UP

JANUARY 2, 1900

*C*harlie swiped at his nose with his shirt sleeve before stomping down the steps onto the snow-strewn walk. There had been a break in the weather. The day was warm, and the sky was that deep, fathomless blue that wants to reach down and pull you up into it. He walked without direction, crossing congested streets gray with slush and turning corners at random, glad to be on his own and away from his miserable family.

The stinging in his cheek faded, and with it, his anger. He'd seen his father drunk often enough to know that, beneath John's bluff and bluster, he was the worst sort of sentimentalist. Always mourning the father he couldn't remember, and the wife who, in every memory Charlie had of her, had scolded him. Once you added the shock of having the police sniffing about, well, the old man could hardly be blamed for going off his head.

As his mood improved, his attention turned outward. The dirty sidewalk was crowded with hawkers and peddlers competing for his attention. A man with a thick black mustache sold hair tonic from a canvas-covered suitcase, while a farmer and his son stood in the bed of a wagon surrounded by crates of cabbage. A little further on, an old Italian beckoned people to a cluttered pine table covered with everything from egg-beaters to sheet music. Their shouting and cajoling usually annoyed him, but today, he surveyed their wares with the critical eye of a man who, at long last, could afford them.

He'd walked this street not a half-hour earlier on his way to Queenie's, but in that short span, the world had become a different place. For one thing, he'd learned that his grandmother was no longer in it, and more importantly, her money was. But how much? He'd given the question considerable thought in the past, and, all things considered, he reckoned five hundred was a reasonable figure.

Five hundred dollars.

Charlie's heart quickened. Strange how the very habits he had despised most in Mémé had been turned to his advantage. She had been the veriest miser to ever pinch a penny, but now, every cent she'd saved would be his to spend. Well, his father's technically, but that was more-or-less the same thing. The justice in this was striking. It was as though the universe had, at long last, recognized the wrongs done to him and balanced the scales.

A vague uneasiness passed, like a shadow, over his happiness. Of course, he had loved Mémé once, one of those undiscerning effusions of childhood, but she had never taken to him, not as she had the girls. By the time he'd turned fourteen, he'd sat through more lectures on what she termed "his failings", personal, moral, and scholastic, than he cared to put number to. He could not, *would not*, be sorry that there would never be another.

Halfway across St. James Street, he stopped to let a Stanley Steamer pass, admiring its red carriage and black leather seats. Maybe he should get one? Why not? Every cent the old lady left would go straight into the South American prospect and, in no time at all, their investment would increase five, maybe even ten-fold. This vision of the future was so potent, and so close to hand, that Charlie found himself blinking back tears. Everything would be different now. Everything.

He reached William's building on Mitre Street and knocked loud enough to sting his knuckles. Mrs. Stapleton opened the door, scowling.

"Yeah?" she demanded.

Several swathes of hair had escaped her bun to curl wildly around her face, and the bone buttons of her blouse were undone all the way to her skirt. He stared a moment too long at her camisole, flushed hotly, and averted his gaze.

"I'm here for Diaz," he told the doorjamb.

She opened the door and shouted "Diaz, visitor" up the stairs before walking away.

Not even the misery of Mrs. Stapleton's could dampen Charlie's spirits today. He climbed the stairs two at a time, ignoring the old oak planks' creaks of protest. He reached the top just as William stepped through the door of his room, buttoning his coat.

"Our troubles are over!" Charlie announced, clapping his friend on the back.

"What're you on about?"

"The old girl is dead."

"What?" William eyed him warily, a ridiculous half-smile frozen on his lips.

Charlie laughed. "I promise you, I'm in earnest. Just heard the news, myself. Fear not, I shan't forget my old friends now that I'm a swell. Come!" he said, turning from William's questioning gaze and heading back toward the stairs. "Let's go somewhere and celebrate."

"When did she die?" William asked, close behind him.

Charlie shrugged. "I haven't the faintest. A detective came to the house today and gave us the glad tidings." He pushed open the door and jogged down the porch steps, relieved to be back outside. The cold air embraced him, and he rushed on with growing enthusiasm. "My first impulse was to write to the Letts for the money straight away, but I think it might be better to wait until after the inquest next week. Don't want to look too eager."

"Inquest?" William now strode alongside him.

Charlie grunted. "Seems the old girl died under *suspicious circumstances*, whatever that means. Maybe she took pity on us and did away with herself." He nudged William and turned to stare after a pretty red-haired girl walking past them. He wanted to talk about the money, not the old woman, and it annoyed him that the conversation kept turning to her.

They walked on in silence for a few moments, Charlie craning his head to look into shop windows. He was admiring a pair of brown Oxfords that would suit him nicely when William's reflection caught his eye. He turned his head to look at his friend more closely. "You've got a new coat."

"Oh, this." William shrugged disinterestedly. "It belonged to Mrs. Malone's son, or husband, something like that. She lent me a few things: this coat, a razor, a few shirts."

"Bessy? From Eastern Avenue?" Charlie's voice took on a knowing quality.

William nodded without looking at him.

"So, that's still on, is it?" Charlie laughed. "You old devil! I don't know how you manage it." Then looking at the coat more closely, he curled his lip and pointed at some dark smears along the front. "What is that?"

"Oh, that. Yeah. It wasn't exactly clean when she lent it me, and then this happened," William held out his left hand, displaying an angry red gash across the fingernails of his middle and pointer fingers. "I cut myself slicing the bread the other day."

"Grisly." Charlie grimaced. "But just think, once the canal deal goes through, you'll have closets full of coats. Then, you won't have to use your charms on old Bessy Malone—unless you want to."

William grinned, and they fell into a companionable silence. The fine weather and exercise got Charlie's blood flowing, and by the time they reached the tavern, he felt hale, hearty, and generally satisfied with himself and the world.

He strolled to the bar, slapped a handful of coins on the smooth wooden surface, and ordered a bottle of gin.

"Not this time." William slid the money back toward him and placed his own coins on the counter. "When you come into your fortune, you can buy."

"Well," Charlie said, eyeing the money appreciatively. "It seems your luck has turned as well."

William shrugged and looked away. "Charlotte gave it to me this morning. The weather's improved and business is looking up."

Charlie laughed, and his voice took on the same knowing quality it had acquired when talking of Bessy Malone. "I don't know how you manage it, Liam, old boy. I really don't."

ACTION, NOT SENTIMENT

JANUARY 2, 1900

"*Y*ou wanted to see me?" Jamie hesitated at the library's threshold, waiting for permission to enter. This room had always been his father's sanctuary, and though the time had long since passed when his jam-sticky hands and constant questions had made his presence there an intrusion, the habit had taken root, and he could no more imagine waltzing in uninvited than he could dancing a jig on his father's desk.

James Lett Sr. looked up from the letter he was reading, his face unusually pale. He waved Jamie toward a chair, took off his glasses, and rubbed his eyes with his palms.

Jamie slid down onto the leather seat, a hard knot already forming in his chest. "What is it?"

"Mrs. Tompkins is dead," his father said quietly. "A burglar broke into our house. She must have confronted him, and the fiend killed her."

"My God," Jamie mumbled, crossing himself reflexively. He didn't know what he had been expecting, perhaps something about Manassas, but not this. People didn't kill harmless old housekeepers.

"The police would like a member of the family to examine the house and take an inventory. Candler didn't notice anything missing, but it's best one of us go and make certain." His father shook his head. "Mrs. Tompkins must have caught him shortly after he broke in. Spooked the fellow, and he ran off with nothing. Senseless, just senseless."

"Of course I'll go," Jamie said immediately. "I'll leave this morning, after breakfast."

Lett Sr. nodded. "The coroner's inquest will be next week and arrangements must be made. Mrs. Tompkins was a faithful servant and a good woman; we can't abandon her affairs to that degenerate son of hers."

"I'll see to everything."

"Thank you, my boy. I know you and Melly were fond of her." His father picked up the letter again, the thin paper fluttering in his unsteady hands. "If you could break the news to your sister—"

"I'll do that now," Jamie interrupted, standing. "Please, leave everything to me."

"Good man." His father smiled weakly.

Jamie walked around the desk and gave his father's thin shoulder a brief squeeze before setting out in search of Smith, his father's valet. He located the energetic little man in his room, polishing boots, and sent him to the library with strict instructions to report back once his father was settled.

Jamie watched Smith's retreating back. Mrs. Tompkins's death, with its mixture of private grief and public scandal, would be hard on Father. There was no avoiding it, and the timing couldn't be worse. Only this morning, the doctor had warned Jamie in the strongest possible language that the Captain should avoid mental and physical exertions. If, as Jamie suspected, his father planned to attend the inquest in Philadelphia, this horror promised to be both.

Jamie walked downstairs. Had it been summer, Melly might

have been out rowing on the lake or off on a ramble, but it was winter, and his sister invariably passed the intemperate months in the old parlor, which she had long since converted into a makeshift painting studio.

He found her there, standing in front of a canvas almost as tall as she. The background had been finished, but the figures in the foreground were still trying to emerge. Some were clearly mounted, and he got the sense of a battle or a hunt.

"Melly," he said quietly. Then, when she didn't respond, "Melinda."

She whirled around, her face taut with annoyance. She hated being disturbed when she was painting.

Jamie walked toward her. "I have bad news."

Her expression changed to one of fear. "Father?"

"Mrs. Tompkins, at Chestnut Hill." He took her paint-smudged hand and led her to a nearby chair. "There was a break-in, and she was killed."

Melly looked incredulous. "Madame Alozia?"

"I'm afraid so."

He waited for the news to settle before adding, "The inquest is next week. I'll see to the house and the police, but I could use your help with the funeral arrangements."

Addressed to someone else, his request might have been insensitive, but he knew his sister. She needed action, not sentiment.

Melly blinked rapidly, but her voice was firm. "I'll attend to it."

"Thank you." He squeezed her hand.

She smiled sadly and looked at their entwined fingers. "Careful."

He turned his wrist. A smudge of the steely violet that darkened the clouds in the painting now streaked his palm. He shrugged, took her hand again and squeezed it tighter.

"Did they catch the person who did it?"

"Father didn't say, and I think he'd have mentioned it if they had."

"Who would do such a thing?"

Jamie shook his head.

Melly raised her tear-filled eyes to his. "You don't think it's connected to that business upstate?"

"No," he answered automatically, even as the question set off an alarm in his brain. What were the odds of two violent deaths occurring around him in the span of only a few months? "At least, I can't imagine how it could be."

Melly was silent a long time, then said, "Have you found anything in the files?"

"Nothing, but I've only looked at about half-a-dozen. You?"

"I haven't fared any better," she whispered, clearly disappointed. "And we have to return them tomorrow."

"No we don't," Jamie said quickly. "I forgot to tell you, Manassas delayed his return for another two weeks."

"Well, that's lucky."

Jamie nodded.

"Even so, I was thinking, maybe we should hire an investigator?"

"A hawkshaw?" Jamie couldn't help smiling.

"Why not?" Melly lifted her chin. "You might ask around at your club for a recommendation."

Jamie frowned. He supposed he could, but there was something distasteful, almost shameful in it. Investigators were, by definition, instruments used to acquire knowledge one very likely had no right to possess. But already, Mrs. Tompkins' death was working a change inside of him. The wild suspicion that had taken hold in Tupper Lake felt different now: weightier, and infinitely more pressing.

"Alright," he said. "I'll ask."

∼

*a*s Melly had suggested, he dropped word at his club that he was interested in acquiring the services of a good detective. It had earned him a ribbing from the fellows, but, in no time at all, he'd received more than half a dozen names. The detective Jamie selected came highly recommended, and the word "discreet" had been used to describe his services more than once. Even so, Jamie was surprised this afternoon when, just five days after meeting with the man, he came home to find a thick manilla envelope addressed to him. Was it, he wondered, a good sign or a bad one that the agent had discovered so much so quickly?

After locking himself in his room, he read the file from cover to cover, once, twice, then a third time, trying to find in it a cipher that would decode the mystery. Jamie was still examining it when the sound of footsteps in the hall informed him that Melly was home from her dinner party. He waited what he deemed a sufficient amount of time for her to change out of her party clothes, then knocked on her door.

She looked mildly surprised when she opened it, cold cream smeared on half of her face, but then she caught sight of the folder. "Is that what I think it is?"

Jamie nodded.

Melly's eyes brightened. "I'll meet you in the upstairs parlor in five minutes."

Jamie took the report to the parlor and skimmed the now-familiar pages while he waited.

"Well?" Melly said, breezing into the room and plopping down next to him on the sofa. She leaned forward and took a cigarette from the Japanned box on the table. "What did your man discover?"

Jamie handed her the report.

"The mustachioed fellow's name was Giovani Souza," he began. "He showed up in New York about a year-and-a-half ago, passing himself off as a high-level executive for a Colombian shipping company."

"*Passing himself off as?* Meaning, he wasn't?"

"Meaning he wasn't."

"Then what was he?"

"A crook."

Melly's eyes widened, and she mouthed a silent "Oh".

Jamie smiled. "Though, to do the man justice, he was a crook on a rather magnificent scale."

Melly raised her eyebrows and waited.

"The report," Jamie went on, warming to his narrative, "picks up with Mr. Souza arriving in New York City. Endowed with a not insignificant bank balance, he started appearing in all the *right* places, you know the sort; he rented a suite at the Astor House, office space on Wall Street, and dined at Delmonico's at least three times a week."

"Not very original," Melly said reflectively, "but effective."

"In very little time, it became known, as such things generally do, that Mr. Souza was in New York seeking financing for his firm. He had been sent, or so he said, to build a headquarters in the US for his company, which expected to enjoy incredible growth once the proposed canal between North and South America is complete."

"And what was the name of this firm?"

"He withheld it for *political reasons*, except, of course, to investors."

"When did you say this was?"

"A year-and-a-half ago."

She wrinkled her nose. "But how can that be? The French abandoned the canal project, why, it must have been at least four years ago. Don't you remember the headlines: *fortunes lost and thousands dead?*"

Jamie did indeed remember the headlines, one in particular, *Twenty-Two Thousand Dead in Failed French Endeavor*. It had been discussed at length at his club, and he remembered thinking that twenty-two thousand was a number too large for the human heart to comprehend. Had it been five, or even a dozen men, such news would have tugged at the national heartstrings, but twenty-two thousand jarred the mind, evoking more a feeling of horrible wonder than of sympathy.

"There has," Jamie said, reaching for a cigarette, "been a good deal of talk about our picking up where the French left off."

"You can't be serious."

He looked up, meeting her gaze. "I'm quite serious. It's all highly speculative, of course, but the consensus is that the canal can and should be built."

Melly shook her head, contempt in every line of her face. "Why would any country take such a risk?"

"Trade," he said simply. "Once the project is complete, we'll be able to move things from coast to coast in half the time and at a fraction of the cost. There's hardly an investor from here to New York who hasn't bought a piece of one sort of canal speculation or another."

"I'm continually astonished by people's stupidity."

Jamie smiled. "When the canal is built, a great many of those *stupid* people will be very rich."

Melly shrugged. "There'll be nothing new in that. You mean to say that people actually gave this Mr. Souza money?"

"Piles of it." Jamie handed her a page from the report. "Within six months of his arrival, our Mr. Souza had borrowed close to a million dollars.

Melly let out a low whistle. "It's hard to imagine so many businessmen investing in such a wild scheme on the basis of one man's word—and a foreigner's at that."

"You are underestimating our Mr. Souza. Apparently, he established his company on paper, producing a number of favorable financials and several letters of introduction from prominent businessmen in Europe and the States. Next, he carefully selected his investors, avoiding banks, and accepting loans exclusively from private concerns. That much accomplished, he had only to keep his investors at arm's length from himself, and as far away from each other as possible. Not one of them knew how many others there were or the size of the sums he was borrowing until it was too late."

"Rather clever, in a horrible sort of way, wasn't he? What did he do with the money?"

"No one knows."

Melly looked at him quizzically.

"According to the report, about six months ago, he just disappeared."

"Had one of the investors grown suspicious?"

He shook his head. "There was some talk, but as long as he kept up with the interest on his loans, no one paid it too much mind. After all, he had provided the very best of references. Once he stopped paying, his creditors took a closer look at his affairs. They discovered not only that no US headquarters was being built, but that there was no record, either in the US or in Colombia, of the shipping company he claimed to represent."

Melly laughed. "That must have ruffled a few feathers."

"You could say that. In fact, you might say that by the time I met up with him, Mr. Souza was the most sought after man in New York."

"What happened next?"

Jamie leaned forward, picking up his glass. "The detective's report ends with Mr. Souza being killed in a freak traffic accident that left his creditors whistling in the wind."

"But surely, one million dollars cannot just disappear into thin air?"

Jamie shrugged and finished his drink.

Melly's face clouded over and her voice became serious. "Do you think Uncle Manny was one of the investors?"

"Possibly, but by the time he and I were upstate, the jig was up. So, why would Souza be looking for him? And why did he ask me about bonds?"

Melly frowned. "Then what do you think this man's connection to Uncle Manny was?"

"Your guess is as good as mine."

"We have to tell Father about this, all of it."

"We can't, Melly."

"Neither you nor I know enough about the business to sort this thing out. I know Father had a bit of a setback, but the doctor was here just this morning, and he told Mother and me that he was feeling much stronger."

Jamie looked down at the rug.

There was a moment of silence, then his sister asked softly, "Was the doctor lying?"

Jamie lifted his eyes to hers without speaking.

"Oh," she whispered. "I see."

"I'm awfully sorry, Mel."

"Why should you be? At least you told me." Melly reached for his glass of cognac, and he gave it to her. She downed it in one swallow then grabbed the decanter and refilled it. "How long does he have?"

"Months. Days. The doctor says it's impossible to say when it's the heart."

Jamie reached for his drink, but she pulled it to her chest. He rose and took another glass from the sidebar, filled it, then rejoined her on the sofa.

She looked at him, her cheeks shining with tears. "I suppose we're on our own then?"

"Yes," he said softly, his own vision blurring. "I suppose we are."

THE INQUEST

JANUARY 10, 1900

*M*arie finished restitching the buttonhole in the thick cotton work shirt and bit the thread to break it. She admired her handiwork before tucking it into her workbasket and hiding it with Mama's moth-eaten gray shawl.

Deception, even one as minor as hiding her mending, didn't sit easily on Marie's conscience, but last year, when she had suggested applying for a position as a shopgirl at Wanamaker's, Papa had flown into a towering rage. He would rather see her dead, he said, than working like a skivvy for wages. When, a few months later, Mrs. Griggs had suggested taking up piece work, secrecy had been Marie's only condition.

The few items of clothing Marie had imagined herself surreptitiously stitching had grown into ponderous work baskets full. But, so far, her secret had held, largely because Papa was so rarely home.

Marie had feared that her grief over Mémé's passing would cause her to fall behind, but, at least so far, the opposite had been true. She had even finished the mending for the Bijou early. There were, it appeared, some benefits to being too miserable to sleep. Marie sighed, then rose and carried the basket to its spot in the corner. She was readjusting the shawl when three loud raps sounded on the front door.

Eliza, who sat reading by the fire, glanced up at Marie, her eyes rounded. "He wouldn't dare. Not today?"

Marie shook her head in disgust. Over the past week, that knock had become all too familiar. At first, Detective Gardiner had satisfied himself with asking a lot of foolish questions: *Does your father own brown shoes? Does your brother often stay out all night? Are you a heavy sleeper?* But in recent days, he had expanded on this routine by requesting various items, which he carefully inspected, labeled with strips of cardstock and butcher's string, then carted away like an archeologist stripping a tomb.

"I'll see to him," Marie said, touching Eliza's shoulder as she passed. "You go and get ready. We have to leave for the inquest in half an hour."

Marie took her time walking the short distance to the door, then waited a few additional seconds before opening it the width of her shoulders. As expected, Detective Gardiner stood in the hall, a uniformed officer behind him.

"You've caught us at a bad time," Marie said crisply. "As I'm sure you know, the inquest is this morning."

"Your father owns a gray coat," Gardiner started right in. "I'd like to see it."

"He's probably wearing it."

"I've seen him. He isn't."

"Well, I haven't time to look for it now."

"I'm afraid it can't wait." Gardiner's tone was professional; that is to say, there was nothing in it that suggested he was capable of feeling either concern or compassion.

Marie hesitated, wondering what would happen if she shut the door in his face and set the bolt. Would he knock again? Order the uniformed officer to put his shoulder to it? She raised her eyes to Gardiner's, his gaze was calm and assured. One way or another, he would get what he wanted, and they both knew it. Of all the reasons she had for hating this man—the way he'd broken the news of Mémé's passing, his continued intrusion into their home and their lives, and the unspoken threat his mere presence contained—none riled her more than this: his comfortable certainty that he had all the power, and she had none.

She turned and walked back into the apartment, leaving the door open.

Eliza sat on the settle lacing her shoes. When she saw him, she covered her leg brace with her skirt and managed an awkward smile. "Hello, Detective Gardiner."

He nodded.

"They've come for Papa's gray coat," Marie said.

Eliza straightened. "Oh, would you like me to fetch it?"

"I'll get it. We'll be leaving in a few minutes." Marie looked pointedly at Detective Gardiner, then marched to Papa and Charlie's room. The coat hung in plain sight, affixed to a hook on the side of the wardrobe. She grabbed it and would have searched it if she hadn't hazarded a glance toward the door and caught the uniformed officer watching her.

Marie folded the coat over her arm and returned to the living room. "Here," she said, thrusting it into Gardiner's hands. "Now, we really must finish getting ready."

"We'll just be another moment." He placed the coat on their dining table and searched it, twisting and pressing the fabric before turning the pockets inside out. His efforts gained him a stained square of foolscap with the name "Gladys" and an address scrawled on it, a cigar stub, and a small silver watch.

He dangled the watch. "Does this belong to either of you?"

Eliza leaned closer to inspect it. "No."

Marie shook her head without bothering to look.

Gardiner continued mauling the coat, mashing the seams, and running his hands over the lining. Once he'd determined there were no secret cavities, he withdrew several labels from a leather satchel he'd brought with him.

Eliza stepped toward the table. "Maybe the watch belongs to Gladys, whoever she is?"

Gardiner looked up.

Eliza shrugged. "Papa often receives those sorts of little gifts from women."

Marie stepped forward and pinched the back of Eliza's arm. Her sister jerked away, stepping toward the detective.

Gardiner faced Eliza. "Will everyone be attending the inquest?"

"Yes," Eliza answered quickly. "We're to meet Papa and Charlie there at eleven."

Marie sighed audibly. Eliza glanced at her and stepped away from Gardiner and the table.

"Then I trust I will see you there." Gardiner picked up his parcels, tipped his hat, and walked out. The uniformed officer trailed him like a shadow.

The moment he shut the door, Marie whirled on her sister. "Why are you telling our business to that awful man?"

Eliza turned worried eyes on her. "He's only doing his job. Besides, it will go easier for us if we help him."

"Help him? Do what, exactly? Throw Papa and Charlie into prison?"

Eliza locked eyes with her, and said softly, "They can't throw a person in prison for a crime they didn't commit."

There was something probing in Eliza's gaze that made Marie uncomfortable. She turned toward the door. "Of course they can. Now go and fetch your hat, that dreadful man has made us late."

Marie understood the question in Eliza's eyes. It had plagued her too, ever since Gardiner had come that first day. Hopefully, today's inquest would bring them some peace.

Marie took a final look in the cloudy glass. Papa had said

that, with all the coverage in the papers, there was bound to be a crowd and plenty of newsmen. The thought filled Marie's chest with an uneasy excitement. She lifted her chin and half-closed her eyelids, assuming the haughty, unconcerned expression of a Gibson girl. Her hair could be piled a little higher, but the defect was not great, and she hadn't the time to fuss with it. Eliza reappeared as Marie was tying the ribbon of her bonnet, and the pair set off.

The courtroom was packed. The "suspicious" death of a prominent family's housekeeper on the first day of the new century had fired the public's imagination. Headlines concerning "The Murder on Chestnut Hill" leapt off the front page of every rag in town.

"There they are!" Eliza yanked Marie to the left, and Papa's bulky frame came into view.

Papa stood encircled by at least half a dozen people and was gesturing emphatically. The moment he spotted them, he broke off and extended his arm. "There you are, my darlings! I was worried sick."

Eliza glanced at Marie, a hint of a smile bending her lips.

Papa closed the distance between them and took Marie's elbow. "Come, my angels. Rest yourselves. You must be cold and weary."

The people nearby bent curious gazes in their direction, and Marie had to resist the urge to pull her elbow free and storm from the room. The crowd parted, and Papa led them to their seats. The moment they were seated, Papa resumed his position in the heart of the semi-circle, his head high and his chest puffed out. In his chocolate striped suit and sapphire-blue silk vest, he looked like a carnival barker.

"What a terrible ordeal these little lambs have endured," Papa announced to no one in particular. "They were very close to their grandmother, and she, poor soul, dearly loved them."

Marie dropped her gaze to the floor, her face burning. How could he be so undignified?

Charlie sat a couple of chairs over. His face was pinched and worry lines creased his brow. Marie moved to the seat next to him and whispered, "Papa is making a perfect spectacle of us."

Charlie shrugged. "At least he's enjoying himself."

"I only wish his enjoyment didn't come at our expense."

"You should try to be more generous. He's had a tough time of it, what with those idiot policemen hounding him day and night."

Marie looked away, abashed. There was, she supposed, no real harm in his theatrics, but just this once, she wished he would refrain from making them conspicuous. Before she could say this, Charlie pointed to a group of men sitting a few tables over. "Do you see that fellow over there? The pale gent in the high-backed chair?"

Marie scanned the crowd until she spotted a likely candidate: an older man with the gaunt, sallow countenance of someone recently ill. "What about him?"

Charlie leaned in to whisper, "*That* is Mr. Lett."

"Oh." Marie straightened to get a better view. According to Mémé, Marie had met the family when she was very young, but, try as she might, she couldn't remember it. They did not seem like strangers, though. Mémé had spoken of the Letts so often, and with such regard, that Marie had developed a great admiration for them. In her imagination, they represented everything that was fine and noble in the world; that is to say, everything that her own family was not.

Several men in dark suits, all holding tall, gleaming hats, stood near Mr. Lett's chair. She wondered who they were and hoped they would disperse once the inquest began. If Mr. Lett were alone, it would be easier to work up the courage to introduce herself.

"I wonder if he brought the old girl's money?" Charlie asked, interrupting her thoughts.

Marie's head snapped toward him. "This is neither the time nor the place for that conversation, Charlie."

Charlie heaved a long-suffering sigh.

"I mean it," she hissed. "Don't you dare disgrace us."

Charlie rolled his eyes and stood. "I'm going to get some air."

Marie glanced at their father, wondering if she should enlist his aid. He remained ensconced in the crowd's center, one arm flung casually around a bald man she didn't recognize, the other cutting a wide swathe through the air as he spoke. No, she thought, Papa would be no help at all.

Her attention was drawn to the front of the room, where several men had approached a scarred oak table. One of them banged a gavel, and the crowd fell silent. Marie returned to the seat next to Eliza. Her sister sat rigid, twisting her hands on her lap. Marie grabbed one of those pale hands and squeezed it. The inquest had begun.

A line of men Marie took to be the coroner's jury entered through a side door and filed to the front of the room. They were an odd mix of factory workers in their Sunday best and bourgeoisie in ready-made suits. A few cast furtive glances at the onlookers as they maneuvered to their seats. A small, dark man seated at the front table asked their names and tapped their responses into a little typewriter-like machine. When he'd finished, the man who had wielded the gavel stood.

"My name," he said, "is Frederick Grimsby, Coroner for the city of Philadelphia."

He paused for the audience to take this in.

"We are here today," Grimsby continued, "to inquire into the nature of the death of one Alozia Tompkins, housekeeper. Detective Gardiner, who was the ranking investigator at the scene, will be the first to provide evidence."

The audience, Marie included, turned to follow the detective's slow progress to the armless wooden chair facing the jury.

Once Gardiner had provided his credentials, Mr. Grimsby asked, "On the first day of the year of Our Lord nineteen-hundred, were you called to investigate a suspicious death at number eleven Chestnut Hill?"

"I was."

"And what did you find when you arrived?"

"The body of a colored woman who we later identified as the housekeeper, Mrs. Alozia Tompkins."

Marie winced at the word "colored". Mémé had been light-skinned, what people used to call "high yellow". Papa, her only child, was so light people generally thought him Greek or Italian, a notion he never bothered to disabuse them of. And Marie's mother, Eleanor, had been a tawny-haired, white woman. Marie was the darkest of their children, and while no one would ever mistake her as Dutch, no one had ever guessed she was part-colored, either.

Mémé always said that being a "colored Creole" was a thing to be proud of and had taken pains to instill in her grandchildren a respect for their storied heritage. But it hadn't taken Marie long to discover that the world outside held other opinions, and that letting white people know you were any part colored was akin to handing them a stick so that they could beat you with it.

The fit wasn't much better in the other direction. When she was little more than a girl, Marie had stood in the colored line at a lunch counter. All around her, conversations had ended abruptly and glances, both suspicious and amused, were aimed in her direction. Finally, a dark-skinned woman approached Marie and told her that she was in the wrong line. Marie explained that she wasn't, and that she too was colored. The woman looked surprised at first, then contemptuous. She shook her head, called Marie a little fool, and walked away. Marie purchased her lunch, but was so uncomfortable she couldn't eat a bite. From then on, whenever Marie was confronted with a similar choice, she chose the white line, but never without a niggling sense that she was letting Mémé down.

"Was the cause of death apparent?" Grimsby asked, calling Marie's attention back to the inquest.

Gardiner nodded. "Her throat had been cut."

A chorus of gasps and stifled exclamations erupted from the audience.

Marie's stomach turned over, and her hand flew to her mouth.

"Did," Grimsby raised his voice and the audience silenced, "you suspect the wound was self-inflicted?"

"That was not my impression, no. We found no blade near either hand. Also, her feet were planted squarely on the floor with her knees raised, suggesting that she was standing when the fatal wound was inflicted, and that she sank down where she stood. In my experience, a suicide, particularly one committed by a woman, would have given more thought to where and how her body would fall."

Marie heard her father stifle a sob. She would have wept too, only none of this seemed real or like it could have anything to do with Grand-mère Alozia.

Grimsby, who had paused to jot a note, pressed on, "In your professional opinion then, the injury could *not* have been self-inflicted? That is to say, you would dismiss a theory of suicide entirely?"

"I never dismiss any theory entirely, but I do think suicide unlikely here. We found evidence of a commotion: an over-turned table and a small workbox with its contents strewn across the floor. A razor case was also found lying just outside the pool of blood, but no razor."

"I assume a thorough search was performed?"

"That is correct."

"Interesting. Proceed."

"There were indications that the body had been searched post-mortem. Her pockets were found inside out, and—" He paused and it seemed like the entire room held its breath. "— there was a bloody fingerprint on her stocking, about three inches above the knee."

Eliza squeezed Marie's hand so tight it hurt, but Marie couldn't even look at her. The room was too hot, too crowded.

When the murmurs died away, Gardiner added, "Finally, every drawer and cupboard in the house had been turned out."

This spurred a fresh flurry of whispering, but this time the voices were tinged with excitement, not shock.

"Was anything taken?"

"Not from the house."

Grimsby looked up from his notepad. "You say nothing was missing *from the house?*"

"That's correct, sir, but several items were taken from the person of Mrs. Tompkins."

"Go on."

"A paperboy delivered a copy of *The Christian Recorder* at seven o'clock that evening. Mrs. Tompkins paid with one of several coins that she withdrew from her pocket. When he gave her change, she returned it to that same pocket, but when we found her, there was no money on her person. We were also reliably informed that she wore a silver watch on her left wrist, but no watch was found either on her body or amongst her possessions."

Marie's pulse pounded in her ears, and tiny pricks of pain blossomed on her face and scalp, like spray from an approaching wave. She couldn't breathe, and she needed to breathe.

Marie stood, ignoring the heads that turned her way. Papa had seated them at the end of a row, and she had only to push past his and Charlie's knees to reach the aisle. Grimsby was talking again, but she ignored him, concentrating only on the exit and getting herself to it before her legs gave way. A quick step sounded behind her, and Eliza gripped her arm.

Outside, the cold air crashed over her, clearing the haze from her mind. Eliza steered her to a bench. Marie sat, grateful to have something firm to hold onto. "A moment," she mumbled, "and we can go back inside."

"Must we?" Eliza asked. "I've heard enough. Besides, it's plain what the verdict will be."

Murder. Marie thought the word and shuddered.

The air smelled of the city in winter, of coal smoke undercut by the musk of the Delaware River, of baked bread and roasting meat from nearby shops, all mingling with the faint stink of horse manure.

"Marie," Eliza began hesitantly, "you don't think the watch Gardiner found—"

"No," Marie said emphatically. "One of us would have recognized it."

Eliza sighed. "When I saw it, I thought it was familiar, but I wasn't sure."

"Don't," Marie whispered.

After what seemed an eternity, a swell of human voices, overlapping and excited, erupted from the courthouse. People spilled out of the doors, jostling and talking energetically, like a satisfied audience leaving the theater.

"I'm better now," Marie said, rising to her feet. "Let's find Papa and Charlie and go home."

By the time they wove their way upstream, the courtroom was almost empty, and they were able to spot Charlie at once. He sat slumped in a chair; his hair and coat disarrayed.

"Where's Papa?" Marie asked.

"They took him," he answered, gazing at a spot on the floor between his boots.

"Who took him? Why?"

"Who do you think? The police."

"Because of the watch?" Marie asked, horror-stricken.

"No, you idiot. He got that piece of junk from a friend."

"How do you know?" Marie asked, her relief overpowering his rudeness.

"*He was arrested,*" Charlie continued, ignoring her question, "Because your Mr. Lett testified that he was always after Mémé for money. The old buzzard said Papa made scenes when she refused him. Said he'd urged her not to give him a cent. Imagine! He freely admitted it!"

"There must be some mistake," Marie mumbled, her mind reeling.

Charlie laughed bitterly. "Mistake? Aren't you listening? The bastard robbed us when Mémé was alive and hopes to go on robbing us now that she's dead."

"Do try to be sensible, Charlie. What need could Mr. Lett have of our inheritance?"

Charlie turned on her, his face dark with scorn. "How do you think the rich become so? Bloody selfish bastards, every one of them." He stood and tugged at his coat to straighten it. "I've had enough of this. I'll see you at home."

"Charlie, wait," Marie pleaded. "You can't leave. We have to do something."

"There's nothing to do," he said. His tone was fierce but his eyes shone with tears. "Don't you understand that? It's over, Marie. Over."

GOING PLACES

JANUARY 10, 1900

*M*arie picked a sock from her workbasket to darn, but every few stitches, her mind wandered back to the inquest. After they'd returned this afternoon, Eliza had settled into the window seat with a book, but every time Marie cast a worried glance in her direction, she found her sister staring out the window. When the sun began to set, Marie placed the sock, still unfinished, back in the basket and rose to light the lamps.

More from habit than hunger, she fetched the leftover cabbage, an onion, and a couple of potatoes from cold storage and began frying them in the old iron pot. Without being asked, Eliza stood and set the table. Marie was spooning their dinner onto plates when Mr. Griggs barged through their front door. He still wore his heavy leather work apron and was waving what appeared to be a folded newspaper before him.

"Did you think I wouldn't see this?" He shoved the evening edition of the *Philadelphia Bulletin* into Marie's face.

Marie glanced at the headline and her stomach twisted. She pushed the paper away and said, "Papa didn't do it."

"He didn't rent these rooms under false pretenses?

Pretending he was an honest white man, when all the time he was nothing but a lying—"

"No one intentionally deceived you," Marie cut in, her heart pounding.

"Bah!" he said, waving his hand at her. "Pack yer things, I want you out tonight."

"We can't leave tonight." Marie said, her head reeling. She sat and wiped her damp palms on her apron. "We have nowhere to go, and besides, we're paid up through the end of the month."

"The good, upstanding white folk I rented these rooms to are paid up, but you ain't that? Are you?"

"But nothing has changed," Marie said plaintively, realizing as she said it that it was a lie—everything had changed "What's the difference?"

"I'd say about a dollar a week."

"What?"

"You know as well as I do this ain't no colored neighborhood, let alone a colored house. If you want the privilege of staying here, yer gonna pay me two dollars and fifty cents a week."

It was nothing short of highway robbery, but what other options did they have?

"Alright," Marie said, mentally tallying their meager savings. "I can have it for you Wednesday."

"You best have it fer me now, girl." He glared at her from beneath grizzled brows.

Marie glanced at Eliza. Her sister's face was bright red, and there were tears in her eyes.

"It's alright," Marie said to Eliza, then turning to Griggs. "I'll go and fetch it."

They kept their savings in an empty can of Old Dutch. Taking care to hide what she was doing, Marie tucked the can into the folds of her skirt and disappeared into her room to count the money. Her hands shook so hard she dropped the can and had to crawl on hands and knees to retrieve the coins that rolled under the bed. When she counted off the sum, her heart sank. With it gone, only a few nickels and pennies remained.

She handed their savings to Griggs, who counted it twice. He glanced up and caught her glaring at him. He stepped forward and shoved a blunt finger in her face. "It ain't no good you lookin' at me like that. The missus and I run a respectable establishment. If'n it were up to me, you'd be in the street already. Understood?"

Marie gritted her teeth and nodded.

Griggs slammed the door as he left, and Marie fastened the lock then stood, waiting for the worst of her anger to subside.

"I hate that man," Eliza said, her voice low and furious. "Plain trash is what Mémé would have called him. Not fit to clean her shoes."

Marie turned toward Eliza. Her sister still stood by the table, her cheeks were flushed with anger, but her eyes were dry. Marie's heart softened. Eliza was right, that was exactly what Mémé would have said.

Marie stooped to pick up the newspaper Griggs had left behind.

Eliza moved alongside her. The headline *Man Accused of Murdering Own Mother* was circled in dark pencil. Deciding it was best to know the worst straight away, Marie began reading. It described how the victim, a colored housekeeper, had been viciously murdered, and how her "venerated employer", Mr. James Lett, had taken the witness box and cast Papa's character in the blackest of terms. The article was long on exposition and short on facts, but Marie's heart lifted when she read the last sentence.

"Did you see this?" Marie asked.

"See what?"

"Here." Marie ran her finger along the newsprint. "'Being in poor health, Mr. Lett departed immediately following his testimony." She slid her finger to the final paragraph. "And here, 'Mr. Chevalier was taken to the police station for further questioning at the conclusion of the proceeding."

Eliza furrowed her brow. "So?"

"*So*, Mr. Lett wasn't there when Papa was arrested."

"How does that help us?"

Marie shook her head impatiently. "Papa *was* always after Mémé for money, Mr. Lett could hardly have said otherwise. But Mémé always told us what a good man—a true gentleman— Mr. Lett was. I'm sure he didn't expect Papa would be arrested. Once he finds out, he might put in a word for us."

Eliza locked eyes with her. "You can't really believe that?"

The words stung. Marie retreated to her chair by the fire. Any other day, she would have argued her point, but today's events had left her shaken. She picked up her sewing, but when she jabbed herself for the fourth time, she shoved her work back in the basket.

It was after nine, so she gathered her toilette and made for the community bathroom. She took her time scrubbing her face with baking soda. The mirror was old, and the silver nitrate had long since started flaking away, leaving the glass cloudy and spotted with dark patches. She stared at herself a moment. Her skin had grown unfashionably pale, and dark shadows ringed her large, frightened eyes.

She had been a beautiful girl once, everyone said so. Eliza was the clever one. During her illness, Eliza hadn't been able to play with the other children, and had spent her time reading and studying. When she had declared her intention of going to college, Papa had surprised everyone by agreeing, so long as Mémé paid for it.

Marie, on the other hand, had only her beauty to recommend her. From childhood, she had known that if she wanted a better life, she would have to marry into it. This had never much troubled her, because by the time she was sixteen, she had grown so lovely that even Papa had said she was destined to wed a wealthy man. Back then, the future lay bright and golden before her, and who could say what might have happened if she hadn't fallen in love?

To her childish mind, William had seemed like a matinee idol. He was handsome, clever, and a little moody. But more than that, when he looked at her, she felt seen, and when he touched her, she felt truly alive for the first time. Besotted as she was, it was easy to believe in his dreams, his potential. How could she not, when a smile or a soft word could empty her head and set her heart to racing? She had shut her eyes to his drinking and carousing, telling herself it was just what men did.

But the forgeries had changed everything. The scandal was so great it not only dashed William's prospects but cost her brother his job and reputation. She'd begged William to explain himself, to tell her it was all a misunderstanding, but he maintained a stony silence. When Papa warned her that if she did not break with him, William would drag the entire family down with him, she'd had no defense to offer.

After William, there had been others; George, the grocer's boy, had taken a keen interest in her, and Papa's haberdasher, Jerome, had as good as asked for her hand. But she had refused them, waiting for a better man, the *right* man, to come along. And now here she was, twenty-one, and already fading. She turned from the mirror and slunk back to the apartment.

Perched on the edge of the bed, she plaited her hair in the dark. With any luck, the morning would bring better news. In the alley below, two cats fought over scraps of garbage, their yowls piercing the thrum and bang of water rushing through rusty pipes. She laid back and buried her head under her pillow, willing herself to sleep.

Papa was innocent, that she did not doubt. Today, at the inquest, her fear had gotten the better of her, but the longer she thought on it, the more she realized there was no reason to doubt Papa's explanation. Silver watches were as common as pearl earbobs or coral cameo pins. You would be hard-pressed to find a woman of any means in this city who did not own at least one. Why shouldn't Gladys, or anyone else, give one to Papa if they chose to?

The police would realize their mistake eventually. But when? And what would become of them in the meantime? This was the thought that underpinned all the others, like a splinter that stabs with every step.

She could ask Mrs. Griggs for more work, though that hardly seemed a solution. The woman would likely follow her husband's lead and reduce her pay. Not that it made a difference. Even if Marie earned twice what she did now for mending, it wouldn't be enough to pay rent. With her father gone, she could apply for a position in one of the factories by the river. That might be enough for a single room in a mixed neighborhood like South-wark, but not groceries. Charlie could not be relied upon, and Eliza was still in school. No matter how Marie turned the pieces in her mind, she could not find an arrangement that kept her family housed and fed. Despair rose in her throat until it nearly choked her. There had to be something she could do, but what?

She bolted upright when the answer came to her. It was so simple, she could hardly believe she hadn't thought of it sooner: rather than wait and hope that Mr. Lett would read about her family's distress, she would go to New York City and tell him of it in person.

Once the idea seized her, she couldn't get it out of her mind. She continued to toss and turn, but now with anticipation. When the first pale rays of sunlight streamed through the cracks in the yellow chintz curtain, she rose and dressed quietly in her Sunday best. She retrieved an enameled trinket box from the top drawer of her vanity and withdrew the tortoise comb Mémé had given her for Christmas. She pressed it to her lips before sliding it into her pocket and slipping silently from the room.

Charlie lay sprawled across the sofa, arms and legs akimbo. Nothing short of a brass band could rouse him when he was in this state, but she still lightened her step as she entered the kitchen and retrieved the newspaper from the kindling box. Ignoring the circled article, she turned the pages until she found the train fares and schedule. She had never taken a train before, but it couldn't be that complicated. After all, thousands of people did it every day.

She tucked the paper under her arm and slipped out of the apartment. A swell of relief, tinged with excitement, washed over her when she stepped into the wintry morning. The sky was a dull gray, and the wind was flecked with ice that burned her nose and cheeks. Despite the gloom, her heart quickened in anticipation of the adventure ahead.

She kept up a brisk pace, stopping only when she reached her destination: a small shop with windows displaying everything from sewing machines to gold watch chains. Marie knew the proprietor well, or rather, he knew Papa. Ten minutes later, she emerged with two dollars and a pawn ticket she knew she would be unable to redeem.

When she turned onto Market, Broad Street Station came into view. A massive structure that dominated central Philadelphia. Its towers, spires, arched windows, and enormous domed shed exuded strength and confidence, an awareness of a distinguished past combined with an openness to new ideas that Marie associated with the city itself.

She pushed her way through the revolving doors and stood stock still, taking it in. For sheer size, she had seen nothing to equal it. The better part of a city block could fit within its walls. Everywhere, people bundled in heavy coats and scarves bustled about. Signs directing travelers to various destinations sprouted from the marble floor and protruded from walls, but she could not make heads or tails of them.

She approached a lanky, chestnut-haired busboy who appeared younger than Eliza and asked for directions. The boy put aside his broom and led her first to the ticket booths, then waited while she paid the fare, before depositing her on the loading platform.

"I can't thank you enough," Marie told the busboy, her heart full of gratitude. "I'd be wandering in circles without you."

He smiled knowingly and held out his calloused hand, palm up. It took Marie a moment to understand what he wanted. Flushing to the roots of her hair, she dug in her purse, located a penny, and pressed it into his palm.

He looked at it, then at her, shook his head and walked away. Marie's cheeks burned, but it couldn't be helped. One day, she told herself, she would have money enough to tip handsomely, but today was not that day.

She looked around. Above the platform rose the domed shed, and, in front of her, a maze of steel rails converged and overlapped. The air was sharp and cold, and smelled strongly of coal smoke, pipe tobacco, and overripe fruit. There were dozens of people standing on the platform with her, they couldn't all be waiting for her train. Or could they? A large clock hung from a steel rafter. Five to nine. Eliza should be getting out of bed now. Marie wished she had left a note.

She was still thinking of her sister when a whistle sounded. A few seconds later, it blew again, much louder, and the huge engine came into view. People who had been seated on the benches rose and came together, pressing toward the tracks. The noise and enormity of the train commanded all of Marie's attention. She had seen trains before, but never this close. The metal wheels were still turning when the doors slid open and the conductor, a stout middle-aged man clad in a navy uniform so dark it was almost black, lowered the stairs toward the platform. Marie joined the press, moving with the crowd until she drew close enough to hand him the ticket.

"To your right, fifth seat down." He punched it and handed it back, his placid gray eyes already searching out the next passenger.

She lifted her skirt so she wouldn't trip and climbed aboard. Inside, the aisle was wider and the seats taller, but it was not unlike a trolley.

People filtered inside, taking their seats. A woman with a flower bonnet and a missing eye-tooth sat down two seats over and smiled a greeting. Marie smiled back, then stared out the window at the workmen and passengers milling on the platform. She was wondering if they were ever going to start moving when a grinding sound filled the air, and the train chuffed slowly forward. She closed her eyes, giddy with nervous excitement. This was really happening. She was on her way.

The train climbed over the Chinese Wall, picking up speed as it traveled toward Schuylkill River. After a while, the buildings thinned, then disappeared altogether, replaced by snow-laden fields and bare-branched trees.

If the train stayed on schedule, she'd arrive in New York City in a mere two hours.

She stared out the window, transfixed by the countryside. She had never been out of the city, and the great humanless expanses filled her with awe, and a little fear. Her thoughts drifted to what she would say to Mr. Lett. Her imaginings varied greatly in the start and middle, but they all ended the same: he would arrange for Papa's immediate release. Sometimes she allowed the daydream to continue, and Papa, grateful and humbled by this experience, would dedicate himself to becoming the respectable citizen she had always longed for him to be; but even in her most optimistic moments, this last scenario seemed rather too much to hope for.

The sleepless night must have caught up with her, because

she woke with a start when the conductor made his way through the aisle calling out, "Next stop, New York City."

The train pulled into a station every bit as grand as Broad Street had been. She located the information desk and asked for the New York City social registry. Her heart beat against her ribs as she turned the pages, suddenly afraid Mr. Lett wouldn't be listed, but of course he was.

Marie took a pencil from her purse and copied the address. When she finished, she thanked the spectacled man behind the counter and joined the crowd moving toward the exits.

Stepping out of the station was a little like stepping off a boat onto a foreign shore. The buildings here were taller; their stone facades, reaching impossibly high into the sky, amplified the incessant clatter of hooves and wheels that traversed the broad avenues below. Even the sidewalks, slick with soot and refuse, bore the stamp of a city far rougher and more chaotic than Philadelphia.

Cabs lined the block. She picked the driver with the kindest face and walked over holding the address up to him. "Is twenty-five cents enough to go here?"

His eyes darted from the paper to her, and she sensed him taking in the expensive but worn shoes, the oft-mended dress.

"It is for you." The gentleness of his smile took the sting from his words.

Ten minutes later, she stood in front of the Lett's house. It was a tall, narrow brick building, much like those around it. Disappointment nibbled at the frayed edges of her excitement. It was a fine structure, to be sure, but not nearly as grand as she had imagined.

She started toward the servants' entrance then caught herself. She had come to see the master of the house, not deliver groceries. Her heart raced as she climbed the front steps. She smoothed her hair and straightened her coat before lifting a trembling hand to the knocker and bringing it down three times.

A sturdy, middle-aged woman in a crisp blue and white uniform opened the door. She looked at Marie without speaking.

This strange greeting, or lack of one, was so disconcerting that Marie almost forgot the speech she had prepared. "M-my name is Marie Chevalier. My grandmother was the housekeeper at Chestnut Hill, and I have a matter of great urgency to discuss with Mr. Lett."

The woman's eyebrows lifted. She thought for a moment, then said, "Wait here."

The door clicked shut, and Marie listened to the woman's heavy tread moving away. In all the times she had pictured her arrival, not once had she imagined being left on the doorstep. The possibility that she would not be admitted occurred to her for the first time, and the terror of it made her dizzy. She tried to steady her nerves by concentrating on the brass door knocker. It was in the shape of a lion's head, its mane gleaming and golden in the winter light. In it, she could see her own reflection, stunted and horribly misshapen.

At last, the housekeeper reappeared. She gave Marie a hard look then said, "Follow me."

FIRST IMPRESSIONS

JANUARY 11, 1900

*M*arie followed the housekeeper through an elegant marble entryway into a large sitting room papered in violet. There, a tall young man stood near a marble-fronted fireplace, inside of which burned a low fire. He turned when they entered. "Good afternoon, Miss... Chevalier, isn't it?"

Marie nodded.

"How may I help you?"

Marie's hopes plummeted. "I'm sorry, sir, but what I've come to say, I must say to Mr. Lett *in person.*"

The man's brow furrowed slightly, but he looked more amused than affronted. "I am Mr. Lett."

Mémé had often spoken of a "Young Mr. Lett", but Marie had always imagined him as a spoiled but good-natured schoolboy, nothing at all like the dashing young gentleman before her.

"I'm afraid my father is unwell," Mr. Lett continued, his voice gentle. "Can't I be of assistance?"

"I'm very sorry to hear that," Marie said, her thoughts racing. She had been confident, or at least hopeful, that Mr. Lett Sr.

would be sympathetic. His son, however, was an unknown quantity.

"Please, have a seat." Young Mr. Lett gestured to a camelback sofa upholstered in cream brocade. Marie's mind went to the dust and dirt clinging to her skirt, and she eyed him uncertainly as she lowered herself onto the cushion, ready to jump up should he change his mind.

He sat in a chair across from her and leaned forward until he caught her gaze. "Allow me to express my sympathy for your recent loss. Your grandmother was like a member of this family. She has been, and will always be, greatly missed."

"Thank you," Marie mumbled. Abashed that her father's arrest had so dominated her thoughts that Mémé's death felt like a distant nightmare.

The door opened and a maid not much older than Marie appeared pushing a trolley with tea and sandwiches. Marie took the cup the maid offered, marveling at its delicate whiteness. It trembled in her hands, so she set it on a nearby table. She examined Mr. Lett as he spooned sugar into his tea. His hair was thick, brown, and wavy, and if his nose was a mite too large and his jaw a tad too narrow, one hardly noticed. He had a strong brow, intelligent blue eyes, and such bearing! He was easily the most fashionable man Marie had ever seen.

He caught her gawking at him and smiled. "I don't wonder at your being uncertain of me. If your grandmother told you but a small part of the grief my sister and I caused her, the damage to my reputation is unrecoverable."

"Oh, no. Mémé would never—" Marie broke off when his grin broadened.

"No, of course not. Madame Alozia was a woman of great discretion, but how we tried her. As children, one or the other of us was forever raiding the pantry or interrupting her inventory with an introduction to the newest member of our menagerie."

He leaned back, his eyes soft, as though lost in a pleasant memory. "Once, a gopher snake Melly and I were nursing back to health escaped the crate we'd put it in. We turned the house upside down looking for it. Two days after we'd given it up for dead, Madame Alozia found it—in the blanket box at the end of her bed."

Marie clapped her hand over her mouth.

"She was a terribly good sport about it," he continued, grinning fondly. "At breakfast the following morning, she informed Melly and I that our doctoring efforts had been a success, and that our patient had been discharged."

Marie laughed.

"But enough of my youthful misdeeds. Mildred tells me you've come on urgent business. It must be pressing to have brought you so far. What is it we can do for you?"

Marie hesitated. Mr. Lett's well-mannered gallantry was of a piece with the surroundings: the sofa, the wallpaper, the teacups—everything elegant and clean. Speaking of her family, of their troubles, felt like letting a sounder of swine loose in the room.

Poverty, she thought, as she feverishly sought the right words to say to the elegant gentleman before her, was a disease. When surrounded by other sufferers, she could ignore her own infection, but here, in this room, there was no mistaking that *she* was the blight.

"My grandmother spoke so highly of your family, of your honor and generosity, I felt I could speak to you of my family's troubles." Marie glanced up quickly. Mr. Lett's face had taken on a guarded expression. Her chest contracted—he thought she was going to ask for money! She rushed on, "As you may know, my father was taken into custody after the inquest. And while Papa can be...*difficult*, he would never do anything like what they've accused him of. You must believe me."

Mr. Lett picked up the teapot and refreshed her cup. "On your account alone, I am prepared to."

Marie exhaled, weak with relief. "Then you will help us?"

Mr. Lett's brow furrowed. "If, as you say, the police have detained your father for questioning, then the matter is in their hands." Noticing her disappointment, he added, "The police know their business. If he is innocent, they will release him."

"But what if they realize his innocence too late? The loss of his income, however meager—" Marie paused, her stomach knotted. It was humiliating to speak of money, but she needed to make him understand. "We will not last long. I tell you truly, we cannot survive it."

"What is it, exactly, you would like my father to do?"

"Mr. Lett is a man of great reputation; his word has weight. If he were to speak for Papa, say that he felt certain he was innocent, I know the police would believe him."

Young Mr. Lett looked doubtful, and Marie hurried on, "They could still investigate, but Papa would be at liberty while they did so. I hate to ask it, truly I do, but you are our only hope."

He looked at her thoughtfully before rising and walking to a window overlooking the icy garden.

Marie's chest was so tight she could hardly breathe.

At last, he turned back to her. "As I told you when you first arrived, my father is ill, but, when he wakes, if he is feeling better, I will plead your cause."

Marie clasped her hands together, tears stinging her eyes. "Oh, thank you! Thank you, Mr. Lett. I'll be in your debt as long as I live."

"None of that." He withdrew a folded cambric handkerchief from his pocket and handed it to her.

Once she'd composed herself, he added, "I must warn you, I make no guarantee about what my father's response will be. Indeed, even if he were to intercede on your father's behalf, it is by no means certain it would have the effect you desire. In recent years, the spirit of reform has descended on our police department, and influence is no longer the passkey it once was."

"Of course," Marie said hastily, "I completely understand." In truth, she was so relieved she hardly knew what he was saying. "But having met the son, I cannot doubt the generosity of the father."

"Well, um, ... yes." His brow furrowed and a little extra color appeared in his cheeks. He gestured to the tea cart. "Now that we have that out of the way, why don't you help yourself to one of these sandwiches? Agnes will be insulted if we don't eat them."

Marie placed two of the startlingly pale triangles on the delicate plate he handed her.

"Did you catch The Four Cohans when they played in Philadelphia?

Marie looked up from her sandwiches, startled. "I did."

"And did you like them?"

"Very much."

"As did I."

Marie placed her plate on the table, so she could turn her full attention to Mr. Lett. The Four Cohans were a hugely popular act, especially with the working class. Was he patronizing her? "And when did you see them?" she asked.

"Last October, and I saw them twice last summer in New York." His smile broadened. "This surprises you?"

"W-well," Marie stammered, wishing her emotions didn't show so plainly on her face. "I suppose, I imagined you'd only care for the *serious* theater."

"And miss all the fun?" He said, his grin infectious. "I enjoy a David Belasco as much as the next man, but I would be very sorry indeed if that meant I had to forego a performance by the great Lillian Russell."

"I see what you mean," Marie said, unnerved by how happy

his response made her. He was just being polite. She picked up her sandwich plate again, grateful for anything that kept her from grinning at him like one of those mawkish porcelain dolls she used to covet in store windows.

He continued chatting pleasantly while she ate, and to Marie's surprise, she soon found herself telling him about the work she did for the Bijou, and what a boon the free admission was, even if she hadn't yet found time to use it. He spoke of his visits to the great playhouses of London, Lisbon, Paris, and Milan. She thanked her lucky stars that she had read enough theater news in *The Inquirer* to follow the thread of his conversation. So rapt was she, that it was not until she heard the clock tolling five that she realized how late it was.

"Oh dear," Marie exclaimed. She placed her nearly empty cup on its saucer and stood. "I'm afraid I've kept you too long."

Mr. Lett looked surprised. "Not at all. I've been enjoying our conversation. Sit, have more tea." He gestured toward the pot.

Marie's heart swelled. She looked at the clock again and, for a fleeting moment, she allowed herself to believe that perhaps it wouldn't be such a terrible thing if she missed the train. If only she had money enough for another ticket—but she didn't. "Thank you, but I really should be going. It's a long walk to the station, and I don't want to miss my train."

"Walk? It must be three miles."

Marie glanced down at her well worn shoes, unsure what to say to this. Clearly, he thought three miles a fair distance, but every grocery day, she walked at least twice that.

"Oh, yes, of course," he said, as though she'd spoken her thoughts out loud. His voice was gentle, understanding. "If you can't stay, will you at least allow me to offer you our carriage?" Without waiting for a response, he reached for the bell and rang it. The maid from earlier appeared. "Tell Niles I need him to take Miss Chevalier to the station."

"You don't have to do that," Marie protested, even as her heart swelled with happiness and relief. She had a fair sense of direction, but did not relish the thought of finding her way back to the station alone. "You have been so kind to me already."

"Don't be absurd. I've done nothing but drink tea with a charming young lady."

He said it so naturally that Marie could almost make herself believe he meant it.

A few minutes later, the maid reappeared and announced that the carriage was ready. Mr. Lett walked Marie to it, giving her his arm for support as she stepped inside. Once she was seated, he handed her a soft fur to place on her lap. She was still tucking it around her, thinking of ways to draw the visit out just a few moments longer, when he called out a final farewell and shut the door.

The carriage jolted forward and rumbled slowly down the street. Marie twisted in her seat and waved like a child to his receding form. Long after he'd gone back inside the house, she stared on, keeping the gabled roof in view until it melted into the white fog of the frosted windowpane. Sinking back into the cushions, Marie pulled the fur close against her, hugging it. On the trip here, she had felt like a heroine in an adventure story, but now she felt more like a princess in a fairytale. She closed her eyes, trying to imprint every detail of the past few hours in her memory.

Once Mr. Lett Sr. spoke to the police, and she was certain now that he would, Papa would be released. Her heart lifted at the thought, and yesterday's terrors evaporated.

Young Mr. Lett had been charming, and Marie felt instinctively that the favorable impression had been mutual. It was as though she had passed a test and been deemed worthy of a great honor, though she was at a loss to say what that honor was. The imprecision of the feeling did not detract from its potency. Her pleasure at having succeeded, at whatever it was, was so keen her chest ached with it.

Far from being the disaster she had feared, this had been, without question, the best day of her life. She sank back into the thick velvet seats, covered her face with her hands, and cried.

REWARD

JANUARY 11, 1900

For hours after Miss Chevalier's visit, she was all Jamie could think about. Beauty in distress is seldom without champions, and Miss Chevalier was very beautiful indeed. That alone was sufficient to recommend her cause to him, but Marie's visit had done something more. It had reminded Jamie of his obligation to Madame Alozia, the loyal and kindly housekeeper who had served his family as long as he could remember.

The carriage had scarcely left the drive before Jamie dashed off a telegram to the Philadelphia Police Department expressing his concern for Mr. Chevalier and his hope that said gentleman would soon be reunited with his family. While he did not share Miss Chevalier's estimation of his family's influence in that quarter, his interest couldn't do the fellow's case any harm.

Once the telegram was dispatched, Jamie was satisfied that he had done his duty, and settled into his favorite armchair to do a little light reading. He picked up the slim French volume he had purchased at Leary's on Ninth. He was proficient, if not fluent, in the language, but no matter how he focused, his thoughts wandered again and again to Madame Alozia's family.

A group of people, he realized with some embarrassment, he had never devoted a solitary thought to.

He was soon thinking of his hastily penned telegram not with satisfaction but with chagrin. What was a telegram but the merest trifle? A thing so paltry it was less aid than insult. Didn't Madama Alozia's long and faithful service merit more than two minutes of his attention?

Jamie laid the novel, a rather convoluted love affair with far less scandalous content than the bookseller led him to believe, on his chest and pondered what more he might do for the Chevaliers. The creaking of a nearby floorboard broke his concentration, and he turned to find his sister in the doorway. He straightened, and, with what he hoped was a subtle gesture, slipped the novel onto the floor. "Melly, I didn't hear you come in."

Melly smiled wryly as she glided into the room. "She must have been even lovelier than Mildred let on."

"What are you talking about?"

"Don't be coy. I know you too well. That flushed, far-away look you're wearing can mean only one thing."

"Ah, I see." Jamie shook his head sadly. "You've been at the laudanum again." He rose, walked to the side-table and poured himself a drink. "I hear there's a good man visiting from Austria. Say the word, and I'll arrange an appointment for you."

"Idiot," Melly mumbled, sauntering past him to perch on the arm of the sofa. "What did Madame Alozia's pretty young granddaughter want?"

Jamie resumed his seat. "It seems her father was arrested and the family is in desperate straits. She wanted to know if we could help."

"And could we?"

Jamie frowned. "I've sent a telegram to the police and await their reply."

"The police! What a rare beauty she must be!"

Jamie took another swallow, stifling his irritation. "Miss Chevalier is a very pretty girl, but had she been plainer than Matsys' duchess, I would still have sent the telegram. It is our duty to help Madame Alozia's family."

Melly raised her eyebrows.

"For God's sake, she's Madame Alozia's granddaughter. What sort of man do you think I am?" The words came out harsher than he'd intended, and he hastened to add, "Sorry, sorry. It's been a hell of a day."

"No, *I'm* sorry," Melly said quickly, sliding off the arm of the sofa and onto the cushioned velvet seat. "Reading those ledgers we took from Manassas's office taxed my patience."

"Did you find anything?"

She shook her head.

"Maybe there's nothing to find?" Jamie heard the hope in his voice and cringed. Impossible though it was, there were times when he could almost believe that his ill-fated trip to Tupper Lake had been a bad dream.

Melly sighed. "It's there. We just have to keep looking. Is Manasses still scheduled to return next week?"

"No. He extended his trip by two weeks."

"Again?"

Jamie nodded.

"For what reason?"

"Didn't say."

"But he's definitely out of state?

"According to his secretary, he is."

Melly shrugged. "Well, at least that makes things easier on us. I'll need more files."

"I'll cable Toby and have him send some over." Not wishing a repeat of their late night excursion, Jamie had negotiated an arrangement with the boy who'd procured the keys for them. What the kid thought of the assignment, Jamie didn't care to imagine, but the extra half-dollar a week had been more than sufficient to secure both his service and his silence.

"What about you?" Melly asked. "Have you finished going through your lot yet?"

"I will tonight." Jamie was bracing himself for the caustic remark he felt certain was coming when the dinner bell rang. He rose swiftly to his feet and offered Melly his arm. She pushed it away, and he trailed her into the dining room.

A dull sadness weighted his chest when he saw the old table with only two place settings. This was the third time in as many days that Father had been too ill to come down. Mother refused to leave his bedside.

The lute-backed chair squeaked against the waxed floor as Jamie pulled it out. Without his parents, the room looked different: darker, older. He picked at the roasted lamb and stuffed tomatoes on his plate without appetite. Melly must have been similarly affected, because they spoke little through dinner, and afterward, she retired to her room. When he returned to the library, he found a telegram on the desk. He tore open the envelope, an unexpected whir of anticipation making his heart beat fast. It read:

Confirming Chevalier's alibi. Once checked, will release.

Jamie folded the paper, a mixture of relief and disappointment swirling through him: relief that he was now spared the onerous task of laying the girl's story before his father, and disappointment because he would not be able to assist the pretty young damsel after all.

He was reflecting on the perversity of the human heart when an idea occurred to him. Grinning, he scribbled off a new telegram addressed to the family attorney, Calvin Duncombe:

*Immediately place 500-dollar reward for infor-
mation leading to arrest and conviction of Mrs.
Tompkins' murderer. Will explain later.*

Jamie rang for Niles and handed him the missive with instructions to be at the telegraph office tomorrow when it opened.
Jamie's satisfaction with this scheme lifted his spirits, and he
decided to make good on his word to Melly and finish reviewing
Manasses's files. Unfortunately, the reading was even duller than
he'd remembered, and if not for his dread of having to admit his
failure the following morning, he would have given it up half-a-
dozen times. At the end of two fruitless hours, he set the last file
in the "completed" pile and leaned back in his chair, exhausted.

He stretched his neck, then looked at the clock. A quarter to
ten—too early for a man his age to retire. He rose and walked to
the side table to pour himself two fingers of cognac. The French
novel was still on the floor next to the armchair. He was considering giving it another chance when the afternoon post caught
his attention.

He set his glass down and picked up the small stack of
letters. All but one were of the ordinary variety. Jamie studied
the outlier. The sender had identified himself as Mr. Charles
Chevalier. The man at the inquest had been named John, so
Charles must be Marie's brother. Charles had addressed his
missive to *The Honorable Mr. Lett, Esq.* Jamie smiled at the
misplaced honorific as he opened the envelope.

Dear Mr. Lett:
*I demand the immediate release of all monies
and properties belonging to your now-deceased housekeeper, Mrs. Alozia Tompkins. We, Mrs. Tompkins'*

rightful heirs and successors, will accept delivery of all said monies and goods immediately, at the time, date, and place of your choosing.

Failure to honor this most legitimate and honorable request will compel my family to take swift legal action against yours.

In all sincerity,

Charles M. Chevalier

Jamie placed the letter on the desk and sat down, amusement competing with annoyance. Had he not met Marie and heard from her lips the abysmal conditions under which the unhappy family labored, such a communication would not have disposed him favorably toward its author.

Determined to give young Charles the benefit of the doubt for Marie's sake, Jamie took a swallow of cognac, picked up a pen, and composed his response.

My Dear Mr. Chevalier:

First, allow me to express my sympathy for your family's recent loss. Your grandmother was a fine woman who was esteemed and respected by all who knew her.

It saddened me to learn of your family's current financial distress. Unfortunately, as executor of your grandmother's estate, my father is not at liberty to disburse your inheritance until your father has been wholly cleared of suspicion in the matter of her death. I realize that, given the immediacy of your wants, this news will come as something of a disappointment.

With your family's need for expedience in view, and as a tribute to your estimable grandmother's long and distinguished service, I have just this day ordered that a notice offering $500 for information leading to the capture and conviction of her murderer be published in every newspaper in Philadelphia. It is my hope that such an incentive will speed the course of justice and hasten the relief of your family's suffering.

Please, give my kind regards to your sister, Marie, and to the rest of your family.

Sincerely,

James Lett

Jamie was tempted to include news of their father's impending release, but his knowledge of the matter was too indefinite. Better to say nothing and allow the mysterious machinations of the police department to run their course.

He smiled as he sealed the envelope. It was addressed to Charles Chevalier, but it was Marie's face he imagined hovering over it, beaming with gratitude.

PIGEON

JANUARY 13, 1900

*C*harlie stood in his apartment building's small foyer and wiped the hazy window pane with his coat sleeve. Leaning forward until his nose almost touched the glass, he scanned the shrubbery for shadowy forms of newspapermen lying in wait.

"Whatcha about, boy?"

Charlie spun around, his fingers tightening into fists.

Mr. Griggs stepped back, both hands raised.

"Sorry," Charlie muttered, relaxing. "These damnable newsmen have me on edge. They're worse than a pack of duns."

Griggs showed his tobacco-stained teeth in what, for him, passed as a smile, and sidled up alongside him. "Can't rightly blame 'em. Five-hundred dollars." The old man whistled appreciatively. "That's a lotta jack."

Charlie grunted agreement. "It's that damned fool Lett's fault. If his plan is for these vipers to drive us away before we get our inheritance, he's got another think comin'."

"Reckoned it was something like that." Griggs nodded sympathetically. "Why, I was saying to the old woman jes' this morning, if'n that Lett's so keen on helping yer family, how is it he didn't give *you* the money? Answer me that!"

Charlie had wondered this very thing since he'd received Junior's letter. Mémé Alozia was dead. Finding her killer wouldn't bring her back, and that five-hundred dollars would do a lot more good in his pocket than in the hands of some grubby stranger. "Whatever he's about, it won't work. We aren't going anywhere till we get what's rightfully ours."

"That's the spirit, laddy." Griggs clapped him on the back.

Charlie forced a smile. He'd almost liked Griggs better when the old man was calling them *colored trash* and threatening to toss them into the street. At least that had been honest. With the inheritance and the reward over their heads, the old fox smelled money in the wind, and would say or do anything to make sure he got his share. Between him and the newsmen, Charlie couldn't so much as take a piss without someone squinting over his shoulder.

"They're either on the roof or McKinley is in town." Charlie gestured toward the empty sidewalk. "Not a sign of them."

Griggs's eyes sparkled. "Aye, I told 'em you an' yer sisters had slipped out the back way to visit yer gran's grave. They couldn't have lit out of here faster if I'd set fire to their drawers."

Charlie laughed in spite of himself. Then, seizing the opportunity, he swung the front door open and strode into the cold afternoon, ignoring the flurry of questions Griggs flung at his back.

When Charlie made it to the street unmolested, he breathed a sigh of relief. The weather was rotten again, but, after being cooped up all day, he enjoyed the sting of icy air in his nose. He sucked in a lungful, barely noticing the tang of manure.

He had advanced only a few steps when a black carriage drew up alongside him, and a tall man stepped out. Charlie stopped whistling and quickened his step. When the man also increased his pace, Charlie spun on him. "I've got nothin' to say to you. So, why don't you take your shitrag of a paper and shove it up—"

"Mr. Chevalier." Detective Gardiner touched the brim of his black bowler, his face impassive. "Glad I caught you. I was hoping to have a word."

The rough apology forming on Charlie's tongue died away unspoken. Arrogance radiated from the detective like stink.

"I'm busy," Charlie said and started walking again.

The detective blocked the path. "Where are you off to in such a hurry?"

"Not that it's any of your business, but I'm going to meet a friend. And I'm already running late. So, ..." Charlie lifted an eyebrow and gestured down the icy walk.

"You won't mind if I walk with you, then. We can chat on the way."

That was the last thing Charlie needed, but some instinct told him that evasion now would only harden the hawkshaw's resolve. Charlie shrugged and started off again at a brisk pace. "It's your time to waste."

"When your father was arrested at the inquest, you said some interesting things in his defense," Gardiner said, his long legs easily matching Charlie's stride, "Gave me the distinct impression that you knew more than you'd been letting on."

Charlie's stomach twisted. "You were mistaken."

"I don't think so. You said that you knew *absolutely* that your father was innocent. What makes you so sure?"

"My father's a gentleman." The words sounded contrived even in Charlie's ears, but what else could he say? The question itself was an insult, and the only proper response a crack on the jaw. "My father is a law-abiding man, and everyone knows it."

Gardiner smirked.

Anger surged through Charlie. Griggs, the newsmen, and now this blatherskite all thought they could treat him like dirt and get away with it. And the worst part of it was, they were right. What could he do about it that wouldn't land him in a cell next to John? He set his jaw and shifted his attention to the narrow, snow-bound path.

"I've questioned a lot of people," Gardiner said. "In time, you get an instinct for it. My instinct tells me you had something more definite in mind than your father's good character. Perhaps, if you think on it for a moment, it will come back to you."

Charlie could have laughed. The man must think him a fool.

The silence stretched on. The only sound was that of an occasional carriage and the rhythmic crunching of half-melted ice under their boots.

It wore on Charlie's nerves after a while, and he was relieved when they drew near Morris's. He stopped a few buildings away and turned to face the lanky cop. "This is where I get off. I'm meeting friends here, and I doubt very much they'd find you good company."

"Why don't we go inside and find out." Gardiner started toward the saloon.

Charlie put out a hand to stop him, but Gardiner pushed past it. The blood drained from Charlie's face, and he rushed forward and grabbed Gardiner's arm, hissing, "Are you mad? They'll think I've turned pigeon."

"Where then?"

Charlie took his meaning at once and nodded in an easterly direction. "We can try the Yellow Cat."

"Lead the way."

Once they'd strode some distance from Morris's, Charlie slowed. The winter sun was on the wane, lost in the haze of the steel-colored sky. Over the stink of Eleventh Street, Charlie could just make out the brine of the river; he wished he were on a ship headed somewhere, anywhere.

The Yellow Cat was half a block from the docks and catered primarily to fishermen and drunkards. Charlie had only been once and would have sworn the barman tried to poison him, but it was small, dark, and he was unlikely to come across anyone he knew.

He ordered Cork Dry Gin. Gardiner asked for black coffee. As soon as they were seated, Gardiner started in, "I'm going to tell you what I know. If you then tell me what you know, we'll soon be finished."

Something about the detective's voice resurrected an emotion Charlie hadn't experienced since his school days: a sucking dread fueled by the awareness that an hour of tedium lay before him, inescapable and unrelenting. He suppressed a sigh and nodded.

"I *know* that you possess information relevant to this case and that you are withholding it. This suggests to me that you are harboring a misguided belief that it somehow benefits you to hinder me in the performance of my duty. Such notions, though not uncommon, are not merely tiresome, they are wantonly destructive to the lives of innocent men and women."

Charlie reached for his drink, nobly resisting the urge to roll his eyes.

Gardiner leaned toward him, catching his gaze. "You say you esteem your father, but if you intended to destroy him utterly, you could do no better job of it."

"You're talking rot." Charlie tried to smile in defiance, but couldn't quite manage it. He took a large swallow of his gin and coughed into his sleeve. "Turpentine," he sputtered.

"Who else would want the old lady dead?" Gardiner pressed. "Who else would be stupid enough to steal personal items from a housekeeper, leaving a whole house full of expensive goods unpilfered? I tell you plainly, we have no other suspects."

Charlie's mouth was dry in spite of the gin. An image of William rose in his mind's eye, the cut on his fingers, the stains on his jacket. No other suspects? What idiots the police were. He set his jaw and motioned for the barman to bring him another drink. Gardiner's staring at him gave him the willies, so he fixed his gaze on the condensation marks his glass had left on the marled oak table.

"The worst of it," Gardiner continued, his tone calmer now, "is that I'm inclined to believe your father is innocent."

Charlie looked up. "You sure have a funny way of showing it."

"I have to do my job, which is made a lot more difficult by people like you."

Charlie's gin arrived. He took a swig. It went down easier this time.

Gardiner pulled his mug toward him. "Of course, I could be wrong. Maybe you're keeping quiet because you know your father's guilty."

"What I know has nothing to do with my father," Charlie's snapped, his temper flaring.

"Who does it have to do with?"

"No one." Charlie's stomach dropped. The gin must be getting to him. He pushed his glass away. "I don't know anything."

Gardiner sighed. "If your father hangs for a crime he didn't commit, it's nothing to me. In six weeks, I won't even remember his name. But you, you'll have to live the rest of your life knowing that you could have saved him and didn't."

The gin went sour in Charlie's stomach. "But, I don't *know* anything."

"Then tell me what you suspect." Gardiner waited a tick, then added, "You've heard about the reward, haven't you? Play your cards right, and you could save your father and earn five hundred dollars in the same breath."

Charlie's heart beat so fast he felt like he'd been running. What harm could it do to mention William? If he was innocent, as he no doubt was, he'd be able to clear himself quick enough.

And if he wasn't—well, then any trouble he came to was his own doing.

"Why don't you shove off," Charlie muttered, scared of his own thoughts.

To Charlie's surprise, Gardiner stood. "Don't say I didn't warn you."

Charlie waited for the detective to say more, his breath coming quick and shallow.

But Gardiner only tossed a coin on the table and walked away.

"Wait," Charlie gasped, his throat almost too tight to speak. He didn't raise his voice or turn around, but he knew Gardiner heard him. Charlie reached for his gin. "Now, mind you, I'm not making any accusations, but I have a friend, William Jones."

Gardiner settled back into his seat.

Charlie kept his eyes on the table. "John and I were trying to get the old girl to bankroll an investment, something Jones had heard about through an associate of his. We agreed that Jones would get a cut of any profits for brokering it. It's a sure thing." Charlie hazarded a glance at Gardiner, excitement warring with his fear. "A real once-in-a-lifetime opportunity. It will make us all rich, sure as you're born."

Gardiner's face remained impassive.

Charlie looked away. "When Mémé turned us down for the loan, it meant the end of everything, for William as well as us. John and I can always find a way to make ends meet, what with the stipend and whatnot." He shrugged. "But for William, this was the end of the line. When I saw him on Christmas, he was flat. He'd pawned his clothes, and was wasting away."

Charlie gripped his glass and forced himself to drink. Every swallow, and every word he spoke, took him further from himself, from this awful bar, this horrible man. None of it felt real. So, what did it matter?

"And?" Gardiner prodded.

"...and... when I saw him after Mémé's death, his situation had ... improved."

"In what way?"

"He had a new coat, for one thing. And money enough to buy drinks."

"Maybe he came into money some other way? It has been known to happen."

Charlie drew a shaky breath. "Sure, maybe...but ..."

Gardiner leaned forward. "But?"

"It's probably nothing, but I noticed he had a cut on his hand. It looked fresh, and there were some stains on his coat that looked like blood." Charlie swallowed hard. "I didn't think much of it at the time, but...it was rather...odd."

"This William, he knew your grandmother?"

Charlie nodded.

"Had he ever been to the house on Chestnut Hill?"

Charlie nodded again. "I took him with me when I went to borrow money once, maybe twice."

Charlie looked up. Gardiner's face remained expressionless, but his eyes sparkled.

"I'm not saying he killed her. William's a good friend of mine, my best friend, and I know he would never murder anyone. He's not like that. He's a good man."

Gardiner almost smiled. "And where does this William Jones live?"

THE TIPOFF

JANUARY 15, 1900

*T*hree loud raps on the front door woke William. He opened his eyes and watched as Charlotte rose from her stool and slid the basin she'd been washing clothes in under the bed. He closed his eyes again, listening to the whispery sound her old house slippers made as she walked to unlatch the door.

"I need to talk to William," a familiar voice said.

William sat up and pushed himself out of the bed. He was running his hands through his hair when Charlotte turned from the open door and said, "It's Mrs. Malone."

"I'll see her downstairs," he said, reaching for his boots.

"No time for that," Bessy Malone said as she stepped into the room. Her gaze traveled over Charlotte and their room with undisguised contempt. "I can't stay long, and neither can you."

"What are you talking about?" William asked, already annoyed. Bessy had a taste for melodrama, and he wasn't in the mood for her antics today.

"You're lucky Charlie told me where to find you, or you and your chit," she said, nodding toward Charlotte who had resumed the washing, "would be plain out of luck."

"Why is that?" he mumbled, rummaging through the ashtray for a stub with some tobacco left in it.

"Because the cops are sniffing around after you, that's why. They came by my place earlier; Charlie showed up right after. Seems they were by his first, and he directed 'em to me."

William turned to look at her, the cigarette forgotten. "You must be mistaken."

"You're William Jones, ain't you? Not Diaz, like you told me."

William didn't say anything.

"Then they was looking for you." Bessy's gaze fixed on him intently. "They say they got a hot tip, and they want to question you ... 'bout a murder."

He tried to laugh, but his heart hammered so hard he was short of breath. He stood and walked to the door. "It's still a mistake."

Bessy, taking the hint, retreated into the hall.

"If you say so." She paused in front of him, her pale blue eyes glinting through sooty lashes. "I just thought you should know."

"Of course." William bit off the words. "But it's nothing to do with me."

"You needn't take that tone with me, Willie, my boy. I'm just lookin' out for you." Bessy placed a soft hand on William's cheek.

He pulled back and glanced behind him to make sure Charlotte wasn't watching.

Bessy smirked. "Guess I'll be seein' you then."

William nodded, and Bessy sauntered down the hall. He followed in his bare feet and watched her plump form, encased in not-quite-enough blue and black striped wool, sway down the stairs. When she reached the bottom, she cast a knowing glance back up at him.

The moment the door shut behind her, William bolted for the room. Charlotte stood in front of the bed, wringing her hands in the folds of her gray check dress. Her dark eyes were wild with fear.

He brushed past her. "If Bessy knows my name is Jones, other people know it too. We need to leave. Now."

Charlotte took a step toward him, her eyes shining with tears. "I never told anyone, Will. Not a soul, I swear."

He shook his head dismissively as he pulled their things out of the small dresser. "If the police know enough to talk to Bessy, it's only a matter of time before someone points them here."

Charlotte hadn't moved; he could feel her eyes fixed on him as he worked. When he could stand it no longer, he turned on her. "Are you just going to stand there?"

"Bessy said the police want to question you about a murder."

Heat flooded his body. "And you believe me capable of that?"

"No, no! Of course not. I would never believe a thing like that about you." Her voice rang with pain.

He frowned, then turned to finish stuffing his other pair of pants into a flour sack.

Charlotte stepped closer, nervously plucking threads from the tattered edge of a blanket. "I only wonder, who do the police think you've killed?"

"How should I know?" He cast the sack onto the bed and glared at her. "But if you keep standing there asking me stupid questions, you can ask them yourself. They're bound to be here any minute."

Charlotte winced, then picked up the sack he'd tossed. "Do you think it might be Charlie's grandmother?"

"For God's sake!" He spun on her. "Why should I kill Charlie's grandmother? I hardly knew the woman."

Charlotte flinched, drawing both hands up defensively. The gesture was pathetic, yet something about it made him want to strike her. He balled his fists and turned away.

"I know," her voice quavered behind him. "It's a mad idea. I only wondered if *they* might think it. The papers are full of her killing, especially now that there's the reward."

He ran his fingers through his hair. An idea came to him, and he turned back toward her. "She was killed on New Year's Eve, wasn't she? I was with you that night."

Charlotte's brow furrowed, and she looked down at her fidgeting hands.

He gritted his teeth to keep from yelling. "You don't remember?"

Charlotte's wet eyes flitted around the room, stopping everywhere but on him. "Of course, I will say whatever you want."

"Say whatever I want? Was I or was I not with you on New Year's Eve?"

She licked her lips. "Not until after eleven."

He blinked, then looked away. "That's right. I had forgotten."

"Were you alone?" Charlotte's small voice was almost a whisper.

"Of course I was alone. Who the hell would I have up *here?*" His eyes swept the room.

"I just thought ... ."

"You don't think. That's the trouble. Any minute, the police are going to cart me off to prison, and what do you do? Stand around asking damn fool questions. If you're not going to help, at least have the decency to stay out of the way—and for God's sake, keep your mouth shut."

She cringed and turned away, but not before he saw her chin begin to tremble. A pang of guilt wormed its way into his consciousness. "Please, Charlotte, not now. We can discuss this later."

They finished packing in a heavy silence. After making sure the hallway was clear, they slipped into the night. Once the immediate need to put distance between himself and Mrs.

Stapleton's had been satisfied, he lost any sense of direction. He didn't dare go anywhere he was known lest the police were there waiting, but he also feared going somewhere new and drawing unwanted attention.

Together, he and Charlotte charted a circuitous path through the Dock Ward, keeping one eye out for the police and another for a hidden place where they might catch a few hours sleep. But even the weather was against him; an icy wind whipped between the buildings, spitting ice in their faces.

They were trudging down Front Street for the third time that hour when Charlotte, who had been silent since leaving the apartment, ran forward and grabbed the arm of a woman on the outskirts of a penny arcade. "Stella!"

"Lottie!" The woman smiled, displaying a wide, gap-toothed grin. "It's been ages. How's tricks?"

Charlotte shrugged. "Same ol'."

"Mm," Stella grunted. "I understand only too well, my dear."

"Charlotte." William tugged at her wrist, wanting to keep moving.

"Who's that?" Stella asked, lifting her narrow chin in his direction.

"My husband." Charlotte turned so that Stella couldn't see her expression, her eyes pleading with him.

"Husband?" Stella dropped her bag and threw her arms around Charlotte. "Congratulations, honey! When did it happen?"

"Last year—and thank you." When Stella released her, Charlotte added, "Say, you don't still have that place on Lombard, do you?"

Stella's grin wilted. "Sure do, why?"

"We're looking for a place to stay, just for a day or two."

Stella looked doubtful. "You know I'd like to help you, honey, but there ain't much room."

"All we need is a corner to sleep in. Our landlord cheated us, and we're in a real spot."

"Sure, sure. I understand." Stella looked William over, her eyes mistrusting.

"You can have whatever I earn, and we can help with the washing, do whatever you want," Charlotte spoke quickly. "You know I wouldn't ask if there were any other way."

Stella looked at Charlotte a long moment, then sighed. "Gladdy is off visiting her sister, so if it's just the one night …."

Charlotte threw her arms around the woman's neck. "Thank you, Stell. You're an angel."

It was a short walk to the old tenement building. Stella's room faced an alley containing a butcher's shop and a bakery; the smell of yeast and death clung to the walls. A shabby couch was squeezed into the corner. It, and everything else in the room, was covered with more clothing than William had ever seen. Lines were strung from wall to wall, and stacks of half-filled laundry bags rose waist-high in spots.

"Gladdy and I do a little cleaning and pressing to earn extra money," Stella explained.

William nodded.

"Well, I'd best get back to work. I won't be home 'till late, but we can catch up tomorrow. The bathroom's down the hall."

William wandered to the window. He was desperate to lay down and end this miserable day. When the door clicked shut, he turned back to Charlotte. Her eyes met his, but neither of them spoke.

He kicked at the rags on the floor until he'd cleared a spot then laid down and stuffed one of the cotton sacks under his head. Thoughts and impressions from the day whirled through his mind until he felt like an opium-eater. He would have to come up with a plan tomorrow. Tonight, he needed sleep.

A wobbling gold light from an ill-placed street lamp danced through a small window over his head, illuminating the tea-colored stains that traversed the walls and ceiling. He turned onto his back, tracing their outlines with his eyes. Charlotte laid down next to him. The room was cold, and he was grateful for her warmth.

After only a few minutes, her breathing grew slow and regular, and he knew she was sleeping. He examined the tiny figure curled against his. Slumber added a softness to her narrow face, and with her lips slightly parted, she looked tranquil, almost pretty. Gently, he tucked a wayward strand of hair behind her ear. Travail suited her, but then it always had.

The night they met, she had been one of several girls plying their trade on Thirteenth Street. One of her friends, a slim blonde with black eyes, was a favorite of his companion. The blonde had waved them over, and after a little back and forth, they'd decided to stop by the delicatessen for some cheap victuals, then the saloon to buy a few pints of rotgut, and make a night of it. Not wanting to be by himself, William had gone along. They invited everyone they came across, and by the time they settled in, there were twenty people or more crammed into the dingy two-room flat.

All of the women, save Charlotte, were smiling and lively. A john had used her badly, and even the generous application of pearl powder couldn't conceal the bruises mottling her face and throat. It had only been a few weeks since he'd split with Marie, and something about this girl struck a chord in him. She looked how he felt: small, miserable, and beaten.

He had a bit of change in his pocket, and, standing there watching her while the others talked and laughed, he had been struck with the strange fancy that he should do something kind for her. Humoring his own whim, they left the party together, and he took her to catch a vaudeville act at the Orpheum, then to a shabby Italian place nearby for dinner. He asked, and she told him the all-too-familiar story of a life governed by the direst sort of poverty. She'd received an education at the city-run orphanage she was raised in, and, for a time, harbored hopes of becoming a teacher. But she couldn't take the beatings and ran away. At just twelve years old, with no money or connections, she'd been forced to earn her bread with her body.

How much of her story she'd made up to play on his sympathy, he couldn't say, but it hardly mattered. His feelings, sensitized by their own suffering, responded to her misery, and he treated her with a tender regard unusual to him. He decided early in the night not to take his pleasure with her. Little and battered as she was, he didn't find her appealing, but that by itself wouldn't have put him off. William had seldom come across a woman that didn't possess some facet or feature that could arouse his interest.

What stopped him was the feeling that lying with the girl would detract from the image of himself he was creating in her mind, and, more importantly, in his own. He liked the reflection of himself he saw in her eyes and was mentally holding it out in defiance of a world that condemned him.

At the end of the evening, he gave her thirty-five cents and told her, truthfully, that she deserved better. Almost as an afterthought, he'd kissed her on the forehead. Her soulful eyes had gazed up at him in wonder, her small, battered face a perfect picture of stunned adoration. He parted from her feeling satisfied with himself and never expecting to see her again.

The following day, after wandering the streets in a futile search for employment, he'd found the girl waiting in his room. She had spent the money he'd given her on food and kindling. The table was set and a pot of stew bubbled on the fire.

The strangeness of the situation was tempered by his loneliness, and he let her stay. The stew had very little meat, but it was hearty and filled him. They didn't talk much, and after dinner, they'd lain together, more for companionship than lust.

The following day he again returned to find her waiting, so too the next. Soon, William forgot that it was strange. He could not say with any degree of certainty when they had started living together or holding themselves out as man and wife. It had just happened.

His not being in love with her did not trouble him. He had known love before and hoped never to be caught in that snare again. Charlotte, he felt, knew this, in the mysterious way that all women know such things, and accepted it.

She never made scenes if he drank or stayed out all night. And if she sulked on occasion, it always ended with her redoubling her efforts to please him. In return, he tried to spare her feelings when he could. They had a quiet, comfortable relationship, and he appreciated the calm and freedom it afforded him.

He studied the peaceful face nuzzled against him. Poor Charlotte. She asked for so little and received even less.

With sleep still hopelessly out of reach, William pulled his body up until he could rest his back against the wall. He moved carefully, but Charlotte woke, crying out and clutching at him.

"Shh, go back to sleep." He stroked her hair.

She blinked and snuggled in closer, laying her head on his chest. He put his arm around her and she grabbed his hand and kissed it. "Would you like me to get you something to drink?"

William shook his head in the darkness. "No. I just want to sit here."

Soon, she was back asleep. His arm, where she rested on it, grew numb and began to tingle, and his legs were so stiff they ached, but he couldn't move without waking her. So, he sat, his limbs resolutely locked in place, and cradled the small sleeping figure until the dawn broke cold and gray around them.

OUT OF SIGHT

JANUARY 16, 1900

One moment, William was examining a splotch on the ceiling that looked uncannily like a dog playing the fiddle, the next, the sound of hushed voices was pulling him back into wakefulness. He opened his eyes. Charlotte and Stella were sitting on the laundry-strewn bed. Charlotte had what looked to be a small cutting board balanced on her knee and was using it as a surface for writing. Both women's heads turned his way as he pulled himself into a sitting position.

Charlotte, still wearing the gray check dress from the night before, rose and took a few steps toward him, her expression tender. She tucked her pencil behind her ear and smiled. "Sleep if you can. As soon I'm done helping Stella write this letter, we're going to see about finding us something to eat."

William stretched an arm above his head and grimaced. His spine was in knots from sleeping on a lumpy pile of laundry. "How much is she giving you?"

Charlotte's face fell and her voice dropped to a whisper. "I can't charge her."

William frowned. "Why not?"

Being the most educated of her set, Charlotte was often

called upon to read letters for her friends. She would then pen their responses in her neat, schoolgirl hand, and, with all the pomp of a magician performing a particularly difficult trick, read their words back to them with the broadest of their errors corrected. Delighted, the women would hand over as much as a nickel per page.

"I can't, Will. Not after she helped us. I just can't."

"Then don't." William lay back down and turned away from her. Charlotte's wounded tone made him feel ungrateful, but he wasn't, not really. He was desperate, and that was quite a different thing. He hadn't the will to argue, not when he'd had such a rotten night's sleep, and a long day ahead. His eyes closed. He meant only to give the impression of sleep, so that Charlotte would stop her hovering, but such was his exhaustion, that he soon succumbed to the real thing. When he next woke, the two women were gone, and he could tell by the light streaming through the window that it was midday.

Panic shot through him, bringing him instantly and fully awake. Why hadn't Charlotte woken him? He'd told her last night that they needed to come up with a plan, and now the day was damn near over. Swearing, he disentangled himself from the piano shawl that had wound itself around his legs, then located the privy and washbasin.

He checked every surface in the room for a note from Charlotte, there was none. What if the police had picked her up, and she led them here? No, she would never betray him, but what of her friend, Stella? If Charlotte had let slip that he was wanted, anything was possible.

William paced the small room, weaving between piles of laundry. Every time a neighbor spoke too loud or banged a kettle, he froze and stared at the door, waiting for the police to smash it in. He had half-convinced himself to set out on his own when Charlotte came flouncing in, a half-full sack slung over her thin shoulder.

She smiled brightly when she saw him. "I have supper."

A torrent of accusations and insults burned on his tongue, but he gritted his teeth and held them in. He knew what that sack had cost her.

Resentment and gratitude swirled nauseatingly in his stomach as he watched her unpack a loaf of brown bread, a wedge of hard cheese, and a small bag of coffee. She had also bought him a bit of soap and a razor, which she handed him.

He gave his bristly neck a scratch and managed a terse, "Thank you."

Charlotte pulled the bread apart with her hands while he sliced the cheese with his pocket knife. Between mouthfuls, William glanced at the fading light coming through the window and mumbled, "Stella is going to have to let us stay another night."

Charlotte shook her head. "That's out, but don't worry, I have a plan."

"Of course you do." Irritation flared inside of him. She was forever making plans for them, then presenting them as though they were gifts.

"We'll leave as soon as it gets dark," she said. "I talked to a friend today, and she told me about a place in Camden, real discreet."

"New Jersey?" William asked, feeling skeptical.

Charlotte nodded. "It's best to get you out of state. You'll have to stay out of sight while I arrange things. We can meet at the old churchyard on Davis Street around nine and go to our new place together. What do you think?"

William chewed the last bit of cheese slowly. It didn't sound like much of a plan to him, but it was too late to come up with better.

The last remnants of the day were still fading when they left the house, sometime around five. The air was crisp and bitterly cold, but at least it had stopped snowing. They walked together to a cab stand. Charlotte smiled and waved when they parted, as though nothing were amiss.

Feeling strangely exposed without Charlotte by his side, William shambled aimlessly down side streets, crisscrossing shabby little neighborhoods filled with garbage and shrieking children, until his feet ached. He made his way to a park and took a seat on a bench. A nearby clock tolled six. Three hours to go. It seemed an eternity.

Yesterday's newspaper lay in a windblown heap on the end of the bench; he picked it up and tried to read by the gaslight. When he tired of this, he turned his attention to the pigeons hobbling about on the ice, looking for food. He remembered the bread Charlotte had wrapped for him, dug it out of his pocket and broke it into crumbs that he doled out. The birds descended in a flurry of flapping wings and thrusting beaks. One bird, in particular, drew his eye, a great fat fellow with a shock of irides-cent plumage. The bird walked gingerly through the ice pecking fiercely at the ground while the slimmer, duller, birds darted around him, snatching crumbs from under his beak. He thought of John Chevalier, and smiled ruefully as he tossed a few more crumbs in the bird's direction.

When the bread was gone, William sat, stiff and shivering for as long as he could bear it. The bell chimed seven. His hands and ears burned from the cold. If he didn't move soon, he would freeze. He rose, stiff-legged, and left the park.

By the time he heard the clock bell ring eight, his mouth was dry and his stomach in knots. The wait and the cold played havoc with his nerves, making his thoughts slippery, like silver fish in a murky stream. He went blocks without really seeing anyone or anything, then someone would step out of a door or jostle him on the sidewalk and jolt him out of his stupor, every nerve electric with fear. On one of these occasions, he became aware that he had wandered onto Perry Avenue and was just steps from The Lemon Tree, one of the few taverns for working men that offered both decent gin and a free cold lunch. It was a favorite spot of his, and one he'd meant to avoid. By the time he realized his mistake, it was too late to turn around, so he tucked his head into the collar of his coat and strode past. As he went by, he hazarded a glance through one of its small windows. It looked as it always did: dark, empty, and welcoming.

He thought of the quarter in his pocket. If he only stayed for one drink, surely that wouldn't hurt anything. The gnawing in his stomach made up his mind. Walking briskly back to the tavern, he pushed inside and was enveloped by the soothing warmth and the familiar, acrid tang of smoke.

William went to the far corner of the bar and when Stanley, the barkeep, made his way over, he ordered a gin. William studied the man, trying to detect the slightest alteration in his tone or manner. There was none.

Perhaps Bessy had got the whole thing wrong? Relaxing some, he piled a plate with salted pork from the lunch table and retreated to a dark corner to eat and nurse his drink. Even if the police were looking for him, it had to be safer here than out in the open. He waited until the clock read eight-forty, paid his tab, and left.

Outside, the air had grown so cold inhaling it burnt his nose and throat. Shoving his hands in his pockets, he strode in the direction of Davis Street. He had advanced only a few steps when a stout, uniformed policeman with hard eyes stepped out of a doorway, stopping in front of him. "Are you William Jones?"

"No." William's chest contracted painfully. He ducked his head and attempted to walk past.

The man stepped in his way. "What's your hurry, William?"

When the policeman said his name again, he knew the jig was up. "No hurry. You just surprised me. Yes, I'm William Jones."

"We've been looking for you." The cop fingered one of William's lapels. "Is this your coat?"

William took a step backward. "No, it belongs to a friend. He let me borrow it."

The big cop stepped in closer. "Take it off."

"I'm afraid I can't." William opened the coat a little, revealing that he wore nothing but an undershirt beneath it.

The cop smirked. "What happened to your shirt, son?"

"I pawned it."

Fat fingers poked his chest. "What are these stains?"

William felt the blood drain from his face. He held out his hand. "I cut myself. Here."

The cop grabbed his hand, examining it roughly. "When did this happen?"

"I don't know—a few days ago."

"Looks older than that to me." The cop squeezed his injured fingers.

William clenched his teeth and sweat started to bead on his forehead.

"Where were you on New Year's Eve?"

"At the theater," William said the first thing that came into his mind.

"Which theater?"

"Walnut Street."

"Anyone with you?"

He was tempted to say Charlotte, but what if they had already found her and she'd said something else? "I ... no. I went by myself."

"A fine looking fellow like you? Alone on New Year's Eve?"

William shrugged and tried to smile. His heart beat so hard, his body rocked with it.

"What show did you see?"

His mind raced. "I...I don't know."

The cop raised a bushy eyebrow at him. "What was it about?"

William opened his mouth and closed it, shaking his head.

A hand closed on his arm like a vise. "I'm going to need you to come down to the station and answer a few more questions."

William didn't bother to protest as he was steered to a patrol wagon. The cop shoved him onto one of the wooden benches. Splinters pierced the flesh of his arm, and he struggled to right himself and get one last glimpse of the world before the doors closed. As the wagon began to move, he thought of Charlotte. It must be nine now. He imagined her standing alone at their meeting place, haloed by the flickering gaslights, and wondered how long she would wait.

THE RIGHT MAN

JANUARY 17, 1900

"*You're* not listening to me." His sister's exasperated voice broke into Jamie's thoughts.

They were in the small parlor. A comfortable fire crackled in the grate, and he was reclining on the divan, legs outstretched and eyes closed. Straightening up, he assumed an expression he hoped conveyed surprise and mild indignation. "Of course I am. You said Agnes Carlton bought a new dress and that it was a perfect fright."

Melly raised her eyebrows. "I said I bought a new dress to wear to Agnes Carlton's dinner next Saturday night."

Jamie smiled. "I almost had it."

Melly laughed and shook her head. "I was just trying to make conversation. You've been quiet ever since you got home today. Too quiet. It makes me nervous."

"Have I? What a bore I must be." Jamie leaned forward, taking a cigarette from the carved rosewood box on the table. He lit it and squinted out the window. The sun was setting in shades of molten gold and rose, infusing the little parlor with a warm glow.

"Well, since you mentioned it, you have been rather dull lately." She reached out her hand for his cigarette.

He looked at her askance. "Mother's still up."

"See what I mean? You needn't worry. She'll be upstairs with Father all the rest of the evening."

Jamie handed her his cigarette and lit another for himself.

Settling back in her chair, she leveled her gaze on him. "So, are you going to tell me what's on your mind?"

He turned the heavy silver table lighter in his hand. "I was going to tell you. I just wanted to get it straight in my own head first."

"And have you?"

"No."

She smiled. "Let's see what two heads can do with it, shall we?"

He placed the lighter back on the table's polished surface and faced her squarely. "I sent Toby, the office boy, into Manassas's office today to return the files we took and get new ones..." He paused, unsure how to proceed.

Melly's hand stopped halfway to her lips; the cigarette's smoke curled around her face like a veil. "Oh God, Jamie, were we caught?"

Jamie shrugged and flashed her a thin smile. "That's the tricky bit. I don't know."

"What do you mean you don't know?"

"Uncle Manny's office has been as good as cleaned out. The boy said most of the files were gone; his desk was bare, and the cabinets half empty."

"Empty? But who would do that? And why?"

Jamie raised his hands in a helpless gesture. "The most reasonable explanation is that uncle Manny noticed his files were missing and decided to destroy what was left of the evidence."

"What's reasonable about that? Uncle Manny wrote Father

last week. He said he wouldn't be back until the first, and that letter was postmarked Vermont—I checked."

Jamie stubbed his cigarette in the ashtray, grinding it until the last glimmer of heat was gone. "Postmarks are notoriously unreliable."

Melly's eyes fixed on his with an unnerving intensity. "You're convinced it was him?"

"I don't know what to think, but it's certainly the most likely explanation."

Melly frowned. "I don't know when you became so suspicious minded, but, as someone who loves you, I feel it's my duty to inform you that it's not a very attractive quality."

He smiled wryly. "Recent events haven't exactly encouraged an increase of faith in my fellow man."

"Perhaps not, but I won't believe Uncle Manny is a villain. Not without proof." Her voice took on an imploring quality. "We're speaking of the man who bought me a Shetland pony on my sixth birthday, and who took you on your first pheasant hunt."

"I don't like it any more than you do, but something's wrong, and he's involved. That much is certain."

"But there's no way of knowing what side of this business he's on yet. He may very well be a victim."

Jamie's heart sank. "You've not realized the worst of it yet. If Manassas's office was cleared out because someone noticed files were missing, there's no way to know when we were caught. Our pilfering could have been discovered the day after we broke in."

Melly nodded, her expression calm. She still didn't see.

He stood up to add another log to the fire.

"Well?" Melly's tone was impatient.

Jamie shifted the kindling with a poker until the fire blazed back to life. He continued to watch the flames as he said, "I was thinking how strange it was that every cupboard in the house was turned out but nothing taken—almost as though someone had been searching for something and hadn't found it."

Jamie turned to his sister to see if she was following his train of thought. Her look of horror confirmed that she was.

She shook her head resolutely. "Uncle Manny wouldn't have. He couldn't."

"I don't know what to think, but I can't believe it's all a coincidence."

"Think what you're saying, Jaimie. That Uncle Manny *murdered* Madame Alozia. It would be absurd if it wasn't so grotesque."

Jaimie turned from the fire. "Alright, if not him, who?"

Melly twisted the gold and emerald ring on her finger, her face lined with worry. "I don't know, but this has gone far enough. If a person looking for those files was responsible for Madame Alozia's death, be it Uncle Manny or someone else, we have a responsibility to go to the police with what we know."

"And tell them what exactly? Up to this point, I have no proof of any wrongdoing, just a handful of deposits from an account I don't recognize, and a strange conversation with a man who was run down the next day. Hell, I can't even say for certain those transactions aren't legitimate."

"If someone was willing to break into our house, *to kill*, for those files, they must contain important information —evidence."

"Maybe, but the only person who knows enough about the business to shed any light on those accounts is Manassas, and I don't see him banging down the door to help us."

Melly sighed.

Jamie took this as an acknowledgment that he was right. "Which brings me to the next reason we can't inform the police. Father and Uncle Manny have been friends longer than we've been alive. If Uncle Manny has betrayed him and involved our mills in some sort of criminal scheme, Father won't survive the shock of it, not in his weakened condition. Face it, Mel. We have no choice but to bide our time and wait for him to make a mistake."

"A mistake? Jamie, we're talking about *murder*. We're well out of our depth here."

"It's no good," Jamie said firmly. "I won't be responsible for rushing our father to his grave, and that's the end of it."

They sat in silence. The sun had finished setting and the only light came from the fire crackling and spitting in the grate. Finally, Melly spoke. "Then maybe it's time we talk to Uncle Manny."

Jamie almost laughed. "The man is very likely involved in something so sinister it has caused the deaths of at least two human beings, and you think we should chat with him about it?"

"You won't go to the police, and we have to do something."

"What makes you think a man who is up to his chin in intrigue would bare his soul to the very family he's betraying? You've had some crackpot ideas before, Mel, but this one takes the cake." Jamie reached for another cigarette, not nearly as convinced by his own argument as he should have been.

"You keep assuming he's guilty, but up until the business with the foreign man upstate, we never had any reason to question his loyalty or his integrity. I can't speak for you, but I'm of the opinion that thirty-odd years of service to our family should count for something."

A knock on the door made them both jump.

"What is it, Niles?" Jamie asked, grateful for the interruption.

"Sorry, Sir, Miss, but this letter came in this evening's post. It's marked urgent."

Jamie took it. The back of his neck prickled when he saw the official seal of the Philadelphia Police Department. "Thank you."

Niles nodded and retreated from the room. Jamie opened the letter, read it quickly, then read it again.

"What is it?" Melly asked, standing to read over his shoulder.

"Someone has been arrested in connection with Madame Alozia's murder. Trial starts next week." Jamie handed the letter to her.

"Well," Melly said, after reading it. "Looks like we're off the hook."

Jamie let out a soft laugh, but his heart remained heavy. "Let's just hope they've got the right man this time."

A TRUE FRIEND

JANUARY 18, 1900

"*I* won't see her!" William spat the words at Charlie as he paced the narrow confines of his cell under the courthouse.

Charlie's eyes followed him through the barred window in the door, his thin face pale and impassive. "You'll have to tell Marie yourself. She's been in a right state since your arrest; it's keeping the whole house on edge."

"What has she to carry on about? She threw me to the dogs long ago." William tried unsuccessfully to keep the hurt from his voice. He hated making an exhibition of himself, especially in front of Charlie, but he hadn't expected this. For the first time in longer than he could remember, Marie had not been in his thoughts. "She has no business here. No right!"

Charlie shrugged. "Then have the guards turn her away. It's your decision to make, but I can't stop her coming. Hell, it was all I could do to keep her from tagging along with me this morning."

Resentment surged through William, but he said nothing. What was the use? Charlie was her brother, a fellow scorpion, immune to her venom.

Marshaling his thoughts along a more productive path, William asked, "Any word on who set the law on me?"

The gas in the pipes sputtered, causing the shadows on Charlie's face to deepen. "Nothing yet."

William bit back his disappointment. When Bessy delivered her warning, she'd said the police had received a tip, but from who? And why? Finding the answers to those questions was the first step to getting out of here. "Keep asking around," William said. "Someone knows. Someone always does."

After that, William kept the conversation light until a guard appeared and ushered Charlie out of the cells. The silence that followed Charlie's departure was so absolute, his ears rang with it. This stillness was broken only by the occasional grinding of iron-bound doors on their heavy hinges. There had to be other prisoners in other cells. William was tempted to go to the small window in his door and call out to them, but he didn't know what to say.

"The tombs", he thought, was an apt name for this place. Those who had the misfortune of being held here were indeed buried alive. When the lamps in the corridor dimmed, he knew the day had ended. Wedged against the wall on his narrow cot, he stared into the awful darkness and felt himself already dead and forgotten.

Sleep came in fits and starts. His thoughts fleeing from one terror to the next, until he could hardly distinguish reality from nightmare. Then he remembered what Charlie had said about Marie. Was she really in a state over him? Charlie had no reason to lie about it. Her distress gladdened William, and he clung to it.

Like a director at a playhouse, he cast her in different roles: Marie the vampire, feeding off his misery; Marie the missionary, piously gloating over his downfall; and, more poignantly, Marie the penitent lover, begging his forgiveness. He despised himself for thinking of her; hated that she mattered at all, but at least these fantasies held his fear at bay.

It was a relief to hear the faint sounds of the change of the guard that signalled morning. Gingerly, he climbed off his cot, stretched his aching back, and tried to sort his hair and clothing. He paced the same seven steps until he could walk them with his eyes closed. An eternity passed before footsteps sounded outside his door. Despite his best efforts to remain calm, his heart took off at a gallop. When the guard appeared with a metal bowl of cold porridge, disappointment tied his stomach in so many knots it was a full ten minutes before he could eat it.

When he finished, William set the bowl back on the tray and resumed pacing. She was doing this on purpose, making him wait. Or perhaps she had changed her mind and wouldn't come at all? That would be just like her: selfish, fickle. This thought made him so angry, he had to resist the urge to bloody his knuckles on the stones.

He had nearly given up when the grating sound of a lock turning at the end of the corridor reached him. An electric sensation, somewhere between fear and hope, surged through him with every thud of his heart. He rubbed his face and tried to smooth his hair with shaking hands. Footsteps approached along the stone corridor, the guards' heavy footfalls overlapping with a shorter, lighter step.

William focused his gaze on the shadowy form that came to a stop on the other side of the barred window. It took a moment to recognize the face staring back at him, and when he did, his knees almost gave way. "Bessy, I didn't expect to see you here."

Bessy brushed a wisp of blonde hair from her face, tucking it into her hat: a feathered straw monstrosity festooned in ribbons of pink and sea green. "That's plain enough by the look on your face. And who were you thinkin' it would be? Or don't you know they got that little tart of yours locked up?"

"Charlotte?" William stepped toward the door, his head swimming.

Bessy laughed, a short, sharp, sound. "You got more than one?"

He ignored the jab. "What do they want with her?"

"Beats me, honey. They're probably just wantin' to ask her some questions 'bout where you were the night the old lady was killed."

"But why? I told them I wasn't with Charlotte."

A wry expression twisted Bessy's face. "You don't expect me to answer that, do you?"

Most of the tension had left his body, leaving him feeling as boneless as a rag doll. He sat on his cot with his elbows on his knees and shook his head.

"Ah, just look at you! Poor darlin'." Bessy laughed again, the same false, grating sound. "Never you fear. They'll ask your Charlotte one question and she'll fall all to pieces. I'll betcha anythin' you like, they'll tire of her snivelin' and toss her back into the street long 'fore they can get one sensible word outta her."

William smiled thinly. It wasn't a kind representation, but it was a fair one.

Bessy took a step closer to the window, her pale eyes seemed almost to glow at him through the bars. "But I didn't come here to talk about your little playmate. I came to tell you who it was informed on you."

William stood and strode to the door. "You've heard something?"

Bessy grinned. "I thought that might get your attention. You can always count on Bessy here to find out what's what."

William tried to smile his gratitude at her, but the muscles in his face had turned to stone. "Who was it?"

"Well, it all came out yesterday evenin', when I was down on Almond Street, buyin' some apples from O'Sullivan's. I was standin' there, mindin' my own business when I hear someone say your name. 'William Diaz,' the voice says. So, I get interested and look to see who's talkin'. It's two fellas I don't recognize, but I take it they're makin' a night of it, as they're dressed common and stinkin' of whiskey. Bein' blessed with a naturally curious disposition, I took to followin' them."

Bessy paused, waiting for encouragement. William bit back his impatience. The story would come faster if he humored her. "You're a true friend, Bessy girl. Tell me, what did you hear?"

She beamed. "Well, the first one, a stocky fellow in a striped navy suit and brown shoes, says to his friend, 'I knew that William was no good, but I never woulda thought he'd stoop to killin' an old woman.'

"To which the second, a lean man in a long gray coat, says, 'Ah, you never can tell what depths a rotter like that'll sink to. There's practically no limit once they start down the devil's path.'

"To which Brown Shoes says, 'And they say his father was a God-fearin' man, too.'"

William glared at Bessy through the bars. "You said you were here to tell me who informed on me, not to waste my time with the slanderous musings of a pair of drunken louts."

"My, my! Aren't you in a pretty mood? I was gettin' to it."

"I suggest you hurry." William's voice held the hint of a threat.

Bessy smiled and her voice dropped, becoming almost sultry. "What's the matter, darlin'? I thought you'd like hearin' what high regard your friends hold you in."

William ground his teeth to keep from cursing her.

She laughed, a more genuine sound this time. "After they got done sayin' all them nice things 'bout you, Gray Coat says, 'Them Chevaliers ain't no better. Neither John nor his Charlie.'

"Brown Shoes has a bit of a laugh at that, and says, 'They say the daughters are right pretty, though, especially the older girl.

Old Jonny Davis saw her once and said she was as fine a piece of—'."

"Get to the point," William interrupted, his voice low and menacing. "Or get out."

Bessy's smile slumped into a pout. "You don't have to be rude. I'm only havin' a bit of fun. So, after Brown Shoes says what a treat the elder Chevalier girl is, Gray Coat says, 'I've half a mind to start courtin' her myself, now that they're comin' into all that money.'

"To which, Brown Shoes responds, 'Then you'd be a fool. Mark my words, that lot'll run through whatever that house-keeper left in less than a fortnight.'

"Gray Coat, real surprised-like, says, 'You haven't heard? It's not just the inheritance they'll be gettin'. Thanks to little Char-lie, once William's hung, they'll have the reward too.'

William staggered backward as though he'd been punched. He didn't hear the rest of what Bessy said. He didn't need to. A blinding light had gone off in his brain, throwing all else into shadow. He could see everything now with such clarity: the forgeries, the murder of the old woman, the reward, and finally his arrest—all of it.

Charlie.

TIME'S UP

JANUARY 18, 1900

*T*ucked behind Independence Hall, the courthouse's stark Georgian exterior loomed bone-white against the steel gray sky. Every step toward the tombs she took increased Marie's anxiety. She dropped her gaze to the wet pavement, and forced herself to think only of the obstacle immediately before her: the marble stairs, the wooden railing, the painted door.

Charlie had given her directions, and she soon located the entrance. Inside, the stale air stuck in her throat. She coughed, and with her hand just grazing the icy railing, descended a long flight of stairs until she emerged into a large, low-ceilinged room. Oak benches lined the walls, graying from overuse. At the far end rested a long, wooden counter with two uniformed policemen positioned behind it. One stood reading a paper, his brass buttons gleaming in the gaslight, while his companion sat hunched over a stack of files, the corners of the pages fluttering in the hot air being piped in through a vent in the ceiling.

Marie approached. The standing policeman chuckled and slapped the paper down on the counter before fixing his laughing brown eyes on her. "Good Morning, pretty lady. And what might we do for you today?"

"I'm here to see Mr. William Jones." The guard's good humor was at odds with the fear Marie felt, and increased her sense of being out of place.

He raised an eyebrow. "You a relation?"

Charlie had warned her that only family was allowed to visit. She held her head a little higher. "I'm his cousin."

His smile broadened. "Of course you are."

Heat blossomed over her throat and cheeks, but she forced herself to hold his gaze.

"Sign in here. You'll have to leave your bag at the counter, and I'm afraid we're going to have to pat you down," the officer continued in the same amused tone.

Pat her down? The words had barely registered when he strolled around the counter and placed his hands on her, running them down the length of her skirt with casual familiarity.

Gasping, she slapped his hands away and stumbled backward until he released her, her heart pounding as though it would burst.

Laughing, he straightened up and winked. "Lively little thing, aren't ya?"

Marie glared at him, her cheeks flaming, and brushed every imaginary trace of his hands from her skirt.

He motioned to the benches. "Have yourself a seat over there, and I'll let you know when I'm ready for you."

Assuming the proudest bearing she could muster, Marie retreated to the bench he'd indicated. Why did everything have to be so complicated? This visit, all by itself, was hard enough. Things had ended badly between her and William, but she had loved him once with all the ardour her soul possessed. Could she have given her heart so completely to a man capable of such a vile act? She didn't think so, but she had to be sure. The need to visit William struck her like a fever, irrational and persistent. If he had killed Mémé, he would hardly admit it, but something in her heart insisted that, if she could only look him in the eyes and ask, she would know.

The guard retreated behind his counter and wrote something in a book. When he finished, he beckoned to her and she followed him down a long hallway with closed doors on both sides. There were small barred windows in the doors, and Marie guessed these were the cells. The stale smell was stronger here and mingled with other unpleasant odors she had no wish to identify. Given that they were underground, Marie felt it should be dark, but it wasn't. Gas lamps hissed along the walls, making it brighter in this gloomy hallway than it was outside.

The guard's cheerful voice broke in on her thoughts. "Except for old Duchaine, Jones has the place to himself. But I don't expect you'll mind that. You and your *cousin* probably have things you want to discuss in private." The guard grinned over his shoulder at her. "For a man accused of murdering an old woman, that Jones fellow sure has a lot of pretty relations."

The urge to slap the grin from his face rose in Marie with such force the fingers of her right hand twitched. She was still trying to master her anger when the guard stopped and thudded his baton against the door to his left. "Jones. Visitor."

At the sound of William's name, a jolt of fear traveled from the top of Marie's head down through her toes.

The guard turned to Marie and, in the monotone sing-song of someone who has spoken just those words in just that way hundreds of times, said, "You have twenty minutes, exactly—no extensions. If you wish to leave before your time is up, come back the way you came, knock on the door, and someone will be along for you shortly."

Marie nodded.

The guard grinned knowingly at her one last time before retreating down the hall.

She heard movement inside the cell, a soft step and the rustling of clothing. Marie's heart beat as though it were trying to burst through her chest. She looked at the number painted on the wall by his cell, twenty-two, and tried to collect her thoughts. Something brushed against the door and when she glanced up, her breath caught.

"Marie?"

Her name, spoken softly, hung in the air between them. William's voice, so familiar, yet so strange, scattered all the speeches she'd practiced on the way there. She stood staring at him, aching and uncertain.

His face hardened. "Why have you come?"

"I had to see you, I had to—" she faltered.

"What?"

Forcing herself to meet his eyes, she whispered, "I have to know—have to ask—."

"I didn't do it." William's eyes bore into hers. His fingers wrapped around the bars in the window, and he pressed his face to them. "Even you can't think me capable of that."

The "even you" of his declaration rang in her ears, pricking at her, but she ignored it. "I just needed to hear you say it."

Incredibly, that was the truth. His innocence seemed so obvious now that she wondered how she ever doubted it. Irresponsible and petty as he could sometimes be, he was no monster. He was just Liam, her Liam.

The lines of strain around his eyes softened.

"How are you faring?" she asked. "Do you need anything?"

He shook his head and the corners of his mouth quirked into something not quite a smile. "My cell is weathertight, and I get three squares a day. What more could I possibly need?"

"Then you'd better enjoy it while you can, because you won't be here long." Marie did her best to sound confident. "They'll soon realize their mistake and set you free, just as they did Papa."

William shook his head slowly, his eyes fixed on hers in a way that made her breath come quick. "No. They're determined to see me hang."

"Never say that. Never. We must hold onto hope."

"Hope." He took his time with the word, drawing it out. "I've not had any of that in a very long time."

The pain in his voice wrung her heart. A warning sounded in her head, urging caution, but it was no use. She slid her hand up the door until her fingertips grazed his knuckles. They were cool and familiar. When he didn't pull away, she wrapped her hands over his. William closed his eyes, his fingers gripping hers so tightly it almost hurt.

They stood like that in silence for several seconds. When he opened his eyes again, they were dark and angry. "How could you have done this to us?"

Marie jerked her hands free. "What have I to do with it?"

"Not this," he gestured toward his cell. "But if you had accepted me as I was, none of this would have happened."

"Accepted you? Liam, being as you were is precisely what led us here."

"Then you do think me guilty."

"You know that isn't what I meant."

"What then? You believe God is punishing me for my sins?" He tightened his grip on the bars. "Then perhaps you'll be so good as to tell me why I should receive such special attention, when there are so many more deserving? Yours is a capricious sort of God, smiting the poor slob who's forced to steal his bread while giving the man who betrays his life-long friend five hundred dollars for his trouble."

"No one said anything about God," Marie said curtly, already tired of the argument. God, and faith in general, had been one of the subjects they argued most about. Not because Marie was particularly devout, but because William was every ounce as passionate in his denouncement of the church as his father was in praise of it. The path of this argument was so well worn between them that it took Marie a moment to realize his words had been specific, pointed. "What are you talking about, Liam? Who was given five hundred dollars?"

"He hasn't told you?"

"Who hasn't told me what?"

William's eyes narrowed. "Maybe you're in on it with him."

Marie placed her hands on her hips, her impatience fast turning to irritation. "In on what? What are you talking about?"

"I'm talking about your brother, *my best friend*, and how he went to the police and told them a pack of lies about me so that he could claim the reward."

Marie stepped away from the door. "Charlie would never do that."

"Is it so hard to believe? Honestly ask yourself, Marie, what wouldn't Charlie do for five hundred dollars?"

Marie shook her head. "Not that. You're his best friend. His *only* friend. He wouldn't do anything to hurt you, not intentionally."

William's eyes shone green and gold in the gaslight. "You think not? Then how do you explain that business with the attorney Duncombe?"

Marie's stomach dropped, and her next words came out in a whisper. "That was your doing."

William's eyes widened. "Mine?"

"There's no use denying it. Papa and Charlie told me everything."

He turned and stepped away from the door. Keeping his back to her, he asked, "What did they tell you, Marie? When?"

"The night before you … the night before things ended between us, Papa took me aside and told me you were being questioned by the police for forging those papers. He said you were trying to shift the blame onto Charlie in order to save yourself."

William spun around, his handsome face distorted with anger. "They told you I was a thief and a liar, and you believed them?"

The intensity of his anger unnerved her. Rallying, she said, "I wish you'd given me reason to doubt it. After Duncombe dismissed you, you never spoke of it. As to the rest, I was all too familiar with your ability to move the line between right and wrong when and as it suited you."

Marie took the silence that followed this as an acknowledgment of guilt, and sighed. She stepped back toward the door. "This is all better left in the past. I don't know what made you believe this terrible thing of Charlie, but I assure you, you are mistaken."

William met her gaze. "Then you're as big a fool now as you were then."

His quiet certainty unsettled her even more than his anger had. A knot of doubt formed just under Marie's ribcage. "And I'm to take your word against my brother's and father's?"

"You needn't take my word for anything. I can prove what I say. When you go home today, tell John I saved his letters, and if he doesn't find a way to get me out of the mess he and his son have dropped me into, I'll make damn sure they both end up in a cell alongside me."

"What letters?"

William moved back to the window in the door. "When your father was first talking me into that accursed forgery scheme, he put the details in writing. I was to memorize my instructions and burn them. But I didn't. So you see, if John and Charlie don't get me out of here, they won't get to enjoy a penny of the money they killed for."

The world shifted under Marie's feet. She put both hands on the door to steady herself, then leaned in to whisper, "Are you saying they killed Mémé?"

William shrugged. "Could be. I know only that I'm innocent,

and if I hang for this, they as good as put the rope around my neck."

Marie continued resting against the door, his words careening through her mind.

William's eyes never left her face, they burned into her. "Are you that surprised? Or is it just that you disapprove of my keeping the letters? With friends like John and Charlie, a man can't be too careful."

She shook her head. "It isn't possible. They told me you had risked our future, and Charlie's life, just to get a little extra money—money you would use for drinking and whoring. Papa swore if I didn't break with you, you would drag our whole family into the gutter."

William laughed, a hard sound. "Drag him into the gutter! That's rich. If you don't know what sort of man your father is by now, there's no sense in my trying to explain it to you."

"But," Marie mumbled, the ground still unsteady beneath her, "that would mean it was all for nothing. That they're responsible for your being dismissed, and for … for the way things ended between us."

"Don't be so modest," William said, again gripping the bars in the window. "You had a hand in it as well."

Marie's head snapped up. "I?"

"I could never please you; nothing I did was enough. You always wanted something bigger, something better. If I'd had the love of a good woman, I would never have been tempted by your father's schemes."

"*A good woman?*" Marie tried to sound amused but was too angry. "Is that what your little friend at the precinct lock up is?"

William looked away.

Marie rushed on, "*Maybe* if you had taken the least bit of trouble under your own initiative, instead of always placing the responsibility for your life on everyone else—" the familiar reprimand sounded dully on Marie's heart, and she broke off mid-sentence. "Oh! Please, Liam. Let's not fight. There's no time and nothing to gain."

His face was flushed with anger, but he nodded. "Will you be at the trial?"

"Yes."

He grimaced. "Of course you will. You'd love nothing more than to see me hanged."

Marie felt as though he'd slapped her. "How could you say such a thing to me?"

"Oh, God, Marie." William ducked his head and covered his face with his hands. "I hardly know what I'm saying."

Forgetting the restraint she'd urged on herself just moments before, she stepped in and reached for him through the barred window.

He encircled her hand with both of his, then lowered his head to it, as though in prayer.

"Don't lose heart," she murmured, her own heart beating so fast she felt faint. "I'll speak to John and Charlie tonight. If what you say is true, I won't give them a moment's rest until they put things right."

He looked up, his eyes shining. "You always were a fighter." Without dropping her gaze, he bent his head over her hand and let his lips brush against her fingers when he said, "It's one of the things I've loved most about you."

Marie's mind emptied as she watched him, tense and expectant. They seemed to be teetering on the brink of something reckless and irrevocable, but she could not turn away. She was drawn to him, like a moth to flame. Her lips parted, and soft words were forming on her tongue, when the door at the end of the corridor opened, and a mocking voice rang down the stone hallway. "Time's up."

NECK DEEP ALREADY

JANUARY 18, 1900

*M*arie pulled the wedding ring quilt tight around her shoulders and settled into the window seat to wait for Papa and Charlie's return. It was a school night, and Eliza had gone to bed hours ago. The fire, which provided the only light in the room, had burned down until only a soft amber glow radiated from the ashes.

After leaving the tombs, Marie had rushed home in a fury. When she found the house empty, it had taken all her strength of will to calm herself enough to bend her mind to the mending and cooking. As the hours passed, chores, and the necessity of putting on a brave face for Eliza, dulled the edge of her anger. She honed it again now by remembering, in agonizing detail, every word William had spoken to her earlier that day.

She had drifted into that borderland between sleep and the waking world when the bang of the house door being slammed shut roused her. Shivering, as much from nerves as cold, she sat up. When Charlie's quick step sounded on the stairs she stood, clutching the blanket around her shoulders like a shawl.

Charlie stopped short when he saw her. "What're you doing up?"

"Where's Papa?"

"How should I know?" He shut the door and hung his coat on the hook before collapsing into a chair. His cheeks were pink, but his eyes were clear as he bent down to unlace his shoes. "What do you want him for?"

"I saw Liam today."

Charlie's face was obscured by shadow, but his hands paused. "How'd that go?"

Marie stood over him. "He says Papa was behind the trouble you and he got into at Duncombe's."

Charlie straightened up and grinned. "And you believed him? Jesus, Marie. You are gullible."

"He says he has proof."

Charlie's smile wavered. "What proof?"

"Letters Papa wrote."

"Have you seen them?"

"No."

"Then how do you know they exist?"

Marie locked eyes with him. "Could they?"

Charlie's gaze dropped to his shoes.

An ache swelled in Marie's chest, making it difficult to speak. "What have you done?"

"It was John's idea."

"By heaven, Charlie. You're going to have to do better than that."

He looked up, his brown eyes defiant. "Well, it was."

"And was it also Papa's idea to frame William for Mémé's death in order to get the reward?"

"Rot! And what makes you think I had anything to do with that?" He sounded defiant, but the fear in his eyes betrayed him.

"He told me it was you."

Charlie's eyes rounded. "Liam told you that I informed on him?"

Marie turned away, hating him and hating herself for not knowing what he was sooner.

"Marie, he told you that?"

"Yes," she said, turning back around. "That's how the business about Duncombe came out. He says if you and Papa don't take back what you told the police, he'll use the letters to make sure you both end up in prison."

"Christ." Charlie stood, took an unsteady step, then sat back down. "Marie, listen; he can't go to the police with those letters. You have to stop him."

Marie recoiled. "*I* have to stop him?"

"He still cares for you. He'll listen to what you say."

The idea would have been laughable if she wasn't so angry. "If you're so afraid of those letters, then you and Papa better do as he asks. Go to Detective Gardiner, tell him you lied. Face the consequences of your actions for once in your life."

"And put my own head in the noose? Not a chance." He stepped toward her. "You realize that if I hadn't given them William, it would have been me or John on trial, sure as you're born."

"And you'd rather see Liam, *your friend*, hang for something he didn't do?"

Charlie shook his head. "It's out of my hands."

"Then I'll go to Gardiner. I'll tell him."

Charlie snorted dismissively.

"I will."

"Tell him what, exactly?"

"That you're a selfish, scheming, no-good liar who framed his best friend for the reward money."

"But I didn't lie," Charlie said with growing confidence. "When I saw William after New Year's, he *did* have money, and there *was* blood on his coat. I never said a word more than that."

Marie stepped toward the chair, suddenly uncertain of her footing. "What are you saying? That Liam really did kill Mémé?"

"No, of course not. But if the police think he did, it's none of my doing." His tone softened, and he looked up at her with wide, imploring eyes. "Which is why you have to help me."

"No, I don't," Marie said sharply. "I don't want any part of this."

His softness vanished. "You're neck-deep already. Once they've calaboosed me and the old man, how long do you think you and Lizzy can survive? Have you given that any thought?"

"Lizzy and I will be just fine."

Charlie cast her a rueful smile. "You think?"

"I *know*. There's the money I get for the mending, and once things have settled, we'll have the inheritance."

"Not after Duncombe gets through with us, you won't. He'll sue us blind just for laughs."

Marie's heart dropped.

"The way I figure it," Charlie went on, "If John and I get sent up, you'll have a week, maybe two, before it's whoring or the river for the both of you. You've got more pride than any woman ought, but I suspect Lizzy's too practical a girl to put rocks in her pockets."

Marie's face went very hot, and tears pricked at her eyes, but she stepped toward her brother. "That was a truly horrible thing to say," she said, her voice low and cold. "What a cruel, contemptible man you've grown up to be."

He dropped back into his chair, the old wood groaning under his weight. "I know it, but that's a topic for another conversation."

Marie turned on her heel and strode toward her and Eliza's room.

"Wait," he called after her. "Where are you going?"

She heard him rise and hurried her steps, but he caught her by the elbow and spun her around. "You don't understand, Marie. He'll ruin us all."

"Let me go!" She wrenched her arm from his grip and

shoved him from her. His eyes were large and almost childlike with fear. She turned away.

"Marie," he said to her back, his voice pleading now.

She stepped into the bedroom and shut the door.

Marie lay in bed a long time before sleep took her. When she did drift off, her dreams were feverish visions of William being led to the gallows, a curse for her on his lips. These horrors clung to the edges of her consciousness even after she woke. Suddenly, everything reminded her of him: a shirt the color of a tie he once wore, a dish that he might once have eaten from, a blanket that would keep him warm in his cold cell. She wanted to scream with the vexation of it. She searched her mind for things she might say to him, or for things she might do to help, but drew the same blank every time.

Papa came home around noon. She could tell by the way he talked incessantly and how his sharp eyes gauged her that Charlie had warned him. He even proffered the house money without making her plead for it.

To her surprise, Marie found that her anger had faded into a deep disgust. When she tried to resurrect the accusations and insults she'd practiced the day before, they made her feel hopeless and ill. What was the use of talking to him? He would only make excuses, tell more lies. It was enough that he knew. It was a relief when he finally shut himself in his room to sleep.

That afternoon, Marie dropped a basket of finished mending off with Mrs. Griggs. In return, the landlady handed Marie a basket of fresh mending with a large stack of mail nestled on top. Marie eyed the letters with trepidation.

Their names and photographs had begun appearing in the newspapers, and Papa had begun receiving all manner of correspondence. Most of it from strangers offering their support or condemnation. Some people even wrote to ask Papa to promote their cause or to send them money. Papa and Charlie found this funny, but it infuriated Marie. The circus-like atmosphere that had begun at the inquest persisted, as though the world were conspiring to turn the tragedy of Mémé's death into a farce.

She placed the basket in the corner and covered it, then sorted through the mail, tossing the bulk of it in the trash bin unopened. She had just finished when Charlie returned from the saloon. In a hushed tone, he asked, "Did you go see Liam today?"

"No."

"Marie, you have to."

"No, I don't."

His brow furrowed. "Marie, please, this is important."

"Don't you think I realize that?" She turned to face him. "How can I ever look Liam in the face again after what you, what *we*, have done to him? I've never been so ashamed in my life—ashamed of my family, and ashamed of myself."

Charlie's face twisted with annoyance. "Well, that's just jolly. Think of it as practice for what's in store for all of us if he goes to the police."

"At least one good thing would come from that," Marie said, matter-of-factly, "I would never have to see you or Papa again."

She turned and strode away, leaving Charlie to mutter curses at her back.

It was fine to exchange insults, but he was right about one thing. Sooner or later, she would have to go and see William. What she would do at that visit, what would be said, she didn't know. She would apologize, certainly, but then what? Grovel and plead for forgiveness? Implore him to go to his death with their secrets buried like a knife in his heart?

She hoped time would unsnarl her thoughts, but she woke the next morning to find everything in the same tangle. When Eliza commented on how distracted she was, Marie pled headache and tried to keep busy. Eliza would, of course, have to be told eventually, but Marie would spare her sister that grief for as long as possible.

After Eliza left for school, Marie went downstairs to rinse the empty milk bottles and put them out for the dairyman. She was surprised when she returned to the apartment and found her father waiting.

"Come here, child," he said, placing the news sheet he'd been reading down on the table. "We need to talk."

His tone was one of command. She considered ignoring him and marching to her room, but she wanted to know what he had to say for himself, so she walked to the table and sat down.

"Charlie tells me that William has some letters of mine that he shouldn't."

"He's going to give them to the police," she said coldly. "Unless you and Charlie find a way to get him out of the hole you've dug for him."

"That *we* dug for him?" Papa shook his head. "He may act like a boy, but don't let that fool you. William is a grown man. Any decisions he makes are his own."

"But you convinced him—"

Papa raised his hand, stopping her. "He convinced himself."

"Even if he did, you still urged him along," Marie said, refusing to get bogged down in the details. "And you lied to me," she added, unable to keep the hurt from her voice.

"I did." He nodded solemnly. "But it was for your own good. You deserve better than a lack-witted crook like William Jones."

"You're no better than he is—probably worse."

"That may well be, but at least I recognize and admit my shortcomings. Can William do that?"

Marie said nothing.

"It's no great feat, mind you, but it helps keep the wolves away." He leaned back in his chair, his full attention fixed on her. "I know my failings and my strengths, just as I know yours. You were meant for better things, my girl."

Marie dropped her gaze to the table, steeling her heart

against his words. "None of that matters, not anymore. Liam will hang if we don't help him."

"And we will," Papa said, "but you need to explain to him that there are no magic bullets. Charlie can, and will, refuse to testify, and I'll do my best for him when I'm on the stand, but the prosecution's case doesn't rest on us."

Marie looked up, startled. "I thought the only thing against Liam was what Charlie told them?"

"No." Her father reached out and took her hand in his. She wanted to pull away, but his hand was so large and warm. It made her feel like a child again, safe in his care. "For them to have proceeded this far, I can guarantee you it's more than that."

She found herself blinking back tears. "How can I believe anything you say?"

"I don't know." He sighed and gave her hand a squeeze before releasing it. "I guess we'll all just have to do our best to trust one another and see what happens."

She shook her head.

"You're my firstborn," he said, standing to stare down at her. "My beautiful little girl, and I'd do anything to protect you. Never forget that."

Marie turned in her chair so that she faced away from him and set her jaw. He was in one of his tender, reflective moods, but it wouldn't last. They never did. When she heard the front door open and close, she dropped her head onto her arms and cried.

What if at least some of what he said was true? Would Papa and Charlie's concessions be enough? She doubted it, but what else could be done?

Once her tears had dried, she felt calmer, but the problem remained. Hoping the fresh air would clear her mind, she set off to pay the butcher. Her thoughts were still circling the same questions, like a drowning man in a whirlpool, when she returned home to find a letter waiting for her. It must have come in the afternoon post. She picked it up and immediately recognized William's handwriting.

Even though the house was empty, Marie hurried to her room and shut the door before opening it, anticipation mingling with her fear.

My Dearest Marie,

After your visit, I received a letter from my mother and sister. My father died three months ago and can no longer keep them from me. They hired an attorney, a Mr. Halford, to defend me. His first instruction is that I cut off all communication with you until after the trial. He fears that if people learn of our connection, they'll say I committed murder intending to marry you and collect a portion of the inheritance. It's a foolish idea, I know, but no stranger than the claims the prosecution already levels against me.

Ah, Marie, I feel like the proverbial lost sheep, willing to follow anyone who promises to lead me back into the safety of the flock. I hope you will not fault me for taking this advice. Even though you've shunned me for so long, I do not relish the idea of this new, forced separation. I have so many questions, so many thoughts and fears I'd like to share with you, but, like everything else, those things will have to wait.

I trust you've spoken to your father and brother about what we discussed. For your sake, I will keep my silence as long as I can. But please, do not mistake my generosity for weakness. Assure them that if I am to rot in prison, I shall not do so alone. This I swear.

Enough of that. I won't be able to write you again until I know not when, and I don't want this last letter to be filled with the ugliness of the past. I will write instead of the future. It may be that they hang me for a crime I did not commit. If so, I shall try to accept my fate bravely, but I could not depart this world without your knowing how much a part of me you are. Even when I felt I hated you, I could not see anything lovely, not a sunset or a spring lark, without conjuring your image. And though I have suffered more than any man alive on your account, I sometimes think I would rather be miserable with you than happy with another. If that is not love, true love, then I hope never to know it.

If I find my way through this, I will endeavor to forget the past. We were neither of us blameless. Mere children, playing at love, but this last year has made a man of me. If I do survive this ordeal, I could wish nothing more than for us to meet again with open minds and unbiased hearts. Until then, know that my thoughts are with you. You have lived in my heart all this time, so that we were never, are never, truly apart.

Yours,
Liam

Marie brushed a tear away with the back of her hand and walked to the bed. From under the mattress, she withdrew an old cigar tin where she kept her most precious items. It contained a swatch of silk from her mother's best blue dress, buttons and snips of ribbon from her and Eliza's childhood, and other letters, also in William's writing. She tucked this new missive away with the others.

She hated the hold he had on her, the way he could say a word or write a letter and turn her feelings upside down. He was not the sort of man who could be trusted with that much power. Maybe he wrote the truth, or maybe he was saying what he thought she needed to hear to ensure that she forced Papa's hand. There was no way of knowing, not that it mattered. Whatever the aim, his letter had worked. She was on his side.

ALL RISE

FEBRUARY 5, 1900

*M*arie smoothed her palms over her black skirt and scanned the court room's wood-railed gallery for an open seat. Row after row was filled to capacity. Even the white marble walls were lined with spectators, a lurid eagerness radiating from their pinched faces.

She suddenly felt very alone. The thought of pushing in and standing shoulder to shoulder with strangers while the most important matters in her life were being discussed was nearly unendurable, but there was no help for it. As a witness, Papa was barred from the trial. Eliza was still at school, and Charlie had flatly refused to accompany her.

Spotting a small opening in the far corner, Marie hurried to it. At the front of the room, a large, highly polished wooden counter rested on a dais overlooking the audience. Two tables, one to either side, stood before it. There were three men seated at the table on the left, and two on the right, and Marie examined the backs of their heads until she was satisfied William was not among them. She was still trying to determine which table was the defense and which the prosecution when a tall man in the audience stood and waved her over. A flush of surprise, and something like happiness coursed through her when she recognized James Lett.

The high, cathedral-like ceilings and cold marble walls of the courthouse made her feel small and shabby, but young Mr. Lett appeared entirely at ease in this setting. As she approached, he bent down and said something to the man in the seat next to him. The man glanced at her, rose hastily, and strode in her direction. She hesitated when he drew near, but the man merely dipped his head and walked past.

"Good morning, Miss Chevalier." Mr. Lett offered her his hand. "I was hoping to see you here."

She took it, flushing hotly, and he guided her to the newly vacated seat. "Thank you. It's very kind of you to think of us, Mr. Lett."

His smile broadened. "Please, call me Jamie."

"Thank you, *Jamie*." His name came out as little more than a whisper. There was something slightly improper about calling a man of his standing by his Christian name, and she flushed with a strange, almost guilty, feeling of pride at his having asked her to.

"Much better." His eyes met hers, his expression open and kind. "How is your family?"

A polite lie was on her lips, but something stopped her from saying it. Inexplicable as it was, this dashing, wealthy young man was genuinely interested in her family's well being. Not only had he helped get Papa released from jail, but he had put up that large reward. Maybe, if she told him their latest trouble, he would help again?

"Not well, I'm afraid." Pride made the words sticky in her throat.

His brows drew together. "I'm sorry to hear it. With your father's release, and this arrest, I had hoped to hear things had improved."

"Oh, they are better ... or they were, at least for a while." Now she sounded ungrateful. Cursing her awkwardness, she pressed on. "I mean to say, things are better, and we are, of course, very grateful to you and to your family for everything. Only, now something new has gone wrong."

His look of confusion softened, and she suspected he was trying not to smile.

Marie swallowed hard and tried again. "Please don't misunderstand me, it's a great blessing and relief to have Papa home, and we're *very* grateful to you. Only, the moment the police freed him, they arrested another innocent person."

"You know this man, Jones, then?"

"He has been my brother's closest friend since childhood, and I can assure you, he's no killer."

"Ah," Jamie said, as if this cleared everything up.

"The worst of it," Marie rushed on, "is that the police aren't looking for anyone else, not since they arrested Liam, which leaves Mémé's killer free to roam the streets."

The lines of Jamie's face sharpened. "And you are absolutely convinced of Mr. Jones's innocence?"

"Completely," Marie affirmed. "What could Liam possibly gain from such a crime?"

"I imagine the police suspect some sort of burglary gone wrong."

"But nothing was missing. That came out at the inquest. Doesn't anyone else find that troubling? That the house should have been turned over, cabinets and drawers emptied out, but nothing taken?"

"Perhaps Madame Alozia caught the thief searching for valuables, and once he'd killed her, he was forced to flee."

Marie shook her head vigorously. "I should think there are very few people who are as foolish as that. William certainly isn't. Consider, if you've come to rob someone, why waste time taking an inventory first? Why create a situation where you're forced to commit murder and then run off empty-handed? No.

There must be something the police are ignoring, some clue that points to the real killer."

Marie paused to gather courage, then said, "Perhaps your family owns something of particular value, and the thief was searching for it?"

Jamie stiffened and looked away. "I can't imagine what."

She was trying to think of a way to tactfully press him further when a paneled door at the side of the room opened and William entered between two deputies.

The air grew thin as Wiliam walked to his chair, head bowed. He glanced up before he sat and scanned the room. For the briefest of moments, his eyes met hers, and the fear in them coursed through her body like lightning.

A bailiff walked to the front of the room. His first sentence was lost to the tumult of her emotion, but she caught: "All rise for the Honorable Judge Hastings."

There was a low murmur and the muted rustling of bodies in motion as everyone in the gallery rose to their feet. Another door, this one at the front of the room, opened and the judge entered, his form obscured by a voluminous black robe.

Judge Hastings gave a brief speech about his commitment to upholding the laws and integrity of the state, after which, the attorneys made their opening statements.

Mr. Adolphus was a tall man with the exaggerated dignity of an undertaker. He wore a fine black suit and was so severe in look and manner that everyone else appeared lax by comparison. This contrast was most pronounced when looking from him to William's attorney, Mr. Halford. Stout and middle-aged, Mr. Halford had a mottled red complexion and wore gold-wire spectacles low on his thin nose. The jacket of his tan tweed day suit pulled at the buttons, and his neck bulged above his unstarched collar.

Both men spoke at some length, then the prosecution called the first witness to the stand: Detective Gardiner. Marie forced herself to listen as the hated detective repeated almost verbatim the information he'd provided at the inquest. When Adolphus wrapped up his questioning, Marie straightened in her seat, eager to hear how William's attorney would undermine the man.

Mr. Halford stood. "Thank you, Your Honor, Counsel, but we forfeit our right to cross-examine this witness at this time."

Marie's chest tightened. She studied William's profile, trying to gauge his mood, but his head was bowed.

Mr. Adolphus rose to his feet. "Your Honor, the prosecution would like to call John Chevalier to the stand."

A preemptive flush of embarrassment warmed Marie's cheeks. She had known this moment was coming, she just hadn't expected it so soon, or that she'd be sitting next to James Lett when it came.

Papa sauntered to the witness box as though he were enjoying a leisurely stroll in the park. He had been gone before she woke this morning, and Marie was surprised to see him wearing a navy frock coat with the crisp sheen peculiar to new clothing, a pumpkin-colored vest, and a cravat of deep forest green—not a single article of which she had ever seen before. With a growing sense of unease, she wondered where the money for his finery had come from.

She dared a glance at Jamie, to see what sort of impression Papa was making. He caught her look and flashed her a quick, reassuring smile. Her answering smile felt more like a grimace, so she turned her attention back to the witness box.

Papa, for his part, seemed to be enjoying himself. He sat on the stand nodding acknowledgments to people, mostly women, in the audience who, with coughs and waving hand-kerchiefs, were vying for his attention. In anticipation of this moment, Papa had forced her, Eliza, and Charlie to pose questions to him while he thought up ever more elaborate responses. After just two days of this, he had succeeded in making himself so obnoxious that even Charlie fled at his approach.

"Good day, Mr. Chevalier." When Mr. Adolphus spoke, the courtroom, which had seemed quiet before, achieved a new depth of silence.

"Good day to you, Sir." Papa's voice rang out, clear and sonorous.

"Do you know the defendant in this case, William Jones?"

"I should say. He's been coming around my place since he was in short pants. Why, the first time I saw him, he couldn't have been more than seven or eight years old. A scrawny little mite he was then, always getting himself into scrapes. Nothing serious, mind you. Just your normal boyhood hijinks: throwing mud balls at the teachers and putting worms down the backs of girls' dresses, harmless little goings-on of that nature."

"What brought him to your home?" Adolphus stepped closer to the witness box, but if this was an attempt to pull her father's attention to him and away from the audience, it failed.

Papa lifted his heavy brow and smirked. "Why, I already told you, he's a friend of my son's. They were at school together. A good school it was too, St. Anthony's. A fine school. I went there myself. Expensive, but, as I always say, you can't put a price on quality. No, especially not—."

"And how familiar was Jones with the rest of the family?"

Mr. Adolphus was standing close enough to the witness box to touch it, but Papa still turned his head to address the jury. "Why, familiar, of course. I practically had to raise him as my own after his father threw him to the dogs. Now that was a damned sorry situation, I can tell you. Called himself a man of God, he did, and then tossed his own flesh and blood onto the streets. And all because William was showing a little high spirits, what is natural to a boy his age. Fortunately, I'm the soft-hearted—"

"And what was your relationship to the victim in this case, Mrs. Tompkins?" Adolphus cut in.

"She was my mother," Papa answered. "And a good mother, too. None better! All this talk of my hounding her, or of her being afraid of me, is poppycock. Pure balderdash. We had our little quarrels, like as what transpires in all families, but it always came out in the wash, and there were never any hard feelings left betwixt us."

Papa's unruffled tone softened the knot that had formed in Marie's chest. For the first time in her life, she was glad her father was incapable of feeling shame. Everything about him, his expression, tone, and manner, all proclaimed that he was more than a match for anything Adolphus, or anyone else, might hurl at him.

"To your knowledge, did the accused ever meet Mrs. Tompkins, your mother?"

Papa nodded. "Certainly. In spite of the lies some of these malicious muckrakers are spreading, we were a close-knit family. None closer! Why, scarcely a week would pass without her dropping in on us, or us dropping in on her. With Jones always being about, he couldn't help but to have met her."

"Close as you were, didn't there come a time when you were forced to distance yourself and your family from Mr. Jones?"

Papa's expression sobered. "I'm sorry to say there was. It was after that nasty business at the attorney Duncombe's."

Marie's heart froze in her chest.

"And what," Adolphus asked, "was this 'nasty business', precisely?"

Papa shook his head. "Oh, there was some question of papers being forged or some such nonsense. Nothing proved, mind you. Pure gossip, that's all."

Marie's throat relaxed enough for her to exhale.

"But it was serious enough to merit a police inquiry, was it not?"

The question was clearly a nudge, and from it, she understood that Papa was not testifying the way the prosecutor had expected him to.

"I believe so, yes. A waste of time and resources if you ask me."

"Yet, you took it seriously enough to distance Mr. Jones, who you say was like a son to you, from your family?"

"An overabundance of caution." Papa continued to speak directly to the jury. "I have two young, and, if I do say so myself, very pretty daughters. I didn't want any of the malicious talk—for I'm sure that's all it was—to attach to their names. A father can't be too careful."

Contempt radiated from the prosecuting attorney. "One last question, isn't it true that you were initially a suspect in this case?"

Marie's heart stopped in her chest. Her gaze bounced from her father to Adolphus then back again. Both men appeared calm, and she soon guessed why. Getting this information in early, and on the prosecution's terms, blunted a weapon that the defense could have used against them. All of the local papers had carried stories about a suspected matricide. Her father's exoneration, however, had been covered with far less journalistic fervor.

Papa pressed his lips into a grim line. "I'm sorry to say that the police were so misguided as to suspect me, wholly without reason, mind you. Thankfully, my alibi was confirmed, and I was cleared of all suspicion in the matter. Which, I might add, is no less than justice demanded."

"No more questions, Your Honor."

Marie exhaled slowly, her body beginning to relax.

The judge finished scribbling a note and looked at Mr. Halford. "Your witness."

"Thank you, Your Honor." Mr. Halford straightened his gold spectacles and walked to the podium. "Good Afternoon, Mr.

Chevalier."

"Good Afternoon, Sir."

"You just told the court that you were forced to separate yourself from the defendant because you suspected him of being involved in untoward dealings. Is that correct?"

"I didn't say that I suspected him, merely that he was suspected. There is a great difference."

"Indeed, but you did say that you were forced to separate him from your family?"

Papa nodded. "Until the matter was resolved, I determined that a certain amount of distance would be desirable."

Mr. Halford smiled. "Very conscientious of you, I'm sure. So, you cut off *all* contact with the defendant at that time?"

Papa frowned. "I wouldn't say *all* contact, no. As I've said, I practically raised him, and I'm not a hard-hearted man."

"So, you did see him then, after he was relieved of his position at Mr. Duncombe's office?"

"From time to time, yes."

"*From time to time.* Wouldn't it, perhaps, be more accurate to say that, up until his arrest, you, your son, and Mr. Jones were constant companions?"

Adolphus stood. "Objection. Counsel is stating an opinion, not asking a question."

"Overruled. The witness may answer," Judge Hastings responded without looking up from his notes.

Papa's face turned red. "That's putting the thing a little strong. If my son and I came across William at a place of public recreation, we wouldn't go out of our way to shun him, if that's what you're getting at."

"When you say 'place of public recreation' you are referring to saloons, are you not?"

The audience tittered, and Judge Hastings looked up in warning.

Marie felt she couldn't breathe again, and wished desperately that Jamie wasn't sitting next to her.

"My son and I have been known to patronize public houses on occasion. There's no shame in that. Plenty of respectable folk like to have a drink at the end of a hard working day."

Mr. Halford nodded. "Indeed, no shame at all. But, you are not currently employed, are you Mr. Chevalier?"

For the first time since he'd taken the stand, Papa turned his full attention to counsel. "Not at the present moment, no."

"And how many times in a week would you say you came across Jones at these saloons?"

"I'm sure I couldn't say."

"More than once a week? Twice?"

Papa shrugged his shoulders.

"Three times? More?"

"It's not the sort of thing I would take note of."

"No," Mr. Halford said understandingly. "I'd imagine it would be difficult for a man such as yourself to keep track of the time he spends in saloons."

The audience laughed. Adolphus jumped to his feet. "Objection, Counsel's snide and unprofessional remarks have no place in this proceeding."

Marie wanted to crawl away and disappear, but between the crowds and Jamie, she was as good as pilloried to her seat.

"Sustained. Counsel for the Defense's last remark will be struck, and," Judge Hastings looked at Mr. Halford, "You, sir, may consider this a warning. Any more of that and I'll fine you for contempt. Understood?"

Mr. Halford bowed to the bench. "Yes, Your Honor. I apologize." Turning back to Papa, Mr. Halford continued, "You say the police suspected you, what were your words, 'wholly without reason', is that right?"

"It is."

"But you knew your mother had a sizable savings put away,

and that, upon her demise, this money was to come to you, correct?"

Papa looked at the jury with a grieved expression. "I wouldn't say that, no. My mother and I seldom spoke of her financial situation."

"Indeed? And was there any particular reason she kept her savings a secret from you?"

Papa's head snapped back. "We had no secrets. Perhaps my mother did tell me of her savings, but—."

"So, when she told you of her savings, did you or did you not believe that you would be her beneficiary?"

"I don't know that I ever gave it much thought."

"Did you have reason to suspect she wished to disinherit you and leave her money to someone else?"

"Certainly not!" Papa's face was scarlet, and even at this distance, Marie could see the veins protruding at his temples.

"So, you did, in fact, understand that you stood to gain monetarily from your mother's death?"

Papa's eyes blazed, and his voice was low and dangerous. "I don't believe I understand your question, sir."

Mr. Halford smiled benignly. "I think you do, but we'll let it pass for now. Isn't it true that your mother owned a silver watch that she was in the habit of wearing every day?"

Marie's mind flashed to the silver watch Gardiner had found the day of the inquest and Charlie's explanation of it.

Papa leaned back in the seat. "Yes."

"And were you aware that this watch was not found on her person when her body was discovered, and that the police considered it stolen, most probably by her murderer?"

"Yes, but, as I explained to them, that was a mistake."

Marie leaned forward, her whole being focused on the two men at the front of the room.

"Isn't it also true that this missing silver watch was found by the police in your possession shortly after the crime took place?"

Papa slammed his fist against the witness box railing. "I tell you, that was a mistake. She gave that watch to me!"

Marie closed her eyes and gripped the edge of the polished oak seat as though it were the only thing tethering her to this earth. Mémé would never have given that watch to Papa. A gift from her first husband, that watch was one of Mémé Alozia's most cherished possessions. Never would she have given it away, not to him, not so long as there was an ounce of breath or fight left in her body.

BEYOND MORTAL AID

FEBRUARY 5, 1900

*M*arie hurried through Penn Square, scanning for her father's bulk. Her face still burned from pleading headache to Jamie and then senselessly refusing his gallant offers of assistance. She'd hoped to catch Papa still in the corridors, chatting with the audience or one of those loathsome newspapermen, but by the time she'd slipped from the courtroom, he was nowhere to be found.

There had to be an explanation, a reason Papa had the watch. Like a curse, Gardiner's description of how he had found Mémé, lying on the floor with her throat—no.. Papa would never, *could* never. But then how did he get Mémé's watch?

Marie stopped at the corner, unsure which way to turn. Her only hope was that Papa would go home to change out of his new finery before going to the saloon. She set off. Every block she traveled without spotting him weighed on her heart. At last, she reached the Griggs's house. Hiking up her skirt, she took the stairs two at a time and threw open the door. The rooms sat dark and empty, just as she'd left them.

Holding back tears, Marie stood in the middle of the living room. What was she to do now? Sitting here, waiting for him, would surely drive her mad. She had to find him. There was nothing else for it, even if that meant searching every saloon in Philadelphia.

Back outside, the wind howled along the alleyways and a light snow was beginning to fall. She would start with Papa's favorite saloon, Morris's, and work her way out from there. Keeping up a brisk pace, she reached the old tavern in less than ten minutes. A group of factory workers, just off the morning shift, stood talking and smoking by the door, their lean bodies throwing long shadows across the icy walkway.

A flicker of fear pierced her resolve when a gaunt young man with a broken front tooth nudged the others and whistled. Someone, she couldn't see who, called out, "Hullo Sweetheart, why don't you come over here? I want to tell you something."

They all laughed.

Her embarrassment increased her anger. They were all the same, these men: drunkards and liars, just like her father. When she grasped the door handle, the man with the broken tooth stepped toward her. "Where do you think you're going?"

Ignoring him, Marie pushed inside. Smoke, thick and choking, stung her eyes. She'd only made it a couple of steps in when another whistle pierced the rumble of male voices. A moment later, a flurry of hoots and catcalls erupted around her. Disoriented, it took her some time to scan the faces at the bar. When she was sure Papa's wasn't among them, she turned to investigate the tables.

Nothing there, either. Her face burned and her eyes watered from the smoke. She blinked hard to clear her vision. A group of men had risen and were standing quite near to her now, their faces sly or solicitous. She approached a bland-faced man dressed like a clerk. "I'm looking for my father, John Chevalier. Have you seen him?"

The man shook his head. One of the hooligans shouted a lewd suggestion, and everyone laughed again.

She turned toward the door. She would have to try Evan's next, there was no help for it, but if she lived to be a hundred, she would never forgive Papa for this. Never.

Marie had just brushed past an old man clenching a half-smoked cigar in his teeth when someone grabbed her arm. She tried to jerk away, but the grip tightened. The catcalls and hoots started up again, and without thinking, she turned to strike out at her captor.

She recognized her father's face a moment before her palm connected with his cheek. Scowling, he yanked her to his side, and she relaxed. He dragged her, unresisting, out into the cold, clean air. After pulling her the length of a city block, he ducked between two buildings and flung her from him. "What in God's name do you think you're doing, girl?"

Marie lifted her chin and rubbed the arm he'd just released. "Looking for you."

Concern clouded his features. "Has something happened to Charlie? Eliza?"

She brushed the question aside with a wave of her hand. "You stole Mémé's watch."

He straightened, drawing back from her. The shadows on his face deepened, and his eyes narrowed. "Don't talk nonsense, child. She gave me that watch."

"She would *never* have given you that watch." Marie's voice gained strength. "You know as well as I, she intended it for me."

He shrugged. "She must've changed her mind."

Blood hummed in Marie's ears and her chest tightened. "If you don't tell me how you came by that watch, I will be forced to believe that you killed her. Do you want that?"

"You wretched, ungrateful little beggar." His eyes flashed a warning as he straightened to his full height. "First, you go gallivanting all over town like some trollop, and now, you're leveling wild accusations at your father? Why, if I were a different sort of man, I'd turn you over my knee here and now."

"I won't be put off," Marie said firmly. "Before this night is over, I will know how you came by that watch, or I swear to you, I will tell anyone who will listen to me that you murdered your mother."

His hand flew up and Marie stiffened, bracing for the blow. After a long moment, his arm dropped back to his side. "All right, you stupid chit. I took the watch. But, I swear on your blessed mother's soul, I didn't harm a hair on your mémé's head."

An undefinable emotion, part anguish, part relief, beat through Marie's chest. "What happened?"

He took her arm, gently this time. "Not here. Come, let's go back to the house. I'll tell you all there."

Despite the cold, Marie did not hurry her steps. Now that the information she'd wanted was forthcoming, she dreaded hearing it. She was relieved when they arrived at their rooms and found them still empty. Marie shook the snow from their coats while Papa set about lighting a fire.

"Well, here goes." Papa, having placed the old iron kettle on the fire, moved the rickety gold chair next to hers. He folded his hands on his lap and looked at her with weary eyes. "Whatever you may think of me, I've got feelings, same as the rest of you. Being cast aside by one's own mother, especially on the most Christian of holidays, well, that's the sort of thing that can cut even the hardest fellow to the quick."

"You mean, when you went to see Mémé at Christmas?" Marie dimly remembered Charlie talking about a failed visit.

He nodded. "With it being the dawn of a new century, I thought I should try to set things right between us. It was on my mind all day, but it wasn't until evening, after I'd had a few drinks, that I got my courage up. It was probably after nine, late for her, but I figured with it being a holiday she might still be up, and might even have been glad of some company."

The boiling pot rattled on the grate. Marie started to rise, but Papa motioned for her to stay. He stood and carefully poured them tea. "When I got there, the door was open, so I went inside. I told myself she must have stepped out for a moment and left it ajar."

"She would never—" Marie protested.

Papa held up his hand. "I know how it sounds, but it's what I thought. After all, she might have popped out to say 'Happy New Year', or to borrow a cup of sugar or some such trifle. And" —he caught Marie's gaze and smiled sadly as he handed her the mug,—"I suppose it's possible I didn't pay much mind to the door because it suited me not to."

Marie placed her cup on the table. "But didn't you think something might be wrong?"

"Not just then, no. It wasn't until I started making my way down the stairs that I realized something was amiss. I could see that the servants' hall was illuminated by the light of a dying fire. You know how stingy—how *careful*," he corrected, "she was with coal and kindling and such. It didn't seem like her to leave a fire to burn out. But, I told myself, it proved she'd popped out not expecting to be gone long."

He paused, and his eyes took on a stony, far-away look.

Marie cleared her throat. "Then what happened?"

"I caught sight of her before I reached the landing. At first, I wasn't sure what I was seeing. She was but a dark massing, backlit by the glow of the fire. When I realized it was her, my first thought was that she must have fainted. I called out and ran to her."

His voice had grown faint, and Marie's heart raced as though she were there, seeing it with him.

"When I drew near, I saw the blood—glistening it was, in the flames."

Marie shuddered.

"I knew then she was beyond mortal aid."

"What did you do?" Marie whispered.

"What could I do?" He shook his head. "I'll spare you the details. Suffice to say that not since the loss of my dear wife, your mother, have I known such sorrow."

Marie shook her head, trying to take in what he was saying. "But why didn't you go for help?"

"She was past help, child. Running into the streets crying "Murder!" would have been of no possible use to her, and would have brought a heap of trouble down on me. After all, it was no secret that she and I weren't on the best of terms, and my having wandered in through an open door was apt to give people the wrong impression."

"But how did you get her watch?"

He raised his head and his face took on the defensive, arrogant, expression she was so familiar with. "I didn't take anything that didn't belong to me."

When Marie didn't refute this, he resumed his narrative, "Well, there I was, neck-deep in it, as it were, and for a moment I thought all was lost. But then a way came to me: I know a certain lady on Moon Street, and she'd let drop that her husband was out of town. I'd been of some little service to her in the past, and knew if it came to it, she'd say a word to the police on my behalf.

"It being New Year's Eve," Papa continued, "there were a great many people out and about, and it struck me I could catch a cab without risking much. My only difficulty was that I didn't have fare. Under the circumstances, this was no small consideration. But then it came to me; the old girl was bound to have some change about her, she always did. So, I took some of what was coming to me."

"You searched her pockets?"

His spine straightened. "It wasn't like it was stealing. Now that she was dead, the money and the watch were mine anyway, that's the law. Besides, it wasn't safe to leave them on her. I know what a lot of bloody thieves those mortuary men are. I've heard tell of them stealing the gold right out of people's teeth. And I'd be damned if I was going to let some ghoul steal one cent of your inheritance!"

Marie was still searching for an adequate response when Eliza returned home. She stopped short in the entryway, her expression a mixture of surprise and concern. "What happened?"

"Your sister can tell you all about the trial," Papa said, rising and making for the door. He kissed Eliza on top of her head as he passed. "It's been a hell of a day, and I need a drink."

Eliza watched him go, then turned to Marie, her face a question. Marie smiled wanly and gestured to the chair their father had so recently occupied. She told Eliza about the trial but not what Papa had told her about the watch. She decided to keep that information close, at least until she'd figured out what to do with it.

It wasn't until later that night, when Eliza had gone to bed and Marie was alone, that she had time to think. Her first thought was that she should go to William's attorney and tell him everything. While not proof of innocence, information that Papa, and not William, had been there that night and taken Mémé's things would undermine the prosecution's argument.

The feeling of hope this gave her didn't last long. After all the interviews Adolphus had given to the newspapers about William's guilt, she couldn't see him abandoning course without something more definite. Besides, after the way Papa had testified that morning, she could easily imagine him arguing that Papa and William had conspired together.

Marie sighed and rested her head against the cool glass of the windowpane. There had to be something she could do, but what? The police were no use. As far as she could tell, the investigation had focused solely on her family and their connections from the start, even though it was the Letts' house that had been broken into.

The brief conversation she'd had with Jamie earlier that day came back to her, and she sat upright, her heart hammering. When she had asked if there was something of particular value in the house, Jamie's whole demeanor had changed. At the time, she'd been too distracted to make anything of it, but now it seemed perfectly obvious. He knew something, something he wasn't telling her.

It was a wild suspicion. One that was in no way consistent with what she knew of the Lett family's integrity and generosity, Jamie's in particular. Still, it was the only clue she had.

Her mind worked quickly now. She would look for him in court tomorrow, ask more questions. If she was very lucky, he would take her into his confidence. If not, he might still let some useful scrap of information slip.

The hope was a slender one, but she grabbed hold of it. She would keep Papa's dangerous secret for now. If the trial went well for William, there would be no need to tell anyone anything. If it didn't, well, she would go to Mr. Halford and tell him all—and God alone knew what would become of them then.

NEFARIOUS ENDS

FEBRUARY 6, 1900

*M*arie unbuttoned her heavy wool coat and wedged her purse into the space between her seat and the small of her back for safekeeping. It was another frigid morning, but the courthouse furnaces were roaring at full, baking the dusty air. After yesterday's crush, she was surprised to find a number of seats still available. She'd chosen a spot in the middle of the gallery, far enough away to be inconspicuous but close enough to get a good look at all of the people involved.

Another quick survey of the room confirmed that Jamie hadn't arrived yet. It was early, she told herself. He would come. To stop herself from staring at the doors, she began examining the people around her.

The gallery was full of strangers. Mostly old women, shop girls and clerks, by the look of them. The attorneys were also present, presiding over their respective tables. Adolphus wore another black serge suit, and Halford sported a slightly rumpled gray flannel. Marie was relieved to note that Halford's hair appeared to have been trimmed and tidied, but even from this distance, she could tell his collar had seen better days.

The man sitting next to Halford looked to the left, and Marie drew in her breath when she recognized William. She had expected him to be led in later, but there he was. His dark navy suit exaggerated the pallor of his face, and his expression was tense. As she watched him whispering to a red-haired young man she took to be one of Halford's clerks, worry filled her chest to the point of aching. For the hundredth time that morning, she wondered whether keeping her father's secret was really the best course of action.

She had just lifted her hand to get William's attention when someone stopped next to her seat.

"Good morning. I hope you don't mind if I join you."

Feeling as though she'd been caught, cookie half out of the jar, Marie dropped her hand to her lap and faced Jamie. "Please do. I was afraid you weren't going to make it today. I know how very busy you must be."

The smile he flashed her was strained as he settled into the seat next to her. "I hope you're feeling better?"

Marie looked away, unable to hold his concerned gaze. "Much."

"I'm glad."

At just that moment, William turned toward her. He looked relieved at first, but when his eyes fell on Jamie, anger hardened his expression.

Embarrassment, and something that felt uncomfortably like guilt, stopped Marie's breath. She met William's eyes, rejecting the implied accusation she found in them. What had she to feel guilty about? William was not her beau, not anymore, and neither was Jamie, for that matter.

Still, she was grateful when a gentleman appeared on the aisle looking to get to one of the center seats. He was followed by three others in quick succession. In only a few short minutes, the room had filled.

By the time she had resettled, William's attention was on his attorney, but now a dull, lingering pain weighted her spirits. Had Jamie noticed the look William had given him? Her heart beat wildly when she thought of it, but her mind rebelled. Such silly, schoolgirl anxieties had no place here. What did it matter what either of them thought? She had a purpose, and she would stick to it.

Marie twisted in her seat to face Jamie. "Have you given any more thought to what we discussed? About whether there might have been an item of particular interest to a thief in the house?"

The strained expression she'd noticed yesterday appeared on Jamie's face again.

"I can see that you have. Please, if you know something, you must tell me." She spoke quickly, before he could think of an excuse.

"If I knew anything that could be of use to you or your family, I would tell you."

"Of course, only...." Marie hesitated, searching for words that would persuade him. "As I'm sure you will understand, anything that could shed even the faintest of lights on that night and what happened to Mémé is of the greatest interest to me, to my family."

"I have nothing to share." His eyes remained gentle, but there was a firmness in his voice and manner that extinguished hope.

Marie looked away before her eyes could fill with tears.

Jamie touched her elbow and she reluctantly turned back toward him.

"I am making inquiries that I cannot discuss, not at this stage. But I swear to you, if I learn of anything that has bearing on Madame Alozia's death, I will tell you."

"Do you promise?" Marie held his gaze, willing him to bind himself to her cause.

Jamie's eyes softened. "I promise."

The words were hardly out of his mouth when the chatter in

the room died off. To their right, the bailiff left his post near the door and walked up the aisle. He stopped in front of Judge Hastings' dais and called out, "All rise…"

Marie stood. Her disappointment at having failed to acquire any new information faded as anxiety for William took hold. The preliminaries were executed, and the first witness was called: Charlotte Brown.

It took all of Marie's self-restraint not to turn her head to gawk as William's "special friend" made her way up the aisle. The newspapers had been full of stories and inferences about the "lady of the night" who had been arrested with her lover.

When Miss Brown finally came into view, Marie's first thought was that there had been a mistake. This infamous "woman" looked more like a girl of Eliza's age. Slight to the point of waifishness, she walked with her head down and mounted the steps to the witness box as though she were climbing the gallows. Indeed, her air was so self-conscious and pained, Marie found herself unsure where to look.

Surprise was soon replaced by a peculiar feeling of disappointment and disgust. Miss Brown, with her girlish figure, mousey hair, and unremarkable features appeared neither beautiful nor bad. And yet, if the stories were to be believed, she had lived with William for months now, had even held herself out as his *wife,* the very position Marie had once coveted.

When the girl was at last seated, Adolphus cleared his throat and approached the stand. "Miss Brown, it is Miss Brown, isn't it?"

The girl nodded.

"Please answer the questions out loud so that the stenographer can record you."

Charlotte nodded again, then caught herself and mumbled, "Yes."

"Do you live alone?"

"No."

"Louder, if you please. I asked, 'do you live alone?'"

The girl's shoulders stiffened, but she called out in a feeble voice, "No."

"Who lives with you?"

"William."

"Do you mean William Jones, the defendant?"

"Yes."

Adolphus moved back toward the prosecution's table and picked up a file. "Do you and William pass yourselves off as a married couple?"

"Yes."

"And were you married?"

"No."

"How long have you been living together?'

"Eight months."

Marie's stomach twisted and her mouth went dry. He must have moved in with the girl a few paltry weeks after breaking with her.

"And, during that time, did you behave as a married couple?"

The girl's terrified, dark eyes darted up at him. "I—I don't understand."

"Did you behave as married couples behave: spending time together, sharing household cares and responsibilities?"

The girl nodded.

Adolphus shot the jury an exasperated look.

Charlotte noticed and blurted, "Yes."

"Did you bring money into the household?"

The girl's head dropped still lower. "Sometimes."

"And what did you do to earn that money?"

Charlotte sagged in her seat, and the courtroom grew so quiet Marie became aware of her own shallow breathing.

"I'll ask you again," Adolphus's voice rang through the still room. "What did you do to earn money?"

The girl looked up. Her chin trembled, and there were wet streaks on her flushed cheeks. "Please, sir. I don't understand."

Marie's stomach lurched, but she forced herself to keep watching.

Adolphus picked a paper off of the desk and brandished it before the jury. "Perhaps this will refresh your memory." He turned to address the judge. "Your Honor, I'd like to submit Exhibit D for the Prosecution. It is a record of the eleventh precinct, night watch, from September 7, 1899. It records the arrest of one Charlotte Diaz for solicitation."

The judge nodded, and Adolphus held the document before Charlotte. "Are you familiar with this?"

Without looking at the paper, the girl nodded.

"You must remember to speak out so that the court can hear you," Adolphus spoke in slow, exaggerated tones.

Charlotte covered her face with her hands and spoke through her fingers, "Yes, it was me."

This time Marie had to look away. She didn't want to feel sorry for this girl. She had troubles enough of her own.

Adolphus pressed on, "Isn't it true that you are, in fact, a prostitute by profession?"

Charlotte groaned. "Yes, yes. I do not deny it."

"Did the Defendant accept money from you?"

Against her will, Marie's attention returned to the witness box. Miss Brown was sitting straight now, her cheeks were scarlet and her dark eyes wide. "Yes, but—"

Adolphus interrupted, "Did he work?"

Charlotte blinked. "No one would hire him."

"So, he did not work?"

"He tried to. I swear he did." Charlotte looked to the jury, her quavering voice pleading with them to believe her. "But no one would have him."

Adolphus frowned. He returned to his desk and shuffled through more papers. The silence stretched to an awkward length before he asked, "Were you and William together on New Year's Eve?"

Charlotte looked dazed by the change of topic. "Yes."

"Remember that you are under oath and that we are already in possession of sworn statements concerning the events of that night. I ask you again, were you together on New Year's Eve?"

"Yes, for most of it." Charlotte's voice was firm, but fear was etched in every line of her face.

"Were you together between the hours of eight and eleven, when the medical examiner has informed us the murder was committed?"

"No, but I know he didn't do it. He's incapable of a thing like that. You must believe me." Charlotte's eyes flashed between the judge and the jury.

Adolphus's voice took on a condescending, almost sympathetic tone. "Your unquestioning devotion to this man can hardly be doubted."

"Objection." Halford rose, startling Marie. He had been so quiet throughout the preceding, she had almost forgotten he existed. "Counsel is stating an opinion, not asking a question."

"Withdrawn." Adolphus returned his attention to the Judge. "Your Honor, I've finished with this witness."

For the first time since Charlotte's name had been called, Marie risked a glance at William. His head was bowed, and she could only see him in profile. The muscles in his face were taut.

"Your witness, Mr. Halford." Judge Hastings finished scribbling a note and turned his full attention to the counsel for the defense.

Halford rose and smiled sympathetically at Charlotte. "You said you've lived with William for the past eight months, is that right?"

"Yes, sir."

"That's a long time for young folks like yourself. In the

course of those eight months, have you ever seen or heard of William behaving violently?

"Never!"

"Has he ever treated you badly? Knocked you around or called you names?"

"Never." The girl looked at the jury, her eyes imploring. "He has never so much as raised his voice in my presence."

Then he certainly must have changed, Marie thought, and immediately felt disloyal. The pang did not last. She had been used to discounting William's indiscretions as unfortunate but unavoidable—something men did that ladies must accept. She had never thought much about the women involved and suspected he hadn't either. But Miss Brown's love for William was palpable, and it filled Marie with disgust, for William and for herself.

"Does he force you to work?" Halford asked, his voice still gentle.

Charlotte shook her head vigorously. "No. He hates it. He's told me time and time again he wishes I'd leave off."

"And what was your line of work when you met William?"

"The same, sir. But he's always treated me with kindness and respect." Her voice quaked.

"On New Year's Eve, when you met with William, did he seem upset?"

"Not at all."

"How did he seem?"

"Like his normal self, maybe a little tired." Charlotte twisted in the chair until she faced the jury. "I wanted to go out and celebrate, but he fell asleep in front of the fire."

Mr. Halford smiled reassuringly. "Not exactly the behavior you'd expect from a man who'd just murdered an old woman for the change in her pocket, is it?"

Marie blanched at this off-hand reference to Mémé.

Adolphus stood. "Objection. It has not been shown that the witness is an expert on the habits of murderers."

Hastings turned in Adolphus's direction and said, "Quite right, sir. Quite right. I apologize to the court and withdraw the question. I've finished, Your Honor."

Judge Hastings addressed Adolphus. "Redirect?"

"Not at this time. If your honor permits, the prosecution would now like to call Mr. Calvin Duncombe to the stand."

Judge Hastings nodded and told Charlotte to register her whereabouts with the court in case they wished to recall her. As Charlotte walked from the room Jamie leaned in and whispered to Marie, "Adolphus was rather hard on the girl, I thought."

Marie clenched her jaw and nodded. He was right, of course. Miss Brown's testimony had been painful to watch, and Marie doubted there was a soul in the room who didn't feel some sympathy for the girl. But this misstep by the prosecution, if mistake it was, was no victory for the defense. Adolphus might appear a bully, but William was something far, far worse.

Mr. Duncombe, who Marie had heard much about but never seen, turned out to be a stout gentleman in his mid to late fifties, well-tailored, with great peppery mutton chop sideburns and pale blue eyes.

"Good day, sir," Adolphus began. "Was the defendant, William Jones, ever in your employ?"

"He was employed by my firm as a clerk for a period of not more than eight months, between September of eighteen-ninety-seven and May of eighteen-ninety-eight, after which, his employment was terminated for cause." Duncombe's voice rang out deep and clear.

"For what reason?"

"Objection. Irrelevant. What has Mr. Jones's past employment to do with the trial at hand?"

"Character." Adolphus said simply.

"I'll allow it." Judge Hastings turned toward the witness. "You may answer the question, Mr. Duncombe."

"Mr. Donaldson, one of my senior clerks, discovered a number of fraudulent letters purportedly issued by my firm in the name of interests we represent. Further inquiry into the matter revealed that the letters in question had been approved by either Mr. Jones, or his friend, Mr. Charles Chevalier."

"What kind of letters were these?" Mr. Adolphus asked.

"Invoices and statements detailing transactions with a foreign shipping company that, as far as we could discover, did not exist. There were also letters of reference guaranteeing the solvency and profitability of the same."

Jamie drew in a sharp breath, and Marie turned toward him. He leaned forward, his eyes riveted on the attorney in the witness box.

Mr. Adolphus continued, "What did this indicate to you?"

"That William Jones and his friend Charles Chevalier were involved in some manner of fraudulent dealing and had used their position with my firm to further their nefarious ends."

"Thank you. No further questions."

Mr. Halford stood.

"Were your suspicions brought to the police?"

"They were."

"And, to your knowledge, was a warrant issued for Mr. Jone's arrest in connection with these charges?"

"I believe so."

"What about for his friend, Charles Chevalier?"

Marie's heart seized.

Duncombe shifted in his seat. "Not to my knowledge."

"Why not? I believe you testified that these suspicious documents passed over Mr. Jones and Mr. Charles Chevalier's desks. If that's the case, why was a warrant issued for only William?"

Duncombe frowned. "Our in-house investigation did not

produce sufficient evidence against Mr. Chevalier to lodge an official complaint."

"But he was let go from your firm?"

"He was."

"Thank you, Mr. Duncombe. Your Honor, we have no further questions for the witness at this time."

Marie's mind raced. Why had Halford brought Charlie into this? Had William told his attorney about Papa's letters?

"That wily old fox," Jamie muttered.

"Who?" Marie's head snapped in Jamie's direction.

"I can't say, not yet," Jamie whispered, already on his feet. "But if I'm right, I'll have news for you, and soon."

ONE DROP

FEBRUARY 6, 1900

*J*amie caught a cab outside the courthouse and directed the driver to Duncombe's office. The worn interior felt like a cage, and he continually craned his neck to stare out the window, willing the road before them to clear.

He needed to see the forged files for himself, just to be sure, but already he felt certain this was the connection he and Melly had been searching for. What were the odds of there being two imaginary shipping companies connected, however tangentially, to Manassas?

Duncombe's firm was located in an eight-story brownstone with neat gold lettering on the windows. The firm had represented his father for as long as Jamie could remember, and he was counting on that relationship to buy him a little flexibility today.

He waved off the secretary who called out to him as he mounted the stairs to the partners' suite. There, a young man typing at a desk stood as Jamie approached.

"Good afternoon. I'm James Lett, has Mr. Duncombe

returned yet?" Having left him on the stand, Jamie knew the answer already, but he figured this was as good an opening as any.

"Not yet, sir."

"Pity, I have urgent business with him and very little time to spare. Is there anyone in the office who might be able to assist me?"

The man's brow furrowed. "Mr. Smythe might, but—"

"Excellent. Please tell him I'm here."

The secretary, still looking uncertain, disappeared into one of the back rooms. He reappeared soon after, following a slight, middle-aged man with a face Jamie recognized as belonging to one of the partners.

"Mr. Lett." The man offered his hand, and Jamie shook it. "Pleasure to see you again. What can I help you with today?"

"It's a little sensitive, Harold," Jamie replied, grateful for his knack of remembering names.

"I understand." Harold gestured to the door he'd just exited, and Jamie walked into an oak-paneled office.

Once seated, Jamie explained what he was hoping to see without saying why he wanted to see it.

Harold templed his fingers and listened, his pale blue eyes impassive. When Jamie finished, he said, "Our office would be happy to accommodate your request, if we could. Unfortunately, I have no personal knowledge of this Jones fellow or the documents you referenced. You see, in a firm this size, there's always a crop of young clerks coming and going, and, not infrequently, their exits are seasoned with varying degrees of scandal."

"Do all of these clerks forge documents for fictitious businesses?" Jamie asked wryly.

"Not exactly." Smythe smiled to hide his irritation. "But the type of investigation that would follow such a discovery would be confidential, and the details would be kept private, even from partners."

"Surely, some record of this investigation exists somewhere? You must have kept copies of the forged documents, at least."

"We may have," Harold said thoughtfully. "Or, then again, we may not have. Once the investigation was complete and a complaint with the police filed, it's quite possible all records were destroyed."

"Well," Jamie said, leaning back in his chair. "I certainly hope you're wrong about that. Fortunately, I'm in no great hurry today, so I can wait while you have one of your boys go and see what they can find."

Harold's face was a mask of polite resentment. "My secretary was under the impression you were pressed."

Jamie shrugged. "I can make time for this."

Harold gave him a look like a man appraising an opponent at the poker table, then stood and walked from the office. The attorney's reticence was hardly surprising. However confident Duncombe had seemed in court, Jamie knew he must be worried. If word got out that the firm had participated in the furtherance of a crime, albeit unwittingly, it was only a matter of time before the victims found their way to his door.

"Good afternoon, Mr. Lett."

Jamie turned at the sound of his name.

"Mr. Duncombe." Jamie stood and extended his hand. "I'm awfully glad to see you."

Duncombe shook his hand and shut the door. "Mr. Smythe tells me you'd like to see the Jones papers."

"That's right."

Duncombe waited expectantly.

"As you know," Jamie said, "Mr. Chevalier and Mr. Jones were hired as a favor to my father, who wished to reward the loyalty and devotion of one of our long-time servants."

Duncombe nodded.

"It has lately come to our attention that the fraud they were attempting to perpetrate may have extended beyond them. In fact—" Jamie hesitated, the man was their attorney and would almost certainly have to know eventually. Still, it was harder than he thought to say the words out loud—"it may have originated with someone at our company."

"Who?"

"I can't tell you. Not yet. Not until I'm certain."

Duncombe nodded and opened the door. The secretary from earlier appeared at once.

"Fetch the Jones papers," Duncombe ordered.

The man scurried away and returned several minutes later with a thick manilla folder in his hand. Duncombe took it from him, looked at it as though he were weighing it with his eyes, then held it out to Jamie.

Jamie gripped the folder, but Duncombe held on for a few ticks before releasing it. The room had an odd atmosphere, both furtive and solemn, almost as though Jamie were being initiated into a secret society.

He walked to the desk and opened the folder. Not two lines down, he found what he was looking for. The imaginary company at the center of the forgeries was none other than the mustachioed man's Zapata y Alvarez.

Jamie looked up at Duncombe, who had remained standing by the door. "I'll be needing copies of these."

"Of course."

Three hours later, Jamie had his own folder of evidence. He resisted the urge to go directly to Manassass's house and confront him. He needed more information first, something directly linking Manassas to the documents.

Back on the street, Jamie waved down a new cab and directed the driver to the courthouse. He held the evidence the entire ride there, feeling numb and anxious in turns. Instead of going through the main entrance, he wound his way along the side of the building until he found the stairs to the tombs.

The trial had finished for the day, but Jamie still had to wait an hour and slip the guard a ten-dollar bill before he was summoned for the visit. The air below ground was so hot and dry it scratched his throat. His fingers tapped a haphazard rhythm on the folder as he followed the guard down the narrow, well-lit corridor. It was a miserable place, no less a dungeon for the gas lighting and piped-in heat.

The guard, a short man with a red, pitted nose, stopped abruptly and rapped on a door with his truncheon. He turned to Jamie. "Twenty minutes. I'll be on the other side of the door we came through if you need me."

Jamie nodded, and the guard retreated down the hall. Jamie watched until the door closed between them, then turned back to the barred window. William Jones stood on the other side of it.

Jamie had formed the opinion that the papers' reports of Jones's dashing appearance were greatly exaggerated. The fellow possessed a good form, regular features, and the carriage of a man well aware of these virtues, but nothing to rate the fuss being made of him.

Up close, however, Jamie had to admit the scoundrel was striking. His pallor was accentuated by heavy brows and curling hair the color of toasted chestnuts. His deep-set eyes were more green than gold, and they gave his face an intense, almost pained expression. His was the visage of a painted martyr, or of a poet. Just the sort of ne'er-do-well who turned young, inexperienced girls' heads.

An unexpected surge of anger made Jamie hesitate. The man was no good, anyone could see that. Perhaps it would be better to allow justice to run its course?

"What do you want?" Jones demanded.

"My name is James Lett," Jamie stated, hesitating only a moment before adding, "and I've come to help you."

Jones lifted his eyebrows, a mocking smile on his lips. "And why should you want to do that?"

Jamie withdrew his cigarette case from his pocket, took out a cigarette and offered the open case to Jones, who shook his head. "I can't tell you, not yet. But what does it matter, so long as I succeed?"

Jones watched him warily but said nothing.

"Suffice to say, I'm on the verge of uncovering something that could prove your innocence, but I need some information from you first."

"What information?"

"The names of everyone involved with the forgeries."

Jones's smirk deepened into a mocking smile. "How does my telling you that help me?"

"Answer the question and you'll find out." With every word he spoke, Jamie's dislike of the man deepened.

"Either you're a fool or you think me one. Whatever the case, you've made a mistake. I never forged any papers, and, if I had, I sure as hell wouldn't be talking to you about it. In case you hadn't noticed"—Jones glanced at the bars separating them—"I have enough to worry about."

"I assure you, no word you speak to me will ever reach the authorities."

"And you think I should take that on faith, do you?" Jones shook his head, then walked back to his bunk and sat down.

"Let's just say, in this matter at least, our interests are aligned."

"How?"

"I can't answer that, not yet. You'll just have to take my word for it."

"You tell me nothing and expect me to give you enough information to keep me behind bars for the next seven years?"

Jones leaned against the stone wall, eyeing Jamie coldly. "Thanks, but help like that I can do without."

"Better to risk seven years than a hangman's noose."

Jones stopped smirking. "I haven't been convicted yet."

"You will be," Jamie said, failing to hold his temper. "I watched the faces in the jury box today when your lady-friend testified. An able-bodied man like you living off the degradation of a poor creature like that? They're prepared to see you hang on the girl's account alone."

Jones was on his feet and at the door in an instant. "You've no right to judge me. With your father's money and easy life, what could you know about me? What do you know about anything?"

"I know that if you don't tell me who was involved in those forgeries, you'll hang. And, as far as I can tell, the world will be none the poorer for it."

To Jamie's surprise, Jones laughed.

"So that's your opinion of me, is it? At least it's honest." Jones looked at him for a long moment, sizing him up. "How about this, if you can't tell me *what* you're doing, at least tell me *why* you're doing it."

For the first time since this conversation had started, an answer he could actually say came to Jamie's mind. "My family has long had a connection to the Chevaliers, and a certain member of that family has expressed a particular interest in your welfare."

"*Marie*," Jones nearly spat her name. "I knew it. Tell me, what has she promised you?"

The man was jealous, Jamie realized with a shock. It explained the menacing look he'd leveled at him in the court-room and his rudeness now. Disgust crept up Jamie's throat, but he swallowed it back. It was better for Jones to think his efforts centered around a woman than to explain his true motive.

"Miss Chevalier takes an active interest in your well-being, and I have an interest in hers." The near truth of this made the blood rush to Jamie's face.

"What sort of interest do you have in her?"

"I don't see how that's any of your business."

"Well, aren't you noble," Jones drawled, his magazine-handsome face radiating contempt. "The gallant son of a rich man turns a pretty, poor girl's head, and then what? Certainly not marriage. Even if we put the fact that she's your housekeeper's granddaughter to one side, she's a colored girl, and that would never do."

"Marie is not *a colored girl*." Jamie's response was automatic, defensive, and he wished at once he could take it back.

"Isn't she? Granted, you can't tell by looking at her, but since when has that mattered? I started at Duncombe's the year after *Plessy v. Ferguson* was decided by the United States Supreme Court. *One drop* of "black blood", that's all it takes in this country for a person to be considered colored, and our Marie has considerably more than that."

"What of it? In case you hadn't noticed, this isn't Louisiana." Jamie had not followed the case closely, but he, and everyone else in the country, knew something of it. Homer Plessy, a Colored Creole man, made headlines across the nation when he boarded a whites-only train car in Louisiana and was arrested. One of the things that made the case so compelling was that Homer Plessy appeared, in every respect, to be a white man.

Some speculated that Mr. Plessy's fair complexion was part of his carefully orchestrated political protest, meant to draw attention to the absurdity of segregation laws. This, it arguably did, but if it was also intended to help bridge the gap between the races, it could not have failed more completely. Homer Plessy lost his case, and the "one drop" rule became the law of the land.

"So, you plan on marrying her then?" Jones demanded. "Is that what you're saying?"

"I'm *saying*," Jamie spoke sharply, "that it's none of your business, and I'd thank you to keep your prejudices to yourself."

"*My* prejudices? I proposed marriage to the girl—and meant it. If she'd accepted, I would have stood by her side though the whole world condemned me for it. But *you*," Jones scoffed, "You can't even admit you like her."

Jamie was stunned into silence. This good-for-nothing had proposed to Marie? At that moment, all of Jamie's anger solidified into a dull hatred of the man before him. Giving this idiot a well-deserved pummeling wasn't an option, and wouldn't have helped matters even if it was. Better to cut his losses now and try his luck with Marie's brother.

"My feelings, about Marie or anything else, are none of your concern. I came here because I thought we might be of some help to one another, but it appears I was mistaken. And now, I will leave you as I found you."

Before Jamie could turn thought to action, Jones called out, "Alright. But if a single word of what I tell you gets back to the authorities, I'll know who's to blame." He met Jamie's gaze. "Make sure Marie understands that."

Jamie waited without speaking.

"There was me, Charlie, and old John Chevalier, but I suspect Marie has already told you that." Jones studied his face for confirmation. "The only other person involved was a connection of John's, an old man by the name of Edmunds."

"Manassas Edmunds?" Jamie's throat was so tight he could hardly speak.

Jones nodded. "Could have been."

"And did this Edmunds tell you what he wanted the letters for?"

"No, not that John told us, at any rate. And to tell the truth, as long as Edmunds paid, Charlie and I didn't much care."

That was all Jamie needed to know. He turned and strode down the stone corridor.

Jones's voice echoed after him. "Wait! What happens now?"

Jamie knocked on the iron-banded door.

"What happens now?" Jones yelled again.

A guard appeared, and Jamie left without so much as a glance behind him.

HOW IT ENDS

FEBRUARY 6, 1900

*T*he horses' pace slowed and Jamie's head lolled against the back of the hired cab's leather upholstered seat. The shabby interior smelled strongly of tobacco smoke and the stables, and faintly of violet-scented hair oil and something he couldn't quite place—formaldehyde? Whatever it was, the bouquet did nothing to help his stomach, which, after spending the better portion of the day in fruitless pursuit of Manassas, had decided to rebel.

When the cab picked up speed again, jolting and swaying, Jamie opened the window, hoping the cold air would ease the nausea. Outside, he recognized the night-black silhouette of the Gloria Dei. He was getting close.

His mind traveled back over today's misadventures. After leaving the tombs, Jamie had rushed to Manassas's house, eager to confront him. Unfortunately, the young maid who answered the door had derailed this plan by informing him that Mr. Edmunds had left early and wasn't expected back until late. The office had been Jamie's next stop, where the old man's secretary, Mr. Loeffler, had insisted that Manassas was neither in nor expected.

Jamie had hailed another cab and continued the search, but, as day wore into night, it became clear that Manassas did not wish to be found. Jamie had paid visits to the old man's club, his friends' houses, and, finally, half the restaurants and public houses in Philadelphia without success.

Throughout the afternoon and evening, Jamie made several unsatisfactory telephone calls checking for Manassas's return. The last establishment Jamie had visited, a dimly lit restaurant on the outskirts of the city known for its *cabinet particuliers*, had been without such modern conveniences. Not that it mattered. By the time he finished there, it had grown so late that the old fellow was sure to be tucked up sleeping. Jamie hoped that was the case. After a day as miserable as this one had been, dragging the old man from his bed would be a pleasure.

At last, the cab rolled to a shuddering stop. Jamie's legs and back joined his stomach in complaint as he pulled himself off his seat and descended onto the icy pavement. He handed the cabbie a five-dollar bill and asked him to wait. Clouds blocked the moon, and Jamie had to strain his eyes to make out the shrub-lined path to Manassas's door. He rang the bell then shoved his hands into his pockets to ward off the cold. It seemed a very long time before the housekeeper, Mrs. Rutledge, answered.

"Hello, Mrs. R. I know it's dreadfully late, but I need to see the old man. It's important."

"I'm afraid he's not at home, Mr. Jamie. He was called away on urgent business this afternoon."

"Was he given the messages I left?"

"Yes, sir."

When nothing more was said, Jamie asked, "And did he leave a message for me?"

"I'm sorry, sir. He didn't."

"And what time did you say he left?" Jamie looked past the

housekeeper, straining to make out the face of the clock in the corner.

Mrs. R pulled the door snug against her side. "This afternoon."

Jamie's attention sharpened. The housekeeper's usually calm face wore a look of nervous strain, and there was an uncharacteristic reticence in her speech. When he tried to catch her eyes, she looked away.

"That's too bad," he said, his heart galloping ahead. "I'll just use the telephone then and be on my way. It won't take a moment."

"I'm sorry, Mr. Jamie, but you can't." Mrs. R looked flustered, her eyes stopping everywhere but on Jamie's face.

"I'm afraid I must." Jamie applied gentle pressure to the door.

The housekeeper hesitated a moment, then stepped aside.

Not wanting to lose his advantage, Jamie made a beeline for Manassas's study. The door was shut. He gave it a rap hard enough to make his knuckles sting then swung it open. His quarry stood hunched over the fire, folders of documents stacked on either side of him.

At the sound of the door, Manassas righted himself and turned to face Jamie. He didn't look surprised, just tired.

"I knew I wouldn't be able to keep you off the scent long." Manassas's eyes moved past Jamie. "It's alright, Ben, Mr. Lett is my guest."

Jamie turned to find a servant filling the doorway behind him. The big man nodded and walked away.

Manassas went to his desk and settled into his chair before motioning Jamie to one across the way. "How's your father?"

"Ailing," Jamie bit off the word. "And he'll be a damned sight worse once he learns how you've betrayed him."

Manassas winced, then nodded. "Well, I don't know about you, but I could use a drink."

Without waiting for a response, Manassas rang the bell, and

Gilroy, the butler, appeared almost at once. "Scotch and soda for me, cognac for young Mr. Lett."

Jamie lit a cigarette and waited until Gilroy had gone before speaking. "I've been to Duncombe's." He paused, his anger choking off the words. "How could you have—"

The old man held up his hand. "I am going to tell you everything. I always intended to. I think I was just waiting until I knew how the story ended."

"And now you know?" Jamie could not keep the contempt from his voice.

"Yes," Manassas said slowly. "Now I know."

There was a long pause, and finally, Jamie said, "Well? What happened? Were you in need of money?"

Manassas shook his head. "It wasn't for myself."

"Then for who?"

"For the company, of course." Manassas's tone implied that this was obvious.

Before Jamie could respond, Gilroy returned with the liquor trolley and began pouring their drinks.

"I may as well start from the beginning," Manassas said, once the butler had gone. "Seven years ago, I was approached by a man named Saunders. He claimed to own a shipping company in prime position to benefit from the French canal project. He showed me a stack of confidential documents, or so I then believed, guaranteeing the canal's completion.

"As you know, we've been losing business to yards in the west for years now, but, once the canal was built, we could ship lumber at a fraction of the cost. Our situation is far from unique. Every industry in the nation stood to benefit from the canal in some way. The scale and difficulty of the project deterred the more prudent investors, of which I had hitherto numbered myself among. But, a man privy to inside information, as Saunders had by then convinced me I was, stood to make a fortune. Within just a few weeks, every penny I had was invested in that shipping company."

"How could you have believed him? The French project was a disaster from start to finish."

"Yes," Manassas agreed. "It was. However, many of the details that are common knowledge today were withheld from the public at the time. Cleverer men than I lost fortunes speculating on it.

"Foolish as that investment was, if it were my only folly, we would not be sitting here now. Believing, as I then did, that I'd seen proof that the canal would soon be completed, I entered into exclusive, long-term contracts with construction enter-prises in California and Nevada. In order to get in ahead of the competition, I promised large shipments of finished lumber at greatly reduced prices, satisfaction of which would be made possible by Saunders' firm once the canal was built."

Jamie's attention sharpened. "And Father agreed to this?"

"No." Manassas held up his hand, preemptively warding off Jamie's anger. "I know how it sounds, but you must try to understand; I believed absolutely that the canal would be built."

"Then why the secrecy?"

"Because I knew your father wouldn't take the risk." Manassas paused, then locked eyes with Jamie. "But I also knew that if something wasn't done, and soon, he would lose the busi-ness he'd spent his life building."

"Things aren't that bad," Jamie said testily. "He would have told me."

"The Captain doesn't know, not the full extent of it. I made sure of that." Manassas nodded at the half-empty glass in his hand. "You think his illness is a recent affliction, but it isn't. He has been visiting a specialist on the Upper East Side for years now. His heart could never have taken the strain."

"So, you deceived him? You deceived us all?"

"My dear boy, I planned to tell him everything just as soon as the canal was built."

"But it wasn't built."

"No." Manassas exhaled heavily. "It wasn't. Not three months after I'd invested, Saunders disappeared. I knew I'd been swindled. My only hope was to cover the difference between the price given in the contracts I'd negotiated and our going rates until the canal was complete. If I could do that, all might yet be saved.

"I sold everything: my art collection, my stable, even mortgaged my properties. Months passed, and the things it had taken me a lifetime to acquire disappeared one by one until nothing remained—and still there was no canal."

"Why didn't you cancel the orders?"

"I tried. The construction companies threatened to sue. If the courts sided against us, the lawyers' fees alone would have forced us into bankruptcy."

"And these contracts still exist?"

Manassas dropped his gaze to the desk. "They do."

Jamie rubbed his face with his hands. "I can't believe what I'm hearing."

"If it had been merely a matter of my own destruction, I would have done the honorable thing at once. But, your father and I have been friends for many years. I owe him everything, and there's nothing I wouldn't do to spare him grief."

"That's hardly possible now," Jamie said bitterly.

"No." Manassas looked away again. "It isn't."

"What about Souza, that man in New York? Where does he fit in?"

"When the French project folded, I grew desperate. Rumors that the United States would pick up where the French left off began to spread before the French had even left Panama. I had traveled so far on my course that turning back was no longer an option. It was then I decided to do to others what had been done to me. I created a dummy company.... but I believe you know about this already, from the detective agency?"

Jamie's spine stiffened. "Yes, but how ... ?"

"I'll come to that. I took on the man you met in New York, Mr. Souza, to be the face of the enterprise. But I needed reliable documentation to ensure the scheme would be a success.

"Then, as luck would have it, your father approached me about getting Madame Alozia's grandson a position. I knew the boy's father was a scoundrel, and it didn't take long to see that the apple hadn't fallen far from the tree. I found him a place at Duncombe's and negotiated a deal with his father. Soon, I had all the documents I needed.

"It was simple after that. Souza played his part, bringing in more investors than I'd dared hope. I created an account at the office and deposited enough money to cover the overage."

Understanding flooded Jamie's mind. "That's what those payments from the Alvarez account were."

Manassas nodded. "It began to seem like the scheme would work, and I believe it would have—if the canal had been built. But the game went on too long. Souza was meant to disappear after six months. I planned to replace him and begin all over again in a different city. Only, Souza didn't disappear. He had a taste for gambling and ran through his share of the money. He demanded more, but, as I told him, that was impossible. He refused to listen, though every day he stayed put us at risk. I had hoped to talk some sense into him on our trip to New York. He was in the lobby waiting when we came in. You were too tired to notice, but I spotted him at once. When you went to your room, I came back down and we spoke. He was raving with fear and threatened to expose me if I didn't meet his demands by the end of the week.

"I promised to sign over a number of bonds, as I had nothing else to offer. But, even as I promised it, I knew such a transaction was impossible. It would have created a traceable link between him and the business, and I could not allow that. That's when I decided something had to be done about him." Manassas turned to Jamie, his tone imploring. "You must see that he left me no other option."

Jamie looked away.

"I checked out of the hotel and hired a carriage," Manassas continued. "I had my handgun on me, the one I use for protection, and followed Souza. I intended to threaten him, force him to board a train with me, and drop him off somewhere far, far away. It was a reckless, desperate plan, but by that time I too was a desperate man.

"It was then that he approached you. I watched from the shadows as the two of you talked in the hotel restaurant. As you may remember, the weather was foul that night, and I lost him shortly after you parted ways. I spent a restless night in a saloon on the other side of town, dreading what he might have confessed.

"It wasn't until the next morning, near the hotel, that I caught up with him again. He followed me willingly enough into an alley, and there, I asked what had passed between you and him the night before. I could hardly believe my luck when he told me he'd revealed nothing. He wanted money, of course. For the hundredth time, I told him that the ruse was up, and it was past time he made himself scarce. That's when he began insisting we go to you for help.

"Well, obviously I couldn't allow that to happen. I drew the revolver and ordered him into the carriage. He looked confused at first, uncertain, but when I raised the gun and pointed it at his head, he bolted. I don't believe he ever saw the carriage that struck him ...."

Manassas's voice trailed off.

Jamie waited a long moment, the liquor sour in his stomach, then cleared his throat.

Manassas straightened and flashed him a tight smile. "It was a grisly business, of course, but, all in all, a tremendous stroke of good fortune. I started following you, just to be sure Souza hadn't revealed more than he let on. When you started sneaking about and taking files, I guessed that you'd started to sort things out." Manassas's eyes warmed with pride. "You've always been a bright lad; you take after your father in that respect."

The soft words were like a punch to the gut. Jamie took a swallow of his cognac.

"While most of my transgressions were well hidden, I had taken less care with the files in my office, and I couldn't be sure how much information you had. I knew you'd be out on New Year's Eve and your Father mentioned that Candler would be visiting his sister. That left only Mrs. Tompkins in the house, and her hearing wasn't what it used to be. I decided it wouldn't be risking much to slip in and have a look about the place."

"Did *you*..." The moment for truth had come, but the words died in Jamie's throat.

Manassas shook his head. "I didn't, my boy. I looked for the files and left without laying eyes on Mrs. Tompkins."

Jamie released a breath he hadn't been aware of holding, but the ache of uncertainty did not leave him. Manassas had been lying to them all for months, *for years*. How could he believe anything the man said?

The pair sat in silence for several minutes, the crackling of the fire and the ticking of a nearby clock the only sound. Finally, Jamie heaved a sigh and looked at Manassas squarely. "How does this end?"

"I turn myself in."

Jamie straightened up in his chair, surprised.

"The money from the scheme is gone, the contracts are past due, and I no longer have the will or the wherewithal to continue the charade."

"But how is that possible? The detective's report said you and Souza stole over a million dollars."

"The detectives, or, more likely, the investors, exaggerate. We took in approximately half a million, and a good deal of that went on setting up Souza and paying Chevalier and a dozen other scoundrels who all had their small parts to play. The rest went not just to cover the contract overages but to make up for the losses the business has been sustaining at an ever-increasing pace. I'm sorry to tell you this, son, but there's nothing anyone can do to save the company."

Jamie nodded, but the words slid over him without leaving an impression. Too much had been said already.

Manassas sighed. "If I admit to embezzling funds and entering into those contracts as part of an independent criminal action, I pray the courts will allow the company to file for bankruptcy and dissolve the debt. It is the last, best action I can take on behalf of the Keystone Lumber Company. I ask only that you give me until tomorrow afternoon to tie up my affairs." He smiled sadly. "There's not much left to dispose of, but I would like to have things in order."

Jamie experienced a disconcerting mixture of disgust and pity. He rose to his feet. "Of course."

Manassas walked over to him and patted his arm. "You and Melly are young and will weather this storm. It will go much harder on your parents. Try and be patient with them. They will need you in the days to come."

THE PATHS OF VIRTUE

FEBRUARY 7, 1900

*W*illiam twisted in his chair, scanning the crowded courtroom. The trial, which had at first seemed to drag on interminably, was fast drawing to a close. Spectators, dressed in their Sunday best, stood two and three deep along the gray marble walls, and the moist air was thick with the stink of stale tobacco, cheap toilet water, and perspiration.

One of Halford's clerks kicked William's chair from behind, and he straightened, forcing his gaze back to the front of the room.

Bessy Malone, the last witness, was on the stand being cross-examined. His former landlady wore a mustard-colored house dress that, judging by the tightness of its fit, was either borrowed or had hung untouched in a closet for years. A small straw hat, adorned with brightly colored silk flowers and no less than two stuffed birds, completed her ensemble.

William tried to focus on Adolphus's questions, but he'd been unable to concentrate for longer than a few seconds all morning. His gaze drifted to the jury. It was inconceivable that these men, not one of whom would have commanded his attention had they passed on the street, now held his very life in their hands. Another kick from behind made him realize he was bouncing his knee. He stilled his leg and gripped his hands together until his knuckles burned with the pressure.

With any luck, he'd be a free man before the sun set today. If not, his only hope lay with Marie. He resisted the urge to shoot a glance in her direction. He'd spotted her this morning, sitting in the back corner with her rat of a brother, her face pale and her eyes ringed. At least she wasn't with Lett Jr. When he'd seen her last week, smiling and flirting with that mollycoddle, he'd been sick with rage. Later, when Lett had shown up at the tombs asking a bunch of questions, William hadn't known what to think.

Marie was plotting something. Of that, at least, he was certain, and Lett was a pawn in her game. But was she working for or against him? He changed his mind about that at least a dozen times a day. Whatever her plan, she was running out of time. Once the verdict came through, he would make good on his threat to her, whatever the consequences.

William's thoughts were interrupted by Halford, who grunted as he pushed off the table and lifted himself to his feet. "Objection, the prosecution is leading the witness. In fact, he's practically testifying for her."

"So he is," Judge Hastings looked disapprovingly at Adolphus, who appeared more flustered than William had yet seen him. "You'll get your chance to make a closing argument later. Now, it is the witness's turn to speak."

"I apologize, Your Honor." Adolphus was red to the ears, but his voice remained controlled. "I will endeavor to keep the questions simple, and pray only that the witness will keep her answers similarly brief and to the point."

Bessy lifted her chin and sniffed with comic effrontery.

"You say," Adolphus continued, "that you lent the defendant a razor, is that correct?"

"My late husband's," Bessy affirmed.

"Prosecution would like to show the witness exhibits G and J." A clerk appeared with a bundle in his hand. He showed it briefly to the judge, then handed one of the items to Adolphus. "And, to the best of your recollection, is this sheath similar in appearance to the one belonging to the razor you lent him?"

Bessy cocked her head and answered thoughtfully, "Something like, but then razor sheaths all look the same, don't they?"

"Please, just answer the question you're asked, Mrs. Malone."

"What do you think I'm doin'?" she shot back.

Mr. Adolphus looked like there was much he could have said in response to that, but he just shook his head. "You say that you also lent the defendant the jacket he wore the night he was arrested?"

On cue, the clerk passed the jacket to Adolphus who, holding it gingerly between his fingers, showed it briefly to Bessy before displaying it to the jury.

"That's right. That's my Matthew's."

"And was it in this condition when you lent it to the defendant?" Adolphus gestured at some dark staining along the front.

"Something like. My Matty's a butcher—damn messy business."

The audience tittered, and Judge Hastings cast them a look that silenced them.

"Did you not wash the jacket before lending it?" Adolphus asked, his nose wrinkling.

Bessy responded with a hard laugh. "It's obvious you've never done no washin'. There ain't enough Soapine in the state of Pennsylvania to get stains like them out. That jacket there was destined for the bin, and I only set it aside 'cause I knew what desperate straights Will, I mean, *the defendant*, was in."

"So, in your opinion, at the time the murder was committed, the defendant was a desperate man?"

Bessy's smirk deepened. "Desperate enough to wear a

stained jacket, sure. Desperate enough to do what you're suggestin', no."

"Objection. Your Honor," Adolphus gestured to the judge imploringly.

"The second half of the witness' answer will be stricken," Judge Hastings said. "Please Mrs. Malone, try and keep your opinions to yourself."

Bessy folded her arms across her chest and gave another sniff.

Adolphus looked down at his notes then back at Bessy and shook his head. "Your Honor, the prosecution has finished with this witness."

"Mr. Halford?" Judge Hastings looked over at their table.

"No further questions, Your Honor."

Judge Hastings nodded. "You're free to go, Mrs. Malone."

Bessy took her time leaving the stand, savoring her moment in the spotlight. As she sauntered past, she flashed William a wide, self-satisfied grin. Sensing the jurors' eyes upon him, he dropped his gaze to the table.

Once Bessy left the courtroom, Mr. Halford rose. "The defense will not be calling any more witnesses, Your Honor."

Hastings nodded and jotted down a note. "Mr. Adolphus, is state prepared to make its closing argument?"

"It is, Your Honor."

"Very well. Let's see if we can finish this by lunch."

William's entire body flushed with heat, then seemed to go numb, as Adolphus rose and rearranged the papers before him.

"Gentlemen," the prosecutor began. "I want to thank you for your patience and careful attention over this past week. I have had the privilege of representing this great state for nearly twenty-five years, and this matter now before you is, without question, one of the most disturbing and—I'll just come right out and say it—evil crimes that I have yet come across."

William looked over at Halford, trying to gauge what sort of a start the prosecution had gotten off to, but his attorney's expression was unreadable. Halford leaned slightly back in his chair, his bland face attentive, his soft, plump hands folded on his chest.

Adolphus's voice rumbled on. "Over the course of this trial, we have seen that the defendant, William Jones, is a man of the lowest moral character. Already a pimp, a forger, and a thief, he decided to add murder to his list of infamies."

William had to clench his teeth, the urge to deny these accusations, to fight back in some way, was so strong. His fury was fleeting. Even if it were not for the armed policemen standing five feet away, he knew that any such demonstration would be fatal, to his case and to him.

Drawing on skills he had honed in boyhood, William withdrew into himself. He hung his head and picked up his pencil, as though taking notes, then shut his eyes tight and pictured the day, it must have been five years ago, that he'd won two-hundred dollars on Ben Brush at Point Breeze. What a day that had been! It had sprinkled off and on all morning, and the officials had almost closed the track. Ben Brush was a long shot, but William had caught sight of the animal trotting behind the stables and just had a feeling. He'd had such feelings before and they'd always come to nothing, so no one was more surprised than he when his pony pulled ahead in the last lap and crossed the finish line first. For three days, William lived like a king. He'd ordered two new suits from a tailor on Chestnut Street, and all of his drinks were from the bottles on the top shelf. It had seemed like a new beginning, one in which anything might be possible—until he lost the remaining one-fifty in a poker game.

He could almost feel the ghostly sting of three-dollar whiskey on his lips when an image of his father intruded, lecturing from his pulpit about the evils of strong spirits. The spark of peace he'd been kindling in his breast was extinguished. It was impossible to believe that his father, the Reverend Archibald Felix Jones, was dead. The man had been as solid an edifice as the rock of Gibraltar. Fixed and unwavering, whether sermonizing to his devoted congregation or looming over young William in the study, Bible in one hand, belt in the other.

William opened his eyes. Now that the initial sting of the prosecutor's words had passed, William could listen to the man insult him with relative aplomb. After all, he had been called far worse in time.

Adolphus lectured the jury on William's many deficits for another fifteen minutes before concluding his speech.

Judge Hastings then looked over at William's table. "Mr. Halford, is the defense ready?"

"Ready, Your Honor." Mr. Halford gave William's shoulder a reassuring squeeze, then leaned in and whispered, "Hold on to your hat, son. You won't enjoy hearing this, but it needs to be said."

William flashed him a questioning look, then dropped his gaze back to the table before the jury could note it.

"Your Honor and Gentlemen of the Jury, I humbly ask for your attention and favorable consideration of the few words I will now address to you." Halford moved out from behind the table, his steps slow and his posture relaxed. "As you know, from the moment this charge was brought against my client, he has denied it; would that I could with equal truth declare him guiltless of all other offenses.

"Mr. Jones was cast upon the world at a tender age. Thrown amidst temptation, and without proper guidance, his life became dissolute, and, as too often happens, dissipation led to crime. I will not insult your intellect by suggesting that my client is a saint. No, indeed, the evidence presented in this courtroom has shown you just how far from the paths of virtue a man may stray. The one and only argument I will present for your consideration is this: though William Jones's sins are many, murder is not among them."

Halford paused, as though to let this sink in.

"My good friend, Mr. Adolphus, would have you believe that a man is either an angel or a devil, but, in my experience, no soul is entirely white or black. In fact, there's not a man of my acquaintance whose character could not best be described in shades of gray. My client is no exception.

"Thanks to the indefatigable gentlemen of the press, and the efforts of my esteemed colleague"—Halford nodded toward Adolphus—"my client's shortcomings are well known to us all. Indeed, in many instances, his misdeeds have been multiplied and expanded upon to such an extent that one imagines he labored both day and night to accomplish so much villainy in so few years."

The gallery tittered, and William hazarded a glance at the jury. Their faces were deathly serious.

"I will not now endeavor to correct the dozens of fallacious accounts printed in the local and national press," Halford continued. "There is not time enough even if I were so inclined. What I will do is address some of the prejudicial and unsupported accusations that have been passed off as truth in this courtroom.

"It has been said that William's use of a false name, and that his and Miss Brown's flight from the police, are indicative of guilt. This is a credible supposition, but guilt of what? We've heard Mr. Duncombe testify that, at the time of Mr. Jones's arrest, a charge of forgery had already been made against him. And just today, we heard his former landlady, Mrs. Malone, testify that he was already using the alias "Diaz" when he lived at her house, nearly a year ago. Unless the prosecution is contending that my client has second sight, it stands to reason that it was from a charge of forgery Mr. Jones was fleeing, not murder.

"Similarly, the prosecution has emphasized the changes in Mr. Jones's story once he was caught and questioned by the police." Halford nodded gravely, as though he had considered this point and found it a fair one. "That sort of inconsistency would be very strange for an innocent man, were he also an honest one. But here I am forced to remind you that my client is not an honest man. Rather, he is, by his own admission, a petty crook and a habitual liar."

This last sentence was delivered with an air of rakish frankness that amused the audience, but this time William could not bring himself to check the jurors' reactions. It would, he thought, almost be easier to hang than to sit here meekly and listen to this.

"In Mr. Jones's mode of life," Mr. Halford went on, oblivious or indifferent to his client's suffering, "police are the natural enemy, and, if questioned, a man such as he will obfuscate and prevaricate as a matter of course. Even mundane information, like his whereabouts, precise occupation, or choice of companionship, is potentially incriminating. His answers, if honestly and plainly given, could expose him not just to public censure, but to punitive legal consequences. While certainly regrettable, there is nothing exceptional about the fact that Mr. Jones lied. Indeed, I think it remarkable that the prosecution can in one breath describe Jones as a compulsive liar, and in the next, declare their shocked disbelief that, when questioned by the on-duty sergeant, he did not unburden the secrets of his soul."

The audience laughed outright this time, and Judge Hastings banged his gavel to silence them.

William clenched his teeth and tried to block out Halford's words just as he had Adolphus's. He was glad he'd asked his mother and sister not to attend. He couldn't bear for them to hear this. A pain shot through his chest as he remembered Marie, sitting in the back corner of the gallery, but the sting soon faded. If, after knowing him as she did, she chose to believe these lies, this infamous slander, then it would be a reflection on her character, not his.

When Halford at last finished and resumed his seat, William's limbs were dull as stone, and his ears rang as though a bomb had gone off. It was some time before he could take in what was going on around him. He was vaguely aware that the judge was speaking, but he was too focused on not losing his breakfast to understand what was said.

It wasn't until the jury rose to their feet and began filing out that William's thoughts regained cohesion. He'd planned to look at them as they exited, to wear an expression of solemn dignity and try to read their decisions in their faces. But now that the moment had come, he stared at the scratches in the polished oak table, too afraid of what he might see.

Judge Hastings dismissed the court, and a flurry of voices erupted around him. The noise and excitement became a physical pressure, pushing on William so that he could hardly breathe. The closeness of the room, and the stink of excited, overheated bodies, choked him. He looked to Mr. Halford for guidance, but the attorney was deep in conversation with one of Adolphus's men. William's heart beat irregularly, and he was seized with an intense longing for all of this to be over, whatever the outcome.

The guards, whose existence he had forgotten, appeared on either side of him. When he failed to stand under his own strength, they wrenched him to his feet. He was almost glad for the physical support.

The crowd pushed around him, some shouting insults, others encouragement. Instinctively, he scanned the dizzying sea of faces, searching for Marie. When at last he spotted her, the chaos faded away. Her face, strained but still beautiful, wore a pained expression and he could just make out the ghostly, irregular path of tears on her cheeks.

She loved him still; he could read it in her suffering, just as clearly as he could see that she thought he would hang. He kept his eyes fixed to hers as they led him toward the door, her face a single point of light in an abyss. All the months of separation and suffering between them faded to nothing, and he knew with a piercing certainty that if he could just hold her to him once more, all would be well.

A tug at his arm and a voice quite near pulled at him. He tried to ignore the intrusion, but the tugging persisted, until at last, with jarring familiarity, the voice registered on his mind.

He tore his gaze from Marie's and found Charlotte at his side, staring up at him. His stomach twisted and his face flamed. He looked back to see if Marie was watching them, but she was already lost in the roiling crowd.

Feeling more miserable than he'd imagined possible, he returned his attention to Charlotte. Her large eyes gleamed with tears, but she smiled shakily up at him. Despite the jostling, she managed to stay close as the guards escorted him out of the courtroom and down the corridor. Her expression was a mixture of suffering and adoration that made him sick to his stomach.

They stopped by a door, and one of the guards stepped aside to unlock it. Seizing the opportunity, Charlotte stepped toward him and squeezed his elbow. "Don't be afraid, William," she whispered. "No harm will come to you, I promise."

The door swung open and he was ushered into the little room. He twisted in the guards' grip, trying to think of something reassuring to say, but his mind was as bare and desolate as the cell. She stood just outside the door, wringing her hands in that nervous way of hers. Mute as a tombstone, he watched the tears stream down her pale, thin face until the door shut between them, and he was left alone.

YOUR LOYAL SERVANT

FEBRUARY 7, 1900

*J*amie searched the darkened room for the pale lines of light between the curtain panels that would signal morning. Not finding them, he dropped his head back onto his feather pillow and closed his eyes.

All night, he'd been plagued by nightmarish visions of his father sinking into the grave under the weight of their disgrace, of his mother's treasured heirlooms being sold at public auction, and, finally, of Manassas himself, dangling like a cloth doll at the end of a rope.

When, at long last, a soft, gray haze filtered into the darkness of his room, he rolled out of bed and shrugged on his robe. If he kept busy, continued placing one foot in front of the other, this too would pass.

After a quick trip to the washroom, he dressed and went downstairs. The tomblike silence of the house was occasionally interrupted by the muted sounds of the servants at work. He thought of Madame Alozia and the ache in his chest sharpened. How many times had she slipped through the green baize door and walked this very hall in the gray half-light of early morning? He could almost see her shadowy form, slipping silently from room to room, drawing the curtains, and overseeing the daily routine.

Goosebumps raised on his arms. He pushed the painful thoughts away, but a deep feeling of unease lingered. Overnight, the house had changed. Not the house, exactly, more his connection to it. The rooms and everything in them were unaltered, and as familiar to him as parts of his body, but were they really his still? How much would remain to his family once the dust had settled? Would they be allowed to keep the little table in the corner, the Staffordshire dogs on the mantel, or would everything have to be sold to clear the company's debts?

In the library, he surprised a maid lighting the fire. She sprang to her feet and curtsied, her eyes on the ground. "Good morning, sir."

"Morning, Lois. Please tell Cook I shan't be having breakfast today, just coffee."

The girl bobbed again and was gone. Last evening's paper rested, unread, on the table. Jamie sank into his chair and skimmed the lead article, yet another about the Boer war. His own troubles rendered him wholly uninterested in those of the British, so he turned the page and was confronted by an image of William Jones.

The photographer had timed the shot well, and Jones appeared to be glaring directly at him. Jamie frowned down at the man. What was it about this fellow that commanded the interest and sympathy of so many? Better men than him died every day, and the papers did not carry their stories, much less their photographs.

Jamie's coffee arrived, and he set the paper aside, watching the sun's continued progress through the sky, and savoring the warmth of the mug in his hands. The coffee helped clear the fog from his mind, but it left him restless. He should have made more definite arrangements with Manassas last night. How long did the old man need to get his affairs in order? And what, exactly, was Jamie to do with him once he had.

How different life had been just yesterday, when he'd thought a comfortable, easy future lay before him. When he'd first started this quest to discover Manassas's connection to the mustachioed man, it had seemed unreal, almost like a parlor game he and Melly were playing to while away the dull winter evenings. He cringed inwardly as he remembered how they had broken into the old man's office and snooped through his files, behaving like the spoiled children they undoubtedly were. They hadn't known it then, but they'd been playing with fire.

For no reason he could name, he thought of Marie. Lately, she had made several of these sudden appearances in his thoughts. He'd be thinking about something quite removed from her when a flash of the last conversation they'd shared, or of something he wanted to say when next they spoke, would light up his mind. Her nature was so excitable, and her opinions so unexpected, it was a pleasure merely talking to her. But instead of the pleasant anticipation he usually felt when he thought of Marie, he felt anxious, and something like shame.

He would have to go to the courthouse and clear up the business about the burglary, that much was unavoidable. Manassas had denied killing Madame Alozia, but the prosecution had based their case around the idea of a burglary interrupted. Learning that it was Manassas, and not William, who had rifled through the cabinets altered things considerably. Beneath Halford's rumpled appearance lurked a keen mind, and Jamie felt certain the attorney would make good use of the information. He didn't give a hang what happened to Jones, but Marie did, and he didn't want her suffering, not if he could prevent it.

The door opened and Mrs. Brewer, the new housekeeper, hesitated on the threshold. "I hope I'm not disturbing you, sir, but this just came by special messenger."

Jamie took the envelope. "Thank you."

She nodded and retreated from the room.

He turned over the envelope. The word "URGENT" had been scrawled across the back in all capitals. With a sinking heart, he tore it open.

Father has taken a turn. Return home at once. Melly.

Jamie stood, his body electric. The urge to harness a horse and ride hell for leather straight home was so strong that for several seconds no other thoughts entered his mind. He forced himself to wait until the first flush of panic receded.

This time of year, and in this weather, he'd have to take the train. His eyes moved reflexively to the grandfather clock in the corner. Six forty. Even if he left now, he would never make the seven o'clock. The next train wouldn't depart until nine-thirty.

Jamie rubbed the fog from his eyes with the flat of his hands. Three hours was an eternity, but standing at the station wringing his hands wouldn't make it pass any faster. Besides, there was no telling what Manassas would do if he left without following up on their agreement. If Jamie made a start of it now, he could tie up the loose ends here and be at the station with plenty of time to spare.

He strode to the desk and scribbled off a telegram.

Leaving on the 9. Love to you, Mother, and Father.

By the time he reached Manassas's house, some twenty minutes later, the sun had finished rising on another cold, gray day. Mrs. Rutledge shook her head the moment she opened the door. "Mr. Jamie, sir. I'm afraid you'll have to come back later. Mr. Edmunds is still sleeping."

"Then you had better wake him." Jamie pushed against the door, forcing the old housekeeper to step aside.

She cast him a dark look before moving grudgingly to the stairs. When all of this was over, he would have to apologize.

He walked to the sitting room and poured himself a glass of cognac from the standing bar. His first belt was still burning in his throat when a piercing scream reverberated through the house. For an instant, Jamie froze in place, then, all at once, he was running through the hall and up the stairs.

At the top of the landing, he hesitated, not sure which way to turn. Blood rushed in his ears and his vision had taken on a sharpness that made everything clearer, yet less real. Mrs. R stood to his right, hunched over in front of Manassas's open office door.

He rushed past the housekeeper and entered the room. There, slumped over his desk, lay Manassas. Jamie ran to him, thinking at first that he'd had some sort of fit. It was only when he drew close that he noticed the pistol on the floor and a dark pool of blood drying on the blotter.

The world contracted around the scene, narrowing until there was only the old man's familiar face, strangely gray, and the angry red wound at his temple. Gently, Jamie extended his right hand and brushed the back of his fingers across the dead man's cheek. His skin was cold. Jamie clenched his hand into a fist to to stop its shaking. He was about to turn away when he noticed two letters propped against the brass desk lamp. The uppermost bore his father's name. He picked them up. The second was addressed to him. He slipped both into his inside pocket, then turned for the door. Gilroy, the butler, stood just past the threshold, pale and staring.

"Has someone gone for help?" Jamie asked, his voice breaking.

Gilroy stiffened. "Ben has."

"Did no one hear the shot?"

Gilroy's brow furrowed. "There was a noise, sir. But we thought it was one of those new-fangled automobiles. Mr. Merced, in the house across the way, bought one for his son last summer. It makes a dreadful racket. We never thought …"

"Of course you didn't," Jamie said quickly, regretting his earlier tone. "No one would. I'll be in the sitting room. Inform me the moment the police arrive."

Back downstairs, his glass lay on its side on the floor, its contents soaking into the paisley rug. He took a new glass from the bar and poured himself a tall drink, swallowed half of it, and refilled it before sitting down in an armchair. The liquor burned reassuringly but did nothing to dull the pain in his chest.

For a long time he sat, unthinking, then he remembered the letters. His hand hovered over his breast pocket for a moment before pulling them out. Jamie opened the letter addressed to him.

Dear Jamie,

You must think me a coward, and perhaps I am. All I know for certain is that I am too old and too tired to face a future such as the one that now lies before me.

Life holds neither mystery nor promise, and I think it better to take my leave like this, on my own terms, than await a jury's pleasure.

You are a young man, and an idealist, (Bless you!), so I do not expect you to understand this, not any of it. All I ask is that, when you think of me, you try to remember the good as well as the bad.

I have enclosed a letter for you to take to the authorities. It provides a full confession of my crimes and the location of documents that can prove the truth of what I write. I sincerely pray that it will spare you and your family further grief.

Give my love to your mother and sister, and tell them that in the last moments of my life, above all things, I hoped that they would one day find it in their hearts to forgive ....

Your loyal servant,
Manassas

WHAT IS NECESSARY

FEBRUARY 7, 1900

By the time the police finished questioning him, Jamie had already missed the nine o'clock. He used the telephone in the butler's study to call in a telegram letting Melly know there had been an accident and that he would be home on the noon train. *Accident.* The word had given him pause, but he would explain later, once he was with her.

Outside, the sun cast a cold, grey light on the snow and ice. The roads glistened menacingly, and Jamie was forced to keep his curricle at a slow trot. When traffic, which had been moving at a crawl, came to a standstill, Jamie climbed down from the box and walked ahead. A cart transporting furniture had overturned, and it looked like a giant had shaken the contents of a doll's house over the road. A mess like this could take hours to clear. Cursing his luck, he returned to his curricle, led his horses to a post in front of the waterworks, and then covered the last seven blocks on foot.

He took the courthouse steps two at a time. The men in the lobby turned to stare after him as he raced through, but, perhaps for the first time in his life, Jamie didn't care about the muddy slush on his boots or the melted snow mingled with sweat that ran down the sides of his face.

His stomach knotted when he rounded the corner and saw the size of the crowd loitering in front of the courtroom. He was too late.

A hasty survey of the faces crowding the hallway didn't reveal Halford's, but he did spot Marie. She sat at some distance from the heavy double doors, her head bowed. He walked quickly to her.

"Good morning," Jamie said perfunctorily. "Have you seen Jones's attorney?"

She looked up. Her eyes were red from crying. "I don't know. We're waiting on the jury."

"Do you have our money?" A young man sitting on the bench next to Marie stood and faced him, his eyes flashing.

"Charlie!" Marie stood too and turned on the man. "This is neither the time nor the place."

"I disagree," Charlie responded coldly. "Father's name was cleared weeks ago. Another man stands on the verge of conviction, and still we've not seen a cent of our inheritance."

"My apologies," Jamie said hastily, piecing things together. "I've had other things on my mind. If you write to our solicitor, Mr. Duncombe, he'll handle the details, but now, I really must—."

"I have written to that windbag, dozens of times. He returns my letters unopened."

"Then write to me, and I will see to it. But now, I have urgent business with Mr. Halford."

"I've tried that too," Charlie insisted, "or don't you remember?"

"Stop it!" Marie rebuked her brother, her face scarlet, then turned back to Jamie. "Do you have news?"

Jamie nodded.

"The attorneys were over there," Marie said, pointing to an empty corner, "but they've gone."

"We must find Halford." Jamie turned, surveying the space. "I'll check the hall here, you check the main lobby."

Marie nodded, and they both set off, her brother glaring after him.

On his second trip down the corridor, Jamie spotted Adolphus stepping through a side door. Jamie hesitated only a moment before rushing to him. "Mr. Adolphus. My name is James Lett, and I have evidence directly bearing on this trial."

The attorney drew back. "I'm afraid the jury is already deliberating."

"Please, hear me out. I have a written confession. It's from a close family friend, swearing that it was he and not Jones who broke into my family's house and ransacked it that night."

At the word "confession" the attorney's eyes narrowed. "Why didn't your friend come himself?"

"Because...." Jamie paused, stumbling over the horrible words. "Because he took his own life this morning."

Adolphus studied Jamie's face, then shook his head. "Wait here."

Adolphus strode down the corridor, and Marie appeared at Jamie's side. "What's happening?"

Jamie steered her away from the crowd and recounted Manassas's confession, at least as far as it pertained to the trial. She kept her head down while he spoke, and he couldn't read her expression. When he finished, she looked up. Her eyes were luminous, but she wasn't crying. "Can we trust Mr. Adolphus? He wants William to hang."

"I think so," Jamie answered, "But if we haven't heard anything in five minutes, I'll start searching the offices for Halford, whatever it takes."

No sooner had he said this than a bailiff approached. "Are you Mr. James Lett?"

"I am." Jamie stepped forward, his heart thudding in his chest.

"Judge Hastings would like to speak to you in his chambers."

"I'd like to come too," Marie said, stepping toward them.

The bailiff shook his head. "The Judge asked for Mr. Lett, no one else."

Jamie turned to Marie. "It's alright. I'll see this through."

Disappointment was plain on her face, but she set her jaw and nodded stiffly.

Jamie followed the bailiff through a side door and down several narrow corridors that appeared to skirt the courtrooms. Finally, they came to a series of doors with frosted glass panels. The bailiff stopped at one and knocked.

"Come in."

Jamie recognized Judge Hasting's distinctive, low voice.

The bailiff opened the door and stepped aside. Mr. Adolphus and Mr. Halford were already there, seated in front of the desk.

"Take a seat." The judge motioned to one of the wooden chairs lining the back wall. "It's good to see you, Mr. Lett— James, isn't it?" Judge Hastings offered Jamie a cigar from a carved wood humidor. Jamie shook his head and the judge took one for himself. "Mr. Adolphus tells me you have new evidence that pertains to this case? A confession, of sorts, is that right?"

"Yes." Jamie took the letter addressed to him from his inside pocket and passed it to the judge.

"The author confessed to me personally last night. It was my intention to come here with him first thing this morning, so that you might speak to him yourself, but he…." Jamie hesitated.

"Mr. Adolphus told me." Judge Hastings unfolded the letter and began to read. When he finished, he handed it to Adolphus. "Do the police know about the rest of this yet?"

"Some of it," Jamie answered. "I hadn't time to explain it all."

"Well, I suggest you make time. There are some serious allegations contained in that document."

"Of course. I would have, only, my father is terribly ill." Jamie fished his sister's telegram from his other pocket and passed it over the desk. "I'm only here because I felt it was my duty to come forward with what evidence I had."

Judge Hastings glanced at Melly's telegram and sighed. "At least he'll be spared what's to come."

Jamie stiffened. He'd had the same thought himself, but there was something hideous about hearing it spoken out loud.

"Well," Adolphus said, handing the letter to Halford. "That's quite a confession, but I'm not sure what bearing it has on this case."

Judge Hastings held up his hand. "Let Myron finish reading first."

They waited in silence. When Mr. Halford finished, he placed it on the desk. "I'm sorry, son. Will you be sending this letter on to Mr. Duncombe?"

Jamie nodded.

"Can I have my clerk copy it first?"

"Certainly," Jamie said.

Halford pocketed the letter and looked back toward the judge. "As for this case, I don't see how a mistrial can be avoided. Unless you want to call the jury back and give me and Amos another swing at them."

Adolphus shook his head firmly. "This letter is hearsay, and its relevance to this case is questionable, to say the least."

"It's a confession," Halford insisted.

"Of crimes that have no bearing on the death of Alozia Tompkins."

"He admits to the burglary."

"Yes, but we have no way of knowing what this man's motivation for such a 'confession' was."

"Perhaps you don't, Amos, but I think the jury will be able to see the letter and accompanying documents for what they are: a guilt-stricken man clearing his conscience as he prepares for death."

"It could just as well be a work of fiction."

Judge Hastings, who had been sitting back listening to them like a spectator at a tennis match, stopped on Adolphus. "What reason could he have to lie?"

"I don't know," Adolphus said plainly, "That's the trouble. The man is dead, and I can't ask him, which is exactly why this letter should be deemed inadmissible hearsay."

Hastings gave a little smile.

Halford cut in. "As my colleague well knows, the last words of a dying man who, were he alive, would have been a witness, are an exception to the hearsay rule. Besides, this young man here," Halford nodded at Jamie, "can testify that the decedent confessed the same to him personally."

"The *death letter rule* is English common law, frequently challenged here in The States." Adolphus responded, leaning slightly forward in his seat. "As for Mr. Lett's testimony, must I remind you of the *dead man's law*, which prohibits perjury against a person no longer alive to defend themselves? Given the content of that letter, and the legal and financial struggles that await this young gentleman and his family, nothing he says about the deceased could be thought objective."

"It's not perjury if the information is true and can be corroborated." Halford pointed at the letter in his pocket. "Further, given the public's taste for sensationalism, I would be astonished if, a fortnight from now, the details of this letter weren't being discussed across dinner tables all over Philadelphia."

Jamie flinched. Halford was undoubtedly right, and Jamie wondered why he hadn't thought of that himself. His mother would be mortified, and his father.... He pushed the thought away. The details would be sorted later. He had come here because it was his duty to clear an innocent man, but all this wrangling and arguing over technicalities was a waste of time, time he didn't have.

"I'm not a lawyer," Jamie said, surprising the three men who seemed to have forgotten his existence. "But I know what Manassas told me, and I know what that letter says, and both are evidence that Mr. Jones did not attempt to rob our house. I sat through the entire trial, and I never heard so much as a hint of a motive other than robbery."

Adolphus started to speak, but Jamie cut him off. "As I said, I'm no lawyer, but I'm willing to bet that what I understand from that"—Jamie pointed to Halford's pocket—"others will too. The headlines from this case have already sold thousands of papers, and if I go to them with that letter, they will sell tens of thousands more."

"This court cannot be moved by public opinion," Judge Hastings said sternly.

"True, but there is the matter of appeal to consider," Halford interjected. "You know how touchy the appellate courts have been of late about judicial overreach and the exclusion of evidence."

"Careful, Myron." Judge Hastings cast him a chilling look. "I won't be threatened."

"That wasn't my intention, John—Your Honor. It's just a plain fact, one you know as well as I. We've got a host of newly appointed judges looking to make a name for themselves. A case like this, already in the public eye, is going to receive a lot of scrutiny. If you allow the jury to reach a verdict here, without formally deciding on the admissibility of this new evidence, they're going to have a field day."

"We're deciding admissibility now," Adolphus added, but he sounded less strident.

"In that case," Halford said, carefully folding his hands in front of him. "allow me to formally request that the jury be recalled so that I can have more time to examine this new evidence, to follow the lines of inquiry it opens up, and to search for new witnesses."

"You know that can't be done," Adolphus said. "Recalling the jury now would place undue weight on any information placed before them, skewing their deliberations."

"I agree," Halford said. "And that is why I think we have to declare a mistrial."

Adolphus shook his head firmly. "Why should the state waste—"

"Enough." Judge Hastings turned to Jamie. "I'm afraid we've forgotten ourselves, Mr. Lett. Thank you for bringing this letter to us, but now I'm going to have to ask you to leave. You've already been privy to things you shouldn't."

The judge rose and held out his hand. Jamie stood, and, fighting back his frustration, shook it. "Of course. I understand."

As soon as Jamie stepped into the narrow hallway a bailiff approached and steered him through the maze of corridors back to the public wing.

After the tomb-like quiet of the judge's chambers, the over-lapping conversations in the hallway seemed chaotic. An urge to get back to his curricle and drive straight to New York seized him, and he may well have acted on it if Marie hadn't appeared.

"What happened?" she asked.

"I showed them my uncle's confession, and they're deciding what to do with it."

"What's to decide? He confessed to the robbery."

"It's a lot of legal back and forth," Jamie said, his irritation stirring afresh. "Nothing that makes sense."

"What do we do now?"

"I've done what I can. Now it's up to them."

"Oh," Marie mumbled, her face flushed and miserable.

He placed his hand on her arm. "It's not as bad as all that. Mr. Halford is putting up quite a fight."

Marie looked up. "And if he loses?"

"We'll get justice some other way," he answered, wanting her to feel certain, even if he didn't. "If the jury comes back against us, I'll go to the police and to the press. Hell, I'll shout it from the rooftops if I have to. Once I start talking, I won't stop until someone listens, you can be sure of that."

Marie stared up at him without speaking, her face a mixture of sadness and admiration. For a long moment, nothing else existed in the world, then she dropped her eyes and whispered, "We will go to the police together then. I too have something of interest to tell them."

The nervous flush that crept up her cheeks, and the way she turned away after saying this, warned him not to ask any questions.

Something in her expression, and how she turned away after she said this, warned him not to ask any questions. They sat together without speaking for what felt like an eternity. Jamie's troubled thoughts kept turning to his father. If things didn't come to a head, and soon, he would have to leave.

He had just glanced at his watch for the fifth time in as many minutes, when the bailiff opened the courtroom doors, allowing the audience back in. Jones, already seated up at the front, turned his head and caught sight of him and Marie as they entered. Jones's face was expressionless, but his eyes were those of a panicked animal. Jamie looked at Marie and saw a similar terror reflected in hers.

They took seats next to Charlie, who had tucked himself away in a back corner. The room was loud with anticipation, but Marie and Charlie sat grim-faced and unspeaking. The silence between them was so laden that Jamie began to feel like an intruder. When Judge Hastings entered the room, the excited chatter died away.

The preliminaries were read out by the clerk. When he'd finished, the judge looked at Halford and said, "Counsel."

Jamie's chest tightened. He glanced at Marie, who was gripping the edge of her seat. Her lips moved soundlessly and her eyes were squeezed shut, as though in urgent prayer.

Halford rose. "Due to the discovery of new evidence with a direct bearing on the facts of this case, my client would like to submit a motion for a mistrial."

Judge Hastings turned to Mr. Adolphus. "Prosecutor? Any objections?

"None, Your Honor."

Gasps of surprise erupted from the audience. Marie straightened, turned to him, then Charlie, then to him again, whispering, "What does it mean? What does that mean?"

Before Jamie could answer, Charlie mumbled, "That lucky bastard," and threw his arms around his sister, who began to sob with relief.

NO POETRY

FEBRUARY 23, 1900

*M*arie reached out a gloved hand and caressed the gravestone's freshly carved letters. Only Mémé's name and the dates of her birth and death marred the ice-white stone. There were no words of love, no psalms, no poetry. It was, Marie thought, too plain a memorial for a woman whose life had been comprised of so many extremes.

The Letts, Marie didn't know exactly which of them, had made the *necessary arrangements* without conferring with either her or Papa. This had disappointed Marie, and enraged her father, but as she had reminded them both, without the Letts, Mémé would have met eternity in a pine box in Byberry, Campbell, or one of the other colored graveyards that were tucked away, out of sight and out of mind.

As it was, Mémé's plot stood atop a small slope in Mount Moriah. A high point overlooking an erratic forest of gray and white marble that reached all the way to the small grove of sycamore that separated the cemetery from the outskirts of Philadelphia.

Marie stared across the quiet, muddy expanse and exhaled slowly, her breath fogging the clear morning air. The chaos of the investigation and trial had kept her mind and emotions full to brimming, so that it was only now, in the strange emptiness that had followed William's mistrial, that grief had found her. It had come without warning, rushing in like floodwater and filling every empty space inside of her. Her only relief came in the form of anger, which she seized and directed at the man she now knew was responsible for it: Manassas Edmunds.

Since that last day at court, when Jamie had shared only a few details, the story of Edmunds' embezzlement and fraud had been printed by every newspaper in town. An enterprising official connected to the investigation had even sold the papers a copy of his suicide letter, which Marie had read with great interest. Taken at face value, it was a confession, but Marie read between the lines and into the character of the man who wrote them. It seemed to her that the purpose of the letter was not to own his guilt, as he claimed, but to avoid it.

He had, of course, denied killing Mémé, but that meant nothing. Responsibility for the death of his accomplice had been carefully evaded as well. Yet, no one could say it wasn't convenient for Edmunds that, in the very moment he was faced with exposure and ruin, the only man who could unmask him had thrown himself under the wheels of a carriage. As for the rest, Marie had recognized it at once for the same sort of self-serving twaddle she'd been hearing from Papa and Charlie since she was first old enough to understand what a lie was.

The only thing that confused Marie was how badly people wanted to believe Edmunds. And because they believed him, the investigation into Mémé's death remained open, looming over her family. Who, exactly, the suspects were, Marie could not say. After being told by the district attorney that he was considering his options, Papa had heard nothing. It was possible Adolphus had quietly come to the same conclusion about Edmunds that Marie had, and Mémé's file was already mouldering in a police station basement somewhere. Or maybe his office was even now preparing a case against William, Charlie, or Papa. She didn't know, couldn't know, and there was no end in sight.

The quiet, so serene just moments before, now stifled Marie. She kissed her gloved fingers and hastily pressed them to the top of the stone before setting off down the wet graveled path out of the cemetery. She would do better to focus on things she could do something about, like today's shopping and chores. Life went on. It had to.

When she reached Kingsessing, she waved at a passing trolley and waited while it rattled and clanged to a heavy stop. She climbed on board, gave silent thanks to Mémé as she paid the fare, and settled onto one of the wooden seats next to an older woman who appeared to be napping.

When the trolley turned on to Wharton, the Fourth Police District Station came into view. The heavy, governmental building caught Marie's attention and held it. Somewhere inside those walls, Detective Gardiner sat, the answers to all of her questions locked in his desk drawer. She imagined standing in front of him, demanding those answers, and getting them.

It was a well-worn fantasy, so it surprised her when, before the thought could fully form in her mind, her hand had darted up and pulled the bell string. The trolley slowed, and Marie had to fight the urge to call out that she'd made a mistake. Could she really do this? March inside the police station and ask Detective Gardiner what his intentions were? It seemed a mad thing to do, impertinent even. But why shouldn't she? If she didn't have the right to know, who did?

Her knees were shaky as she stepped onto the road, but they had steadied by the time she entered through the station door. The air inside was warm and dry, and smelled vaguely of antiseptic, as though it had been recently cleaned. More than a dozen chairs, most of them empty, were bolted to the walls to the left and right, while an enormous oak paneled counter ran along the back. This ungainly edifice was manned by two uniformed officers. One of them, a young man with fair hair, hastily set aside a mug he'd been drinking from as Marie approached. The other, a swarthy man with dark, curling hair, glanced up from his paper, then continued reading.

"Good morning," she said to the fair one, cringing internally at how brittle her voice sounded. "I've come to see Detective Gardiner. I would like to inquire about the status of my grandmother's case."

"Happy to help." The officer pulled a well-used pencil and leatherbound notebook toward him. He had wide-spaced blue eyes that made him look even younger than he probably was. A brass nameplate, the sort with individual letters that slide in from the sides, was planted on the counter in front of him; it spelled out, "Sgt. Peterson".

"What's your grandmother's name, and what sort of case is it?

"Alozia Tompkins, and … murder." The last word came out in something close to a whisper, as though she were communicating a terrible secret to him, and maybe she was.

Sgt. Peterson glanced up from his notepad. He shook his head, and his light blonde hair, which he wore a little longer than she was accustomed to, swayed. "I'm sorry."

Marie nodded gratefully, some of the tension leaving her shoulders.

"Gardiner isn't in the office today, but let me go and check with our homicide division. See if someone there can help you."

"Thank you."

"My pleasure." Sgt. Peterson flashed Marie a self-conscious smile before disappearing through a door on his side of the desk. Marie's gaze wandered to the remaining officer. The nameplate in front of him read "Sgt. Sullivan". He was also young, but he wore a bushy mustache that made him look older. When he didn't look up from his paper, Marie looked away.

Sgt. Peterson returned a few minutes later, his manner and

expression so altered that Marie's heart froze. "What is it?" she asked. "Bad news?"

"You didn't tell me your grandmother was colored." The softness in his eyes was gone. Instead, he looked knowing and angry, as though she were a naughty child who had tried, and failed, to prank him.

Marie shook her head. "I'm sorry. Does that make a difference?"

Sgt. Peterson lifted his eyebrows and said nothing, as though the question was too stupid to merit a response. She glanced over at Sgt. Sullivan. He was looking at her now, his expression unreadable.

Marie turned back to Sgt. Peterson. "May I leave a message for Detective Gardiner?"

"Gardiner isn't lead anymore. Your grandmother's file was transferred to Detective Smith. Him and Filpot handle the colored killings. "

"May I speak with Detective Smith then?"

"He's busy, but if you leave your name and address, he'll get back to you."

"My name is Marie Chevalier, and I live at—" Marie broke off as a pair of uniformed policemen entered the station supporting a wino between them. The wino was singing at the top of his voice in a language Marie didn't recognize.

Sgt. Peterson grinned at the trio. "If it isn't Mr. Johansson again. You keep this up, you're going to have to file a change of address with the postal service."

Mr. Johansson stopped singing long enough to mumble something incoherent, then started up again. Sgt. Peterson laughed. The officers led their charge into one of the backrooms and Sgt. Peterson turned back to Marie. "Alright. I'll give Smitty your details. Have a good day."

"I haven't given them to you yet."

"Haven't you? Well, I'm sure they're on file."

"Perhaps I had better wait here until Detective Smith can see me," Marie said, her chest tight with restrained emotion. The logical part of her mind told her she should leave, that talking to this officer was useless. But something stronger held her firmly in place.

"You'll be waiting a long time. In fact, now that I think on it, Detective Smith didn't come in today either."

Marie glanced at Sgt. Sullivan again. He was wearing a frown now, but he said nothing.

The door behind the desk opened, and one of the officers who'd brought in the wino came through it. He nodded at Peterson and Sullivan then smiled broadly at Marie. "Good morning, Miss. I'm Sgt. McKenzy, and it would be my pleasure to assist you today."

"She's colored." Sgt. Peterson declared, like a man warning of a snake in tall grass.

"Is she?" Sgt. McKenzy's eyes widened. He turned back to Marie, a half smile playing around his lips. "Well, I'll be damned. I'd never have guessed."

"My grandmother was murdered," Marie said stiffly. "I've come to speak to the detective in charge of her case."

Sgt. McKenzy leaned on the counter and studied her as though she were a specimen behind glass. "Colored, you say?"

"That's right," Sgt. Peterson confirmed.

Marie clenched her teeth. The urge to pick up Sgt. Peterson's mug and fling its contents in McKenzy's face was so strong she had to look away. She caught Sgt. Sullivan's gaze as she did. His expression was pained, almost embarrassed. He dropped his eyes and reached for the paper, and she knew he would not help her. That's when she noticed the notepad and pencil. Standing on tiptoe, she reached across the counter and pulled them to her.

"Woah, now. That's police property." McKenzy said, his tone mocking.

Marie scribbled her name and address then pushed the pad and pencil back toward Sgt. Sullivan. "Please, have Detective Smith contact me just as soon as he's able."

Without waiting for a response, she turned and walked away.

"Isn't that something," McKenzy said behind her. "Normally, I can spot a colored blindfolded. Seriously, I can smell 'em."

"Get out of here," Peterson replied, his tone encouraging.

"I mean it."

"And what do they smell like?"

"Fertilizer and watermelon. No, it's true," McKenzy insisted, raising his voice to be heard over Peterson's laughter. "Must be all those generations working in the fields."

Marie dashed outside. The fresh air soothed her face, which was so hot she felt as though her blood were boiling. When she was again calm enough to think, she realized that she'd gotten the answer she wanted after all. The investigation, though not officially closed, may as well have been. As far as the police were concerned, Mémé was just another dead colored woman.

It had never struck her before, but Marie now realized that the only reason Mémé's case had received the attention it had was because of her connection to the Letts. But in the few months that had passed since the murder, Mr. Lett had passed away, and the remainder of the Lett family had far more pressing matters to contend with than the death of a servant.

Marie should have felt relief, but her indignation was stronger. She wanted Mémé's case resolved, not swept aside because no one cared enough to solve it. Marie told herself she was asking for too much: she knew who did it, and should be grateful for anything that kept people like Peterson and KcKenzy out of her family's lives. Her chest, however, was still aching two hours later as she mounted the front steps to her apartment.

No sooner had she stepped inside the foyer, a sack full of

groceries slung over her shoulder, then Mrs. Griggs appeared and stopped squarely in her path.

"The Bijou found another girl to do their mendin'," The older woman declared flatly. "And Mrs. Lewis is fixin' to do the same. Mebbe with that inheritance of yours comin', you don't need the money no more, but you coulda at least thought of me, 'specially after I done so much for you."

Marie's spirits, already low, sunk still further. "Tell Sam that the trouble I had has passed, that I'll catch up. I'll work twice as hard, whatever he wants."

"I was pleadin' with that bastard all mornin'. He's hearin' none of it," spat Mrs. Griggs. "Best you focus all that energy on holdin' on to what we've got left. That is, unless you's too good to work fer your money now."

"I want the work," Marie insisted, meaning it. The inheritance, while unquestionably a blessing, was Papa's, not hers. And who knew how long it would last?

"Then you best git to stitchin'" The landlady shot Marie a hard look meant to drive her words home, then turned and swayed unsteadily back to the door she'd come from.

A lump rose hard in Marie's throat. She swallowed it back. What use was crying?

Feeling as low as she ever had, Marie checked the cubby where Mrs. Grigg's placed their mail. There was one letter, and it was addressed to her in a hand she didn't recognize.

When Jamie had sent word to collect their inheritance through Mr. Duncombe instead of writing himself, Marie had tried not to be hurt. With the death of his father, and all the rest, the man was clearly busy. But now that the fever of the trial had passed, her friendship with him, if friendship it had been, seemed so improbable that she began to wonder if she had imagined it. Charlie may have gotten the particulars wrong, but his overall assessment of their connection had been accurate enough: there could be no true friendship between someone like her and the young Mr. Lett. A part of Marie wanted the letter to be from him, but she didn't think it was.

William was a different matter. Every day, she had waited for the morning and then the afternoon post, hoping for word from him. None came. Desperate for news, she had written to his attorney, Mr. Halford. That was three days ago now, and she suspected this letter was his response.

She tore the envelope open.

> Dear Miss Chevalier:
>
> I'm in receipt of your communication dated February 20, 1900. In answer to your questions concerning my client, Mr. William Jones, I can inform you only that the district attorney has decided not to renew the murder charge against him. Any further information will have to be provided to you by Mr. Jones himself. As I understand it, he remains in his cell at the courthouse awaiting the state's pleasure concerning the accusations of forgery.
>
> Sincerely,
> Myron P. Halford, Esq.

Marie's mind reeled. Her initial feeling was relief that the murder charge had been dropped, but a mixture of confusion and hurt soon followed. If he was no longer a murder suspect, then his connection to her could no longer harm him, so why hadn't he written? Her heart sank as an explanation came to her: he was negotiating with the district attorney, and using her father's letter to do it.

No. She rejected the idea. William wouldn't go back on his word like that. Or would he?

She looked at the small hanging clock on the far wall. If she hurried, she could still make visiting hours.

Her mind was blank as she walked, but a dull pain had spread through her chest and settled just under her ribs. Rainwater remained pooled on the roads, and when crossing the street she had to lift the hem of her dress and balance on the rough planking that had been placed over the puddles to avoid the mud. Overhead, the sky was clear and blue, offering no hint of the storms that had wracked the city for the past three days.

The stairs to the cells were steeper than Marie remembered, and she was slow going down them. The same insolent guard she'd met last time manned the counter. He looked up when she entered and grinned broadly. "Look who's back."

"I'm here to see William Jones," Marie said stiffly.

"I'm afraid you'll have to wait your turn. Mr. Jones already has a visitor."

Marie looked up sharply. Her mind conjured an image of that slip of a girl from the trial.

The guard grinned. "His sister, Julia, I think it was. S'pose that makes her a cousin of yours, or don't it?"

Marie smoothed her face into a look of cool disdain as the tension left her body. *Julia.* William had often spoken of his sister, but, because of his feud with his father, Marie had never met her. These weren't exactly the circumstances under which she'd hoped to be introduced, but if Julia was as kind as William had intimated, she would understand.

"Have a seat over there." The guard nodded at the graying oak benches lining the far wall. "I'll go and tell them you're here."

Marie paced the perimeter of the room, studying the fliers and broadsheets that had been pinned to the bare plaster walls.

When she'd first read Halford's letter, Marie had let her fear get the better of her. Now that she could think more clearly, she realized that William probably had a very good reason for not writing, just as he had during the trial.

Their last meeting had been strained, but that was because they hadn't seen each other for so long. It would be different this time. In his letter, he'd said he'd changed, well, so had she. And she would do everything in her power to see to it that he had his new beginning. For both their sakes.

A door creaked open and Marie turned with rising excitement. The guard came out first, his large body filling the doorway. Marie stepped toward him, a warm smile and words of greeting on her lips, but it was not Julia who followed the big man into the waiting room; it was Charlotte Brown.

PLAYING AT LOVE

FEBRUARY 28, 1900

*A*ware of the guard watching them, Marie pasted a cordial expression on her face and stepped forward, holding out her hand to Charlotte. "Good morning, cousin."

Charlotte wore a light gray cotton dress with tiny cream dots. The style was simple and the material notable only for its plainness. An unlikely choice, Marie thought, for a woman in her profession.

"Good morning, Miss Chevalier." Charlotte flushed, then touched, rather than shook, Marie's hand. "It's so very thoughtful of you to remember William like this."

The girl's fingers were limp and slightly damp, and Marie had to resist the urge to fish out her handkerchief and scrub away the feel of them. There was a flush of color in Charlotte's cheeks, from exertion or strong emotion, Marie could not guess. Marie wasn't even certain of her own feelings. The second she'd recognized Charlotte, a curtain had descended over her heart.

"There's no need to thank me." Marie kept her voice polite, if not friendly. "William has been close to my family since childhood. He knows he can count on our support."

"It makes me so happy to hear you say that," Charlotte said, but if she was happy, she didn't look it. A flush still rode high on her pink cheeks, and as Marie studied her, she dropped her dark eyes to the floor.

A flutter of irritation beat against Marie's ribs, and she turned toward the guard. Any hopes Marie may have had for this visit were gone, but there was plenty she wanted to say to William. In his letter, he'd said they'd been children *"playing at love"*, and here he was, a grown man, still at it.

Before she could wave the guard over, Charlotte touched her arm, then withdrew her hand as though she'd been burned. "Actually, Miss Chevalier, it's amazing good fortune that we've met like this. I've been hoping for an opportunity to speak with you."

"About?"

Charlotte leaned closer and whispered, "About William, of course."

Marie took a step back, her face flaming. The implication that William was a secret the two of them shared was as strong an insult as Marie could imagine.

"Could you…," Charlotte spoke tentatively, before dropping her voice back to a whisper, "perhaps spare a moment now?"

Marie glanced at the door leading to the cells.

"I promise I won't keep you long," Charlotte implored, her dark eyes desperate and gleaming.

Marie turned toward the guard while she considered. He had resumed his place behind the counter where he stood watching them with undisguised interest. Stiffening her spine, Marie faced Charlotte. "Of course. Only, I think it would be better if we spoke outside."

"We can go to the park across the way," Charlotte volunteered. "There are benches there. We can sit and talk as long as we need."

As long as they need? The words, though spoken softly, were ominous. How much could they possibly have to say to one another?

Outside, Marie cast a wary glance at the puddles lining Chestnut Avenue, but the girl had already stepped off the curb and was striding carelessly across the filthy street. After a few steps, Charlotte turned and noticed Marie wasn't beside her.

"Do you need a hand?" Charlotte asked.

A swell of indignation rose in Marie's breast. "No, thank you."

Marie stepped onto the muddy road and walked with a quick, light step toward a secluded bench under a large white oak. By the time she sat down, mud was spattered as high as her knees in some spots, and the hem of her blue dress was a solid ring of brown.

She turned toward Charlotte. "What would you like to speak to me about?"

"I... I hardly know where to begin." Charlotte studied her hands, which she turned nervously in her lap.

"I generally find the beginning to be as good a spot as any." Marie softened the remark with a quick smile, but her heart thudded sickeningly in her chest. Now that they were alone, a profound sense of dread had taken root. What did this girl, *William's girl*, want to say to her?

"Of course." Charlotte flushed, her eyes darting up then dropping back to her lap. "William has told me so much about you. He's always saying how like brother and sister you are."

The idea was so incredible Marie could have laughed.

Charlotte continued, "Which is why I felt I could come to you with, with our problem."

"Problem?" Marie's throat was so tight, it was a miracle she could speak.

"Well, you see, William and I would like to be married and start a family, but that's impossible if we stay here. I'm sure you'll agree that there can be no future for William in Philadelphia now—not after the trial. We hope to move out west, maybe Washington or Nevada, somewhere we can start a life together where no one has ever heard of him."

Marie turned away, her heart hammering. Her first feeling was relief, grateful at least that their *family* was as yet a future prospect, but confusion and a deep sense of betrayal were not far behind.

"There's so much opportunity out west for a man like William; I just know he'd make good," Charlotte went on, too absorbed in her own emotion to notice anyone else's.

"You seem quite decided on the matter," Marie said at last, with a calm that surprised her. The entire conversation felt unreal, like something written for the penny theater. "I take it you've discussed your plans with William, and that the two of you are in agreement?"

"Oh, yes. Actually, it was his idea for me to come to you."

Marie recoiled as though she'd been slapped. *This* was William's way of conveying his feelings to her? He had been careless before, but *this*, this deliberate cruelty, was a new development. "Sounds like it's all settled then," Marie said, her voice tight. "What is it you require of me—of my family?"

Charlotte hesitated, dropping her eyes again. "Moving takes money, and we haven't any. We were thinking, now that the trial is over and you have the inheritance, you might help us to our new start. It's an awful lot to ask, I know, but seeing as you're like William's family...."

The girl's voice drifted off, but her eyes held Marie's, pleading for reassurance. Marie had none to offer. The sheer effrontery of the proposal was dazzling, even for William.

"After all," Charlotte resumed, tentatively. "It was Will's connection to your family that made life so impossible for him, first with Duncombe, and then with your grandmother's trial. Not that it was anyone's fault, not really, but still, there it is."

Marie had an overwhelming urge to stand up and walk

away, to run. Only her pride, or what was left of it, held her there, sitting, hands folded, on a park bench while a slip of a girl tore her heart to pieces.

When they'd sat down here, Charlotte had been the interloper, but in just a few short minutes, their positions had somehow reversed. Marie studied the woman next to her with freshly opened eyes. Could it really be that William loved this girl? *Preferred* her?

To be sure, Charlotte did not possess the striking good looks Marie had been praised for, but there was a delicate loveliness to her that gradually impressed itself on the senses. Her diminutive size gave her a lightness, which was accentuated by the fineness of her features: her small, straight nose, perfectly formed pink mouth, and soulful, dark eyes.

Marie rose hastily, afraid that if she stayed any longer she would strike out in a fit of violence, or worse, cry. "I must discuss this with my family. If you keep Charlie informed of your whereabouts, you'll have an answer soon."

Charlotte stood as well, her face radiant. "I knew you'd understand—a woman always does."

"I must be going," Marie said. Charlotte said something in response, but Marie had already strode away, indifferent to the state of her shoes or her mud-stained dress. When the courthouse came into view, she turned down the first path she came to and walked without direction.

A feeling of illness, of decay, grew inside her. What a fool she had been! That girl had as good as said that her family was to blame for all of William's troubles. That was just like the William she remembered, always blaming someone else for his own mistakes.

Marie stopped abruptly, her fists clenched at her sides. An urge to go back to the courthouse, to scream her hurt at him surged up inside of her until she was nearly choking with it. Only her shame stopped her. The guard would smirk at her again, and it would hurt in a way it hadn't before, because now she knew he was right. Every fiber of her body wanted to strike out, to inflict on William some measure of the pain he had caused her, but what if he was indifferent to her misery, or, worse still, enjoyed it?

William had another woman now: someone who would never criticize or blame him, no matter what he did. Charlotte had sold herself to support him. Happy, apparently, to walk the streets while he loafed and drank gin with her brother. How could she compete with that? And why would she want to?

Marie started walking toward home again, but her thoughts gave her no peace. She should have known this would happen. How had she sat through the trial and not seen that it would end like this? What an unmitigated fool she was. No wonder Jamie had cut ties with her as soon as he could; even the William Jones's of this world did not want her.

When she reached her building, she found the apartment empty. With a growing sense of urgency, Marie strode to her bed and yanked the keepsake box from under her mattress. Flinging open the lid, she withdrew several letters. Clutching them in her fist, she hurried back into the living room and fell to her knees before the fireplace. Nearly frantic now, she arranged scraps of newspaper and coal in the grate with her free hand.

Her fingers were shaking so much that she dropped the first match and had to strike two more before the kindling ignited. The flames were low and blue, but steady. Seizing the poker, she prodded until the fire roared to life. She watched it dance a moment before thrusting the letters into the heart of the blaze, singeing her fingers.

The room was filled with a fearful crackling hum, and the heat burnt her face and arms, but still she remained on her knees, kneeling on the stone hearth. For the first few agonizing moments, the paper seemed impervious to the fire; orange and blue flames darted around the letters' sides without harming them. Finally, the edge of one caught, then another. A moment later, they erupted, swelling the fire into a dizzying display of smoky wisps and leaping sparks.

An eradicating blackness sped over the cream of the parchment. Marie watched, nearly wild, as the darkness raced toward the center of the uppermost envelope, where the words "To My Dearest Love" were written in William's neat hand. An urge to snatch the letters from the fire, to save whatever scraps remained, seized her, but by the time the thought writ itself in her mind the inscription had been consumed, and every trace of her and William's love was destroyed.

BEFORE YOU GO

MAY 1, 1900

*J*amie glanced at his watch. Alfred, the desk clerk at the La Pierre House Hotel, was speaking at great length to a white-whiskered gentleman and his wife about the many fine dining establishments near Broad and Chestnut. Jamie sighed and looked around the lobby. Despite obvious renovations, an aura of yesteryear emanated from the thick oriental rugs and the towering potted palms. This feeling of a bygone elegance was heightened by the guests themselves, the youngest of the dozen or so who loitered amidst the velvet armchairs and carved mahogany side tables, was above sixty.

Duncombe, whose office had made Jamie's travel arrangements, had apparently thought that a room here, as opposed to at the more fashionable Hotel Walton down the street, would better suit Jamie's reduced circumstances. In truth, the La Pierre was well beyond Jamie's current means. Not wishing to embarrass Duncombe, or himself, Jamie had mitigated the cost by staying in Philadelphia only one night, instead of the initially contemplated two, before starting back to Tacoma. This meant catching the last train out of Broad Street station this afternoon and spending eleven nights, instead of ten, in the spartan berth of a second-class "tourist sleeper".

Jamie had spent this week wrapping up loose-ends in New York and Philadelphia; this morning's hearing had been the last of it. *Bankruptcy*. The word still made Jamie's skin crawl. His father had been dead less than a week when, in his new role as both head of the family and owner of Keystone Lumber Company, Jamie had made his family's ruin official by filing with the federal district court. Just a few years ago, before the Bankruptcy Act of 1898, he would have been able to negotiate things privately, but now, thanks to Senator Nelson, the whole sordid business had to be aired in a national forum.

At least the filing had convinced his more suspicious-minded creditors that his protestations of poverty were genuine. Duncombe had persuaded the judge, an old friend of the Captain's, to allow negotiations to continue outside of the courtroom. That, apparently, is how "restructuring", as it's known in the legal parlance Jamie was becoming all too familiar with, is accomplished. Though, if you asked Jamie, *butchering* was a more apt name for it.

The Keystone Lumber Company, a family business reaching back three generations, was now a corporation. He and his sister each owned a forty-five percent share. The remaining ten percent was in the hands of Manassas's creditors. But before those creditors could be induced to accept scraps of paper in lieu of payment, they had required Jamie to take a comprehensive inventory of his family holdings, personal and professional, and sell everything that was not essential to their survival. This had meant parting with the houses in New York and Philadelphia, and most of the furniture and items inside of them, along with almost all of the company's mills, timberland, and cutting rights in the northeast.

At least Uncle Manny had been right about one thing: the future of lumber was in the west. Shortly after his father's funeral, Jamie had traveled to Washington to take stock of their undeveloped holdings there. What he found both surprised and heartened him. The forests along the Pacific were vast and untapped: acre upon acre of timberland, containing millions of board feet of redwood, douglas fir, and red cedar. It was good news—the first his family had received in a very long time. A fact he had to continually remind his mother and Melly of as he packed them, and the few possessions they still owned, off to Tacoma.

Jamie's attention was brought back to the present when the couple in front of him thanked Alfred loudly and started toward the hotel doors. Jamie stepped forward. "Hello again, Alfred."

Alfred, a man in his early thirties with neatly slicked brown hair and a side part, looked first left, then right. Once he had established there was no one else to serve, he faced Jamie stiffly and said, "Good afternoon, sir. How may I assist you?"

"Do I have any messages?"

"If you give me your name, I will be happy to check for you."

Jamie smiled to hide his irritation. Alfred knew his name. Just as he had known it when he asked last night, and again this morning. "My name is James Lett, Suite 3B."

Alfred turned to a wall that had been sectioned into dozens of wooden cubbies. From one of these, he withdrew a small white business envelope. Wordlessly, he handed this to Jamie, then turned to tidy a stack of receipts.

"Thank you," Jamie said, with practiced courtesy that Alfred pretended not to hear.

At first, Jamie had been too occupied with work to notice that the invitations to dinner parties and for weekend excursions to the Poconos had stopped arriving. When, at last, it came to his attention, he met the discovery with the same resigned forbearance he would have greeted an unsavory, but expected, house guest. Scandals, though not common, weren't unknown in his circle. Nor was he too young to remember the

Panic of 1893. If he concentrated, he could still conjure the faces of friends whose families, unable to weather the crisis, had disappeared from the social register, never to be heard from again.

These consequences, and more, he had expected. What had surprised him was the way strangers, common folk, had reacted to the news. Factory workers and secretaries would cast side-long, disapproving glances at him in the streets, and sales people, or clerks, like Alfred here, would go out of their way to be rude to him. This "moral imperative" to punish his family for their misfortune baffled Jamie. It stung what was left of his pride, but had it impacted him alone, he would have waited it out. The public's interest, never fixed in one direction too long, was sure to move along to the next scandal. But the idea of shop girls, and the servers at lunch counters, looking down their noses at Melly and his mother was unendurable. That, truth be known, was the true reason he'd rushed the move to Tacoma.

This morning's court hearing was a formality, one that Duncombe had warned him he needn't appear for. But Jamie, who had been planning to tie up some loose ends in New York anyway, thought it best to be on hand, just in case something went wrong. As it happened, nothing did. The entire proceeding lasted from nine in the morning, to nine fifteen, leaving Jamie with the rest of the morning to spend as he chose.

He'd normally go to his club, but, today of all days, the prospect did not appeal to him. Still, the weather was fine, and no sane man preparing to spend eleven days on a train would willingly spend the morning bottled up in a hotel room. He was thinking these thoughts, and more like them, when it occurred to him that he had one friend who he could see without fear of causing embarrassment: Marie.

Jamie opened the envelope, read the address written there, and smiled. God bless Duncombe!

Forgetting all about the annoying Alfred, Jamie strode

through the lobby and nodded to the doorman as he passed. Three cabs were lined up in front of the hotel, waiting for business. He approached the first, and read the address aloud. The cabby, a dark complexioned man with a deeply creased forehead, did an admirable job of hiding his surprise.

Twenty minutes later, Jamie's cab pulled up in front of a house with chipping paint and a patchy lawn. He had seldom traveled through neighborhoods like this, let alone stopped in one, and he briefly experienced the same species of mental unsteadiness he'd felt when he'd first traveled abroad.

Plucking up his courage, Jamie walked up the short path and knocked on the front door. To his surprise, an unusually large middle-aged woman opened it. Based on what he knew of Marie's family, he hadn't expected them to have servants. Had Duncombe gotten it wrong? Had he? "Good afternoon, Ma'am. I've come to pay a call on Miss Chevalier, is she at home?"

If Jamie was surprised to see the woman, the woman was astonished by him. "Just a moment, young sir." She tittered, her wide blue eyes blinking rapidly. "I'll go and see if she's in."

Leaving the door wide open, she turned and lumbered up a narrow set of stairs. That's when Jamie realized that Marie's family did not occupy the entire house, but only rooms in it. That foreign feeling returned to him.

"Marie," The woman called out, followed by a loud banging. "Are you at home, dear?"

Jamie waited, a prickle of anxiety starting just under his collar.

There was the sound of rusty hinges, and then he heard Marie's confused voice. "I'm here, Mrs. Griggs. Is everything alright?"

There's a *gentleman* at the door for you." The woman, Mrs. Griggs, said with meaningful emphasis.

Jamie heard footsteps, then Marie's face peeked over the

stair rail. His heart stopped beating for a second. My God, but she was beautiful! How had he forgotten that?

Marie's eyes widened, and her face disappeared from view.

Should he say something, apologize for his sudden appearance? He hadn't yet made up his mind when Mrs. Griggs's generous body appeared at the head of the stairs, pulling Marie behind her. "Ah, fortune's smilin' on you, young sir."

"Indeed it is," Jamie said, his eyes locked on Marie's flushed face. She wasn't happy to see him.

Puffing, Mrs. Griggs reached the bottom of the stairs and practically pushed Marie in front of Jamie.

"Mr. Lett," Marie said, dipping her eyes. "What a surprise."

He took her hand, the soft warmth of it made his chest tighten. "You must think me terribly rude calling on you like this. I'm only in town for the day, and I very much wanted to see you."

Her face softened until she glanced at Mrs. Griggs, who was standing just a few feet off with a rapt expression on her face. Marie withdrew her hand from his and walked to the door, opening it to step onto the porch.

Jamie followed her outside. It was a bright blue spring morning. A group of neighborhood children shrieked with joy as they played "kick the can" in the empty lot across the way.

"I really can't apologize enough," Jamie said. "I was in town finishing up some business, and I hoped you might have time for an early lunch."

For the first time since she'd come downstairs, she looked at him directly, and an expression of surprise flashed across her face.

"What is it?" He asked, bringing a hand to his cheek.

"I'm sorry, it's nothing. You just look so ... different."

Jamie nodded, understanding what she meant at once. Between the travel and the long days of work and worry, he had changed, in every way. He'd lost weight, which he didn't mind, but he'd lost more than that. The easy manner, that undefinable something that he'd worked so hard to master, had gone from him. Fine lines appeared around his mouth and eyes, giving him a strained, almost pained expression. "As it turns out, bankruptcy is no beauty treatment," He said lightly. "But how about that lunch? I'm famished."

Her brow furrowed, and he knew she was going to say no before she spoke. "That sounds lovely, but I'm afraid I've just eaten breakfast."

"Have you? What a pity," he said, his smile fading. "My own fault, of course, for leaving things to the last minute. Terrible bad manners, I know. Only, I so wanted to see you."

"You never wrote to me," she said, and there was a flash of anger in her voice, and hurt. "Not a word, even though I wrote to you. Twice."

"Did you?" he said gently, understanding her coolness toward him better now. "I never saw those letters. And if you only knew what an ungodly mess my life has been since I last saw you, you would understand why I didn't write, why I couldn't."

"I know it must have been hard. One of my letters was condolences, after I read that your father had passed."

Jamie breathed deeply.

"You say you're only in town for the day?" Marie asked, her manner softened. "Where are you going? New York?"

"Washington."

"Washington?"

Jamie nodded. "We've moved shop. The business, family, everything. My life is in Washington now."

Jamie regretted the lightness of his tone as he saw Marie's face fall. So, she did care after all. For a brief moment, this realization made him terribly happy, and then just as sad.

"What about the house on Chestnut Hill?" Marie asked.

"Sold. You must have read about my family's difficulties? The papers can talk of nothing else."

Marie looked away and nodded.

"There is one good thing about all of the attention we've received," Jamie said wryly. "It saves me the trouble of explaining our situation."

"The papers grow rich printing lies, everyone knows that," Marie said, her voice sympathetic.

"It would seem the greater the calamity, the less the need for exaggeration." Jamie leaned against the banister and stared down the road.

"And to think, it's all because of that awful man."

Jamie looked up, surprised. "You mean Uncle Manny—Mr. Edmunds?"

Marie nodded.

"Well," Jamie said, considering, "He certainly didn't help things for me any, but a change was inevitable. Business had been on a decline for some time. I was just too wrapped up in my own petty troubles to notice."

To his surprise, Marie reached out and tentatively placed her hand on his.

He clasped it warmly as he turned to look at her. "Don't you go feeling sorry for me now. I've lived a charmed life, a little work won't do me any harm, or so my sister keeps telling me."

Marie smiled weakly. "Do you think you'll ever come back?"

A chord in his heart sounded. He waited a moment before answering, choosing his words carefully. "Once I've sorted out the business, I'll be back."

"You promise?" Marie turned bright pink as she asked this and quickly looked away.

She was so sweet, so lovely. In that moment, he would have said, *done*, almost anything to see her smile. He squeezed her hand gently. "I promise."

A rich silence settled over them, one that Jamie was reluctant to break. She seemed to feel the same, and it was several minutes before he worked up the self-discipline to say, "I should be going. My cab is waiting, and I don't want to give your neighbors more to gossip about." He tipped his head toward Mrs. Griggs and another woman who were staring at them over the low fence between the yards. The neighbor, embarrassed to be caught spying, feigned interest in a flowering shrub. Mrs. Griggs waved.

"She must have gone around the back," Marie said, her voice both amused and annoyed.

Jamie waved back at Mrs. Griggs, then straightened up. "Would you mind if I wrote to you?"

Marie blinked in surprise, then flushed a becoming shade of pink. "I'd like it very much."

"Good." Jamie picked up his hat, which he'd placed on the railing and turned toward the path to the street.

He hadn't gone more than a few steps when Marie called after him, "Jamie!" He turned back toward her. "Before you go, there is something I've been wanting to ask you, that I need to ask you."

"Oh?" He said, retracing the few steps between them.

"When..." she hesitated, then rushed on, "When that Mr. Edmunds told you what he'd done, did he say anything about why he killed Mémé?"

Jamie hesitated, the now-familiar queasy feeling he experienced whenever he thought of Uncle Manny already stirring in the pit of his stomach. "He said he didn't."

"Why else would he have..." Marie spoke quickly, then paused, before finishing in a whisper, "*killed himself?*"

Jamie stared down at his hat, which he turned slowly while he considered his answer. "It's hard to say, exactly. I think by that time, he'd done any number of things he couldn't live with."

"I read about that South American gentleman in New York," Marie said hesitantly.

Jamie nodded. "That's just what I mean. He'd dug himself into such a hole, I imagine he felt there was no way out."

He glanced over at the waiting cab, almost eager to leave now.

"I'm sorry to have brought this up," Marie said, as though she too felt and regretted the change between them. "I know how painful it must be. It's only, the police have given up the investigation, and that man admitted he was in the house. It's hard to imagine an entirely different person breaking in on the same night with the sole intention of murdering a harmless old woman."

Jamie sighed and gave his hat another turn. "I've thought about it myself. Maybe it's just sentiment on my part, but I'd like to believe that Uncle Manny told me the truth in the end. After all," he added with a shrug, "it is *possible* someone else was in the house that night."

Marie's face paled, and she shook her head. "No. It had to be him."

She stepped back, away from Jamie, as she said this. Only a few feet separated them, yet the distance seemed greater than when he'd been in on the other side of the country.

"You may be right," Jamie said, smiling sadly, "but I hope you aren't."

He nodded a last farewell, before walking toward his waiting cab and his new life in Washington.

AN UNFINISHED CANVAS

AUGUST 10, 1900

*M*arie sat in the window seat, her needle paused in midair, the thread dangling like a stray thought. Outside, the late summer haze clung to the rooftops, thick with heat and stillness. Inside the apartment, the silence was absolute. Eliza had been gone a week now, packed off to Miss Hershaw's Institute for Young Ladies, a boarding school in Connecticut with a reputation for turning out first-rate teachers.

When Marie and Eliza had approached Papa with their plan for Eliza's future, they had expected a fight, but he'd surprised them, saying only, "Of course Lizzy will go to school! Didn't I promise Maman she would?"

Since Eliza's departure, their little apartment had taken on a closeness, a weight. Papa's voice echoed louder, and Charlie's jokes grated more readily. The horror of Mémé's death, and all that came after, had receded enough to allow the more mundane difficulties of life, such as tradesmen's bills and the exorbitant cost of beefsteak, to resume preeminence in her thoughts. But there were still moments when memories of

Mémé, or of William, caught her off-guard and destroyed the equanimity she'd worked so hard to achieve.

Today, it had been an article in the newspaper about the Tagalog Insurgency. One of the soldiers in the grainy photographs had looked a bit like William. Her heart had frozen while she inspected it, only thawing once she'd confirmed that the man's nose was too long and his chin too pointed. But now, an hour later, she still felt sick and angry, as she always did when she thought of him.

When she'd returned home with Charlotte's message, Papa had sworn he'd rather be hung in the town square by his unmentionables than give William and Charlotte, or, as he phrased it, that "grousing pantywaist and his whore" a single penny. It was only after Marie reminded him of the letter William still possessed, and the charges the district attorney was considering, that he determined fifty dollars was, perhaps, a small price to pay to be rid of a no-good fool forever.

Arrangements had been made, and, not long after, they received word that the district attorney had dropped all charges, leaving William and Charlotte free to set off for parts unknown. Apparently, it was Duncombe himself who was behind the decision not to prosecute. Defrauded investors were clamoring for someone to blame, preferably someone with deep pockets, and the last thing the lawyer wanted was a trial drawing his firm deeper into the scandal.

The money they gave William came from the inheritance, which had turned out to be six-hundred dollars, a sum substantially more than anyone had anticipated. Marie had expected Papa to spend the money on horses and drink, as was his way, but instead, it had fired him with a single-minded determination to increase his fortune. This he aimed to do by finding a man in possession of a good idea, but without the means to bring it to life. Each night, a new hopeful, usually a middle-aged man with slicked hair and polished boots, would take them out to supper and pitch his scheme. To Marie's astonishment, Papa had taken to asking Marie to accompany him to these dinners. It hadn't taken her long to realize that Papa hoped to secure both his financial success and her marriage in a single transaction.

Marie pricked her finger on the needle and hissed. A bead of blood bloomed on her fingertip, and she reached into her sewing basket for a strip of cotton to dab it. When she did, she caught sight of a scrap of shimmering gold material, a remnant from her work for the Bijou. She picked it up, admiring its sheen in the changing light. Her mind drifted back to the long hours she'd spent bent over sequins and embroidering hems. The work had been hard, but it had been hers.

She set the shirt aside and stood. The air in the room was still and the heat stifling. A walk was what she needed, or maybe a show, anything to shake her doldrums. Marie put her sewing away, tidied herself in the mirror, and stepped out into a golden summer afternoon.

The Bijou was staging a musical production of The Prisoner of Zenda, complete with corsets, swordplay, and a gallant hero who warbled love songs as he rescued a maiden in distress. Marie watched with distant amusement, noting that the pleats in the heroine's gown weren't as even as they should have been.

After the show, she was standing in front of the theater, wondering if she should hail a cab or walk home when a man approached her.

"Marie Chevalier, isn't it?"

She looked up. "Mr. Sam," Marie mumbled, both happy and embarrassed to see her old employer. "I've been meaning to come by and explain...to *apologize*."

"Are you in a hurry?" Sam asked.

Marie shook her head.

"Come."

Marie followed him through the narrow space behind the

theater, past discarded props and crates of costumes. Backstage, there was a swirl of noise and action. Marie tried to absorb the myriad sights and sounds without losing track of Sam. He led her to the wardrobe he was master of, where she used to drop off the finished orders. When the door had closed behind him, he gestured to a chair, and she sat in it, curious what he wanted. He couldn't still be angry she'd fallen behind on her orders, or could he?

"I read about your grandmother's death in the papers," he said, his tone direct but not unkind. "You should have come to me, told me. We could have made arrangements."

Marie's throat tightened. "You're right. I should have."

Sam nodded. "Did the police ever catch the bastard who did it?"

Marie shook her head.

"No surprise there." Sam leaned against the brick wall, arms crossed. "Did I ever tell you, I used to work at the Standard?"

Marie looked up sharply. The Standard was a well-known colored theater.

"That's right," he said. "You'd be surprised at how many colored folk are in the theater. It comes natural to us, I suppose, since we spend so much of our lives playing a part. We've got to be better than the white folk think us, but not so good that they feel threatened."

Marie opened her mouth, then shut it. She hadn't known. She hadn't even guessed.

"And people like us," he continued, gesturing at Marie, "live between worlds. Unless we announce our ancestry every time we walk into a room, or wear signs saying "colored", people assume we aren't. And if it goes on like that long enough, you start forgetting that you aren't really a part of their world yourself.

"But the folks that run things, them that make the laws and mete out what they like to call justice, they *never* forget. Because it's them that hold most of the money in this world, and all of the power, and they mean to keep both. It's as simple as that."

Marie stared, wide-eyed, as her heart thudded in her ears. All her life, she'd walked a line she couldn't see, only feel. Now, here was someone else who knew the shape of it. She wanted to thank him, to tell him she understood, but the words stuck in her throat. She could only stare as the tears that had welled in her eyes began to roll down her cheeks.

"Yes," he said thoughtfully. "I'm sorry about your grandma, but I'm not surprised." Sam studied her face a moment, then added, "It's a funny thing, but you've caught me at just the right time. There's a company heading west. All the way to California. They need someone to do costumes. Might even be room for a few lines here and there, if you're interested. You got the looks for it, and I know more than one leading lady who got her start with a needle and thread."

Marie blinked, like someone coming out of a dream. "California?"

Sam nodded.

"I don't know," she said, her thoughts racing so quickly she could hardly keep up. "I never dreamt …. Do you really mean it?"

"If you want the spot, best let me know quick. They're scheduled to play St. Louis next week."

"That soon?" Marie shook her head. "I don't know."

He straightened up and walked to the door. "Go home and think on it, but think fast."

Marie thanked him and walked home in a daze.

Papa or Charlie had come and gone while she was out. On the kitchen table lay a crust of toast, a half empty mug, and a letter. She picked the last item up, surprised to see it was addressed to her. Her name was written in a neat, schoolgirl script, and the postmark read Nevada.

She squinted at it, wondering who it could be from, then

tucked it in her pocket and cleaned the mess left on the table, her mind full of Sam's offer. It was, of course, impossible for her to accept. Papa would never let her go. But she couldn't resist thinking about it. What a life that would be! Traveling to different theaters, and even acting. Acting! Her, on a stage. The idea was too fantastic.

Her excitement was so great, she couldn't sit still and spent the next hour tidying a kitchen that she had already cleaned that morning. She had completely forgotten about the letter until she took her apron off and felt it in her pocket.

She took it out and stared at it again. She didn't know anyone in Nevada, did she? Mentally, she conjured the blurry shapes on maps from her school days, trying to remember exactly where Nevada was. It was close to Washington, wasn't it? The thought excited her, and she slid her finger under the seal of the envelope and withdrew the letter.

Marie:

This is Charlotte. William's Charlotte. I reckon I'm the last person you expected to hear from. Lord knows, I never thought I'd be writing to you myself, but some of that Catholic learning I got back in my school days must've stuck. I think of you and your grandma most every day, and have come to believe that if I want to move forward, I must first square my past.

The first thing I want to make clear is that I did not intend to kill your grandmother. Nor was it an act of jealousy, as you probably think. When I went to Chestnut Hill that night, I didn't know that you and William had been lovers. I knew there was a woman in William's past. Once, when he'd drunk too much, he told me about her. Not by name. He's too much a gentleman for that.

He told me how, in order to purchase an affection his hard work and devotion had failed to win, he had turned to crime. He ended up losing both his job and his reputation, but worse than that, at least for him, was the loss of this woman, who cast him off when he needed her most.

From that night forward, I despised you, for William's sake. But it wasn't until that final day of the trial that I learned who you were. When William looked at you, his heart was written on his face so plainly that any fool could read it.

Even then, when his life hung in the balance, that look tormented me. It destroyed the happiness I should have felt when a mistrial was declared, and gave me no rest thereafter. I wanted him so bad I ached with it—and he wanted you.

That same night, I began to plan.

I'd noticed the way you hung on young Mr. Lett whenever he came to court, and guessed that William would've too. The day after the trial, I paid William a visit. I told him you'd offered us money to go somewhere, anywhere, so long as it was far away. I said you didn't want him around, embarrassing your family and spoiling your prospects with the young sir.

Hurting him like that was hard, but it had to
be done. You won't understand this, but if I
believed for one moment you could make him happy,
I'd move heaven and earth for him to have you.
But you are too greedy, too selfish. Your believing
me as readily as you did proved that. You wanted
what I said to be true, because it cleared the way
for you and your fancy man. In that sense, what
I told William was not a lie, not really. I just put
your hopes into words.

I know you think I'm scum. Saw it in your
face every time you looked at me. And maybe I
am, but at least I have the sense to recognize a
rare good thing when I see it. From the first day
I met William, I knew I'd never let him go.

This past Christmas, William was lower than
I'd ever seen him. Your brother, Charlie, stopped in
to tell us that your grandma had refused your pa
another loan. After his visit, William seemed to give
up completely. I'd leave for the day and come back
to find him lying just how I'd left him. If something didn't change, and soon, I was going to lose
him.

I went to work as usual, but the cold and fog
drove everyone but the police away. I thought I'd
go mad with desperation, and that's when it came to
me. Charlie was forever boasting about your grandma's money. Saying how he and your pa could

invest it and how they would all get rich. He always included William in their plans, saying that William had earned his share.

I started thinking about this loan more and more, and how different things could be if the old woman would just give in. Her money would go to your pa once she was dead anyway, so why not let it do some good while she was alive?

Mind you, I didn't have much faith in Charlie's scheme. I don't know much about business or investments, and care even less. What I did know was that having the money would give William hope. Hope would buy us time, and time was all I needed.

New Year's Eve is always busy in my line of work. William wouldn't expect me home until late. Before I stepped out, I slipped a razor into my purse. I told myself it was for protection, but I've since wondered if I didn't already know how things would end.

I'd been to the house before, waiting outside with William while Charlie secured a fiver, so I knew my way well enough. It was already dark when I rang the bell. I spun a yarn about being a friend of yours and Eliza's. Said we'd agreed to meet there on our way to the theater.

She invited me down to what I later found out was the servants' hall. We sat near the fire, as it was very cold. She was bent over her needlework, yammering on about you and your sister, while I waited for the right moment to say what I'd come for. After a while, she started to wonder why you had left me waiting so long, and I knew my time was up.

When I told her the true reason I was there, she looked at me like I'd grown horns. I forced myself to keep talking, telling her how much that loan would mean to all of us, William and myself included.

That really got her ire up. She started talking a lot of gibberish, insulting William in English and French. I may not have understood all of the words, but I caught her meaning well enough. When I defended him, it made things worse. She said she was going to write to your pa and Charlie, and if either one of them so much as spoke to William again, she'd cut them off without a penny.

I was struck dumb. If she wrote that letter, William would never forgive me. I tried pleading with her, not for the money, I knew that cause was lost, but to forget that I had come, to let things go on as they had been.

She ordered me out of the house.

If I'd done as she said and walked away, she'd have lived a few more years, but I would have lost William forever, and he's the only good thing I've ever known.

My head was whirling like a top, and my knees were shaking so hard I could barely keep on my feet. In that moment, I knew only one thing: she had to be stopped.

My hand found the razor in my purse. She bent over, picking up a spool of yarn that had fallen from her lap when we were arguing. Still, she was talking, warning me about the dangers of bad men. Truly, I do not believe I knew what I was going to do until I did it. In a moment, a mere fraction of the time it now takes me to write this sentence, the deed was done.

William was in our room, waiting for me, just as I said at the trial. I cleaned the razor and washed up before going to him, as usual, and he never suspected a thing.

I never imagined the police would arrest him. And they wouldn't have, if it hadn't been for your brother. I must say, the selfishness in your family is without limit.

When they came for William, I was off my head with fear, but I knew he was innocent and that a fair trial would show that. Of course, if anything had gone wrong, I'd have come forward straight away. Luckily, it didn't come to that.

It goes without saying that it would be better if none of this had ever happened. I can't tell you how many times I've wished your grandma had been more reasonable, more generous. But it seems those traits do not run in your family.

You should also know that I was as surprised as any when, at the trial, the prosecutor said the house had been turned over and your grandma's pockets picked. That might have been the work of a greedy cop, I can't say. I know only that I didn't do it.

There, now I've told you all. I'd like to believe you could profit from my story, that you will see the harm your selfishness and vanity have caused and be the better for it, but I suspect that is too much to hope for. In my experience, people don't change. Not really.

You can take this letter to the police if you like. It won't do you any good. Out west, life is different. There are vast stretches of desert, unfinished canvases of sky and mountain, with only a few shrubs and shacks in between. Anonymous, uninhabited places that give adventurers, failures, and even criminals a chance to start over and create new lives for themselves. Here, in a land of strangers, your past is whatever you say it is, and the future what you make it.

This life is perfect for William and me, and you made it possible. For that, at least, I thank you.

Sincerely,

Charlotte Brown

Marie sat frozen long after she'd reached the final line. Her whole body trembled, and her breath came fast and shallow. She stood abruptly, as though motion could dispel the weight crushing her chest and lungs. Her stomach churned, and she stumbled to the washbasin and gripped its sides, certain she was going to be ill.

When the feeling passed, she looked behind her. The letter lay on the table, taunting her, like a living thing. It had been Charlotte all along. Not William. Not Manassas. Not Papa. But Charlotte, with her downcast eyes and timid smile.

Marie had been taken in completely, and all the while, Charlotte had seen her clearly. Her vanity. Her pride. Even the secret dream, unacknowledged even to herself, that William would leave so that Jamie could take his place. The girl had read her heart and made a weapon of it.

Marie staggered back to the table and picked the letter up. She wouldn't get away with it. Marie *would* go to the police. The over-confident fool had condemned herself with her own hand.

Marie was halfway into her coat before she thought of Sgt. Peterson and McKenzy, and remembered Sam's words from earlier today. The police hadn't cared before. Why would they care now, especially with Charlotte on the other side of the country?

Marie pressed a hand to her chest. *Jamie.* He would help. He had always listened to her, always believed. But he was in Washington, thousands of miles away.

Marie sat down, her mind whirling. That's when Sam's offer came back to her, but now it had a different weight, a new purpose. What had he said about the company going west, all the way to California?

All this evening, she had thought of it as she would a

daydream, a wild fancy, but now she forced herself to entertain the idea in earnest. She looked around the apartment: the faded wallpaper, the damp patch near the ceiling, and the larder that was always empty. What had she to stay for? Eliza was gone, and Papa and Charlie were never home. The only thing she had to look forward to was marriage to an old man Papa would select for her.

Or, she could accept Sam's offer. It was a life of risk and uncertainty, to be sure, but also one of adventure and *hope*. Not just of finding Jamie, Charlotte, or William, but of making a life worth living for herself.

Marie folded the letter and slipped it back into her pocket. Her hand lingered over the fabric, sealing the moment into her mind and heart. Then, with sudden clarity, she strode to her room and began to pack.

www.ingramcontent.com/pod-product-compliance
Lightning Source LLC
Chambersburg PA
CBHW050030120726
47903CB00006B/1980